She Looks Like Fun

Special Thanks

To my family and to all my teachers.

SHE

LOOKS

LIKE

FUN

Constantinos Koumontzis

WHITECHAPEL TRADING CO.

WHITECHAPEL TRADING CO.

constantinoskoumontzis.com

"If I had a world of my own, everything would be nonsense. Nothing would be what it is, because everything would be what it isn't. And contrary wise, what is, it wouldn't be. And what it wouldn't be, it would. You see?"

— Lewis Carroll

For Helen

Three Beers, One Vodka-soda

School locks are simple. I wiggle my makeshift pick, which is nothing more than a few bobby pins secured with a hair tie on a red grading pen. With a slow turn, the bolt pops, the lock gives way, and the door creaks open. Before entering the lab, I glance over both shoulders, surveying the vacant halls. I can't wait until school completely empties - Mr. Walter will rot by then. And I can't risk that. My neighbors will report the smell. It's happened before. No, it has to be NOW, while the slow burn of last period distracts the student-teacher body. I glide the door shut behind me, holding the handle down until it returns to its frame. No loud slam or violent click from the latch. Silence.

Rows of stools sit flipped, four on top of each table. I leave the lights off. The smell of preserved tadpoles still lingers, causing a waft of faint chemical vapors to breeze into my nostrils and burn my tongue. Middle and high school classes primarily use this room, conducting labs and dissecting amphibians and birds. My nose wrinkles from the sour, fruity, yet fishy aroma, reminding me why I chose to teach fifth grade, and not secondary science.

I slip between the tables to an overhead cabinet lining the back of the room. I only need two plastic jugs of sodium hydroxide–perfect for bodies–each a little larger than a gallon of milk. I stuff them into a reusable grocery bag and conceal them with my rolled-up black sweater. Chicago fall has bloomed, so the crisp air justifies my extra layer. I escape the room as though never there. I'm coming for you Mr. Walter.

The clock in the hallway reads 2:15 pm as I depart from the lab. My shoes squeak on the tile floor not yet crowded by a sea of students. My pounding heart mimics my quickening pace as the bag scuffs against my leg. My eyes scour the classrooms to make sure no one spots me through the windows.

I don't really consider taking the chemicals to be stealing. I consider it giving them purpose; a higher purpose than sitting on the shelf. At least I'm going to use them for a worthy cause.

Nearly there, I think to myself.

I feel a buzz from that soon to be victory–the victory of knowingly getting away with it. A rush I never can seem to comprehend. As I approach my classroom, I slow my pace, easy and calm, with controlled breathing. At least that's how I try auditioning my movement. But as I turn the corner of the hallway, the calm sprints from my bones. Panic.

She stands in my doorway. The worst possible person to discover what I've done. Her arms are crossed, and a sneer slopes along her face. I see it in her eyes; I'm definitely not making it inside my classroom.

"Principal Salem's office," Angela Greene says, with a stern tap of her off-brand low-heel loafers, "...now."

A few of my students peep from behind their books. Each classroom door has a window on it. The students who sit in the front see everything happening in the hall. Those kids are always part of Ms. Greene's fan club. The volunteer hall monitors, the grade grubbers, the ass-kissers. I prefer the students who keep to themselves and sit in the back.

"Let me just drop this off inside," I say, trying to squeeze by her.

"No," she snaps. "Bring it with you. We need to go right now."

Angela snatches my wrist. An authoritarian grip. Skeletal knuckles that pulse red. Knuckles you'd expect to see attached to an almost dead nun. The veins in her hand are so blue. My mother had a grip like that. The kind of grip that makes you wonder how someone so fragile, as if constructed by nothing but brittle twigs, could have a vice so unbreakable. The type of grip fortified by years of wear and tear on the battlefield of the heart.

Eventually she lets go of my wrist. Though I'm not about to argue with her. Still new to the school faculty, I'm a novice when it comes to the power hierarchy. Angela Greene is my peer. Yet she acts like my superior. What differs between us is twenty-five years, a bitterness the likes of Folgers coffee, and poor fashion sense. But, hey, I'm not judging.

In his office, Amir Salem's annoyance beams from his copper-tinted cheeks like a neon sign above a nightclub. He spins a pen between his tan fingers, pointing it when he wishes one of us to speak. On his desk sits a composition notebook, the name Danny Hilton on the front.

"I just don't see how we can tolerate this type of behavior." Amir slouches as Angela Greene, my fifth grade co-teacher, rattles on. Angela wears high socks and a pullover or cardigan buttoned up to her neck every day. The colors she dons rotate from white, to off-white, to gray, and to today's outfit, a beige that isn't quite yellowish, but more so the flush of a frozen custard. And so far, my least favorite. "How are we supposed to promote safe spaces when boys in her class draw death symbols on their homework? Just look at it. Look!" she continues.

The clock ticks above my right shoulder - 2:30 pm. I need to get home, I think to myself. Anxious leg pulses ensue, bouncing so fast some of the trinkets on Amir's desk shake. I fixate on the minute hand, anticipating it to spin wildly out of control and reach past the three.

"Bonny, what are your thoughts?" Amir finally asks, sitting up as he takes a glance. I don't know why he insists on using my last name. I prefer Ann.

"I'm sorry," I say with a tickle in my throat. "About what, exactly?"

"Are you even listening?" Angela again. To be fair, I'm not. There's a lingering of resting shock. The whole time before I saw the notebook, I assumed I was in here for stealing or something important. Amir raises his brow and sinks back into his chair, unamused at my disinterest. "One of your students is seriously deranged," proclaims the prim and proper Ms. Greene. I lean forward, studying the notebook. She opens to a page littered with doodles of skulls and knives with a few smears and scratches of red pen ink to give the impression of blood dripping from triangular pointed blades.

"Looks like he has an imagination to me."

"That's what you call imagination?"

"You're right, people with imaginations only draw rainbows and bunnies, never anything emotional or violent." I flip through some of the writing passages from homework assignments. A big, red letter A or a PLUS MARK top each graded entry, graded by me, of course. "I think he's being bullied. What are you proposing?"

"Have you addressed the other students? The ones bullying him?" Amir asks.

"I've tried," I confess, "but he refuses to give names. I think everyone's a little guilty."

"You can't assume everyone is so terrible, can you? Especially not without proof." Amir sheepishly attempts to offer an authoritative comment.

"I don't need proof. I believe him. Are you suggesting that he should be expelled? If you ask me, it's the rest of the kids that deserve punishment."

"So, what do you suggest? That we punish everyone because he claims to be bullied?" Angela sarcastically adds.

"Punishing the entire student body is hardly a solution," Amir states.

"They'd deserve it," I say under my breath, but loud enough so that Angela can hear.

"If you think so little of Pearcey—"

Amir extends his arm with his palm facing backward and stops her.

He sits back, creating a piercing squeak from the tendons of his chair. "Miss Greene, would you please?" His hand beckons to the door. I do my best to mask my grin as she stammers out, irate that she's being sidelined. After a brief silence, Amir lets out a long sigh.

"Danny stays, for now. But I suggest you keep an eye on him. Pearcey is one of the top-rated schools in Chicago. You know where that starts?"

I shake my head.

"Look, I know it's only your first year here, but parents notice when their children are happy. And when the children are happy, the parents are happy. It's always my throat. With the board, with the parents... you get it, right? I want to preserve our donations and funding, along with our reputation. It's the only soul a school can have. If we have students who divert from the culture here at Pearcey, then we need to reevaluate what we're doing. Do you understand where I'm coming from?"

To be clear, Pearcey is not one of the top-rated schools in Chicago. Amir wants it to be, and refers to it as such, as if saying it out loud makes it true. Funding is short and admission is down. At least that's what I'm told. But as long as he says it's great... then it must be great. Like most men, he lives in his own lie.

"Perhaps you should sit down with his parents," he says, repositioning his glasses.

"I've only met his mother," I confess. I don't know the whole story about his parents. I try not to pry about that information, with kids or adults. I fear the return question of 'So tell me about your parents.' Nope, not going there. I nod to be a team player and finally leave the room.

After the questioning in Amir's office, I rush back to my classroom, grab my belongings and sling the bag around my shoulder. I make a break for the door, racing against the bell, forgetting for a second that I'm still a teacher. All I can think of is getting home to Mr. Walter.

"How was Principal Salem?" Seriously! I freeze at Rebecca's perky voice. My hands squeeze the frame of the door and my eyes clench as I grind my teeth. I don't have to turn around. I see her image in my brain. Her smile stretched from ear to ear like a slit throat and her pigtails dangling like suspended corpses on coat racks. Whenever she sucks-up to me, she props herself above a book far beyond her sixth grade reading level, dimples deep from her playful smirk.

I spin around and offer a pseudo smile, as if happy to see her.

"It was great," I say, submitting to the brown-noser. I turn to the rest of the class, "You are all free to go. Call it early today. You're welcome!" A drumline of closing books and crescendo of giggles and high fives follow. I can't deny the feeling that sparks in my chest as they cheer for me. For a micro moment in their lives, I mean more to them than anyone else. Not because I teach them prepositions or describe Lois Lowry's colorless world, but because I just gave them time. Time to be free.

But I'm not free. Because just as the last student steps out, the bell sounds.

I blame Rebecca. Had she minded her own business, I would have been gone before the other teachers had a chance to snatch me. I blame Angela for confiscating Danny's notebook. The bell's deafening tone unleashes a charge of students. The halls flood with racing children and a tide of runaway backpacks, preventing my escape. The other teachers attack so swiftly, as if they'd been planning their assault throughout the day; scheming to corner me at the exact moment of opportunity and take me off guard. I don't stand a chance.

"Ann!" I shudder. The ambush from Sonya's joyful voice is so sudden I nearly drop character." Keep it together, Ann. "You ready for happy hour?"

Happy hour. The worst two-word phrase created by the cruel gods of the English language. Don't get me wrong, I enjoy a discounted drink, not to mention the therapy of alcohol after a day spent around hundreds of kids. It's the company I don't care for– the forced social interaction. And I'm already late.

I take an involuntary step back from Sonya. Beside her stands Mr. Douglass, who everyone just calls Douglass, even the kids. His loosened tie dangles from his neck. His breath an unpleasant concoction of cannabis and coffee. Sonya must have taken the last period to change into her "after school clothes," though she keeps them hidden under her jacket.

"Nick and Ang are already in," Douglass says as he tosses his gum from one side of his teeth to the other. "Trying to get a headcount."

"I know you don't have plans, sweetie." Sonya doesn't let me get a word out. They definitely planned this. "You need to come; it's gonna be so fun."

"She has plans. She's coming with us," Douglass says. They aren't even looking at me. Do I exist at all? I can never really tell.

Douglass has one of those infomercial voices. "I doubt she'd forget she's up this week." No, I remember. They want me to go for one reason. It's my turn to pay. Not something I can't handle, but for sure the reason they need my presence so badly. "C'mon, Municipal is a short walk, happy hour goes from 4 to 7."

"Well actually I—"

"So, it works? Great!" Sonya wraps me in a hug, tight enough that I feel the silicone in her breasts her husband had given her for Christmas last year.

Without fail, I succumb to happy hour. Not because they are my friends, but because happy hour functions as one of those things I have to do to conform, to feel like I fit in somewhere. No one suspects anything if I'm willing to occasionally swallow the pill of social influence. Everyone questions the loner, the introvert, the mysterious anti-socialite... and the last thing I want is my co-workers prying into my personal life. I cannot risk being exposed.

I avoid Angela the entire walk to the Municipal. When we arrive, we are greeted by the bar's pre-existing buzz. It seems like all of Chicago gets off work at the same time each Friday. No matter how swiftly we race down the street, we never seem to get a good seat. I loathe walking into a crowded bar. A hundred eyes suffocate me with their gaze. I look at the floor. I don't want to be here. Too many people. Too many eyes. And two jugs of stolen chemicals.

Our group gets stuck behind a gaggle of young corporate ducklings in their blue button downs and khaki slacks, the uniform of the urban financial douchebag. I watch them waddle in with their steam-pressed trousers and their baby-smooth faces. They nudge to the front, their ringleader tossing his head back to get a drink count. Always the same. In a group of four, two order beer right off the bat. They set the tone for the rest. If it's Blue Moon, then they all follow suit. If it's an IPA, the third changes things up. No duckling wants to look like a pussy, but even number three can't pretend to like IPA. So instead of a margarita, because he loves fruity, or an old fashioned because he doesn't want to sound pretentious knowing the difference between rye and bourbon, he orders a vodka soda. The fourth in line plays the drums on his Calvin Klein's, staring along the sentried rows of glass bottles as if he has any clue at all what he is looking for.

"Bryce, what'll it be?" The head duckling says. The fourth replies, "What are you having?" The ringleader is always under the most scrutiny, so whatever he orders, the fourth finds solace in ordering. Inevitably, it will be one of two things: Blue Moon or IPA.

The squabble of thirsty teachers pushes past me, breaking my focus on the ducklings. Sonya and Douglass take to the bar, while Nick goes to score a table and Angela waits behind. She doesn't want to "go anywhere near that filthy bar."

I squeeze my way up to the bar to order, overhearing the ducklings, lingering now as they take recon for potential 'tail'. They argue about fantasy football picks. Oh, their fantasy lives. How tragic. One complains that hotties don't come to this spot anymore and they should bail. The door is to your left, asshole. Waiting to order my own drink, I peek down as the bartender delivers to the ducklings. Three beers, one vodka soda.

An involuntary chuckle slips, and I gloat.

"You need something? Holy shit, me? I pretend to ignore him. "Hey, bitch."

Time to play innocent teacher.

"I'm sorry?" I squeak. Heads begin to turn; eyes fix on me - sandwiched. People's intuitive nature to smell the scent of brewing conflict amuses me. How they lust to watch from a safe distance.

"Is something funny?"

Yes, in fact. "No." I play with a strand of hair, keeping eye contact. His Dartmouth green eyes narrow, and his nostrils flare as he tries to hold his smolder. There's a small red scrape on the edge of his jawline, I guess from his razor, and a patch of hair pomade on his earlobe that his "friends" are probably too afraid to inform him about.

"She's kind of hot," one of the foursome elbows him. Another plays with his straw, making blow-job motions. God it's so loud in here. "What're you drinking?"

"You're blood."

He leans in with a "what?". I'm not sure if he wasn't paying attention or if the high-pitched frequency of the happy hour blitzkrieg drowned me out. From the bar's mirror, I see Nick shuffle between tables, working his way to my rescue. As if I need it. Ducklings don't fight. Not before 1 am, anyway, and then their frat senses hit them like a werewolf's curse. I don't respond to their antics. I just stand there, staring.

They chuckle and nudge one another, making jokes that I no longer hear. The sounds from the bar disappear. The music fades and voices fall to a frozen whisper of white noise that vanishes into thin air. It's just me and the ducklings. Frozen in time. I imagine how I could filet them and use their skin as new wallpaper.

"Hey." Nick's voice snaps me out of it. His hand rests gently on my shoulder. "We got a table."

I shake off the ducklings; but before I follow Nick I notice it's gone. Where the fuck is my bag? The bar hook where I originally placed it is vacant. Did I put it on the floor? - No. I scan the room. Would someone have taken it? – No.

Then I catch it in my sight, being carried away from me and towards the table of teachers. In Nick's hand.

"Nick, hey, you have my bag." I snag his arm before he gets too close to the others.

"It's no big deal. I can carry it for you."

"I'd really rather carry it myself."

"It's fine, Ann. I'm happy to. What's the big deal?"

"Please, just give it back."

"Ann, I was just walking it to the table–" He notices the daggers in my glare.

"I got it."

His face deflates and he surrenders the bag. Somehow, I offended him, at least that's how it seems because he turns away and helps himself to a chair without saying another word. I can carry my own bag. I must carry my own bag. A bag filled with chemicals I stole from the school. Of course, men always have an ulterior motive. No thanks, Nick.

I sit at the table, enough room for a comfortable four–two chairs and a small booth. The ducklings had their moment, but my curiosity gets the better of me. About a half hour later,

I look over to their table, smiling to myself as I picture their heads on a plate in my freezer.

Nick and Douglass talk about the game on Sunday while Sonya asks Angela about her husband, a hotshot professor at Northwestern. I play a game that keeps track of how far Douglass' hand gets up Sonya's skirt. She has a talent for hiding the small fire of horny glee from his wedding ring grazing the flesh of her bare thigh. Two months ago, I walked into him bending her over a table in the teachers' lounge. They didn't even notice me. Somewhere inside myself, I envied it. Sex that erases all reality and propels two unhappily married people to fuck in the first place. And they could care less who knew.

"They raised their prices again," Sonya rolls her eyes while glancing through a hand-sized menu booklet.

"You say that every time we come," Angela mocks.

"I do not." She holds the booklet in front of Angela's face. "Look for yourself."

The grocery bag of sodium hydroxide sits between my legs. I could always say I have a shower drain problem. What girl doesn't anyways? I keep checking it, looking under the table and feeling underneath the sweater. I do my best to keep it out of their view. I can only think about getting home. Home to Mr. Walter.

I've never been one for kicking it with a big friend group. I catch morsels of their argument about Dickens' Great Expectations. When I'm asked to chime in whether I believe the theme is revenge or materialism I say I believe that "people are the material nowadays. Manipulated strings. And as for revenge... The novel dissuades it as a consuming force in one's life. Some things are good in moderation." I suppose they like what I say because there's a nice pause in their blabbing for a few moments. Just open-mouthed glares.

There's a cushion for people to blend with the rest of society. A masturbational repetition that people crave to just exist. Not me.

Nick eyes me from across the table. They have a hint of kindness to them. But the kind that wears an innocent, charming shield in front of something skeptical and mysterious. It's not that I don't trust him. Nick is a nice guy. But that's the point. Nice isn't a personality. Nice is a way a person behaves. Nice is a platform to showcase the misconstrued elements of one's identity. He sets his drink down and says my name as if he caught me at my game.

"Ann," he repeats.

He has a nice head of hair. Dark brown with a slick wave in the front going from his right to left, which he plays with the end of. Cute. But cute in the way you look at a small puppy your friends bring over for attention, not the kind of cute you want to wake up to in the morning.

I turn my focus away from his hair to his mouth.

"My cousin is giving me an extra ticket this weekend," he tells me.

"That's nice." I don't give a shit. I return to my drink, emptying the last drop of whiskey from the glass. I only take it straight. No ice. Neat.

"Would you wanna go?"

"To what?"

"The game, silly." His white teeth glisten as he smiles. He has a habit when he speaks to me. A short grin that leads to a heartfelt laugh and smile. Then he'll nervously run his hand through his hair and down the back of his neck.

"You don't wanna go watch the Bears get their asses kicked by the Lions?" Douglass takes a break from his quest up Sonya's thigh to apply eye drops.

"It could be fun." Nick lifts his glass. I can tell he's nervous from the way he fools with his straw. He hasn't ordered anything to drink, milking the same iceless glass of water for the past thirty minutes. The others had all ordered some cinnamon flavored Moscow Mule. "And it's not the Lions this week," he says, talking to Douglass now, "it's the Vikings."

"Oh yeah, our Minnesota girl," Sonya gives a small cheer. "You should go!"

"Still don't think she looks like a Minnesota girl." Sonya smacks Douglass on his arm for that one. "Right? You know what I mean." His view pans over to me. "It's a compliment."

"Where did you say you taught before coming to Pearcey?" Angela is suddenly interested in our conversation.

"Oh, it was a small prep school in this little town…Bridgeton Prep."

"You know," Angela says, "my cousin lives in Minneapolis. Was your school far from there?"

"It was a little further south. I'd go up to Minneapolis sometimes on weekends. I needed to get out of that small town oppression, you know?"

"From what my cousin tells me, the whole state seems like a small town." She takes a sip, eyeing me strangely.

"Fuck," Douglass says, "this city is one big small town, too. I had a friend who was sleeping with these two women – turned out they were cousins and roommates."

"A friend?" Sonya raises her eyebrows.

"Yeah, a friend. Michael Richardson."

"Doesn't he teach tenth grade at Pearcey?" Nick asks.

"No, no, that's Tim Richardson, different guy, but has a similar story, swear to god."

"So," Nick's eyes switch to me, rolling off Douglass' absurdities, "would you go with me to the game? See your team get their butts kicked by the Bears?"

My team? Ha.

"I don't think I can," I say blankly. I would actually consider it, if it was a match between real lions and bears. That would be something worthy of a Sunday afternoon date. Nick has asked me out three times this month. Three times he's asked, and three times I said no. Each time I give the same reason. "I have to visit my uncle. He is still very sick."

So what if I lie? Doesn't everyone fib when they're trying to avoid going out with men? If I lie to him now, I should probably never date him. I noticed that when I started lying to Kitty it was the beginning of the end for us.

What I hate most about happy hour is being trapped. You're either stuck in a booth or pinned at the bar. Teachers don't sit at the bar unless it's a hotel, so we are always at an awkward half booth, half chair contraption. Two of us start a conversation while others rest their head on their elbow diddling the straw with their tongue, offering an occasional comment or two. Meanwhile, whoever is left sits there sipping the mixture of melted ice and whatever alcohol remains at the bottom of their glass, awkwardly looking at the door every time someone walks in, begging for freedom.

Nick gives a volley of understanding nods; his eyes linger on his water glass. He downs the final sip as the waiter asks if we want another round. Everyone hesitates so as not to presume anything.

"Isn't it Ann's turn?" Sonya says–as if she doesn't remember.

We have a rotation. Every week the teachers go out and every week there is a selected one of us that pays. It's easier than five or so underpaid educators fumbling over how much each person owes to the cent. I despise going no matter what, but today I have someone waiting for me at home. And of course, today is my turn to pay. Say what you will about criminals, but these teachers are diabolical.

"Yes," I say, standing. I fumble in my bag, pulling out a wad of cash. "I need to go."

"Where are you off to in such a rush?" Douglass winks at the waiter as he signals for another round.

"I have...plans." Damn, all those questions wiped out my good excuses. I flip through the cash.

"Quite the stack there," Angela remarks. "Bridgeton must have paid well."

"Or been a front," Douglass jokes. I think he's joking. "Why would you move to another cold as hell city? Why not California or Florida?" He pours the final remnants of his first drink down his gullet.

"I moved because I didn't have a choice. I'm all my uncle has, really. The nurses at his care facility don't have that familial touch that keeps a man young and healthy."

"That's why Amir hired her," Douglass says. "She has that familial touch." Only he doesn't mean familial by his raised eyebrows and hand gestures.

Sonya laughs, tapping my ass. "Like he could ever get her."

"Amir?" I say, my face blank. He wishes.

Angela scowls as Douglass crunches down on a piece of ice.

"I'm kidding," he says, raising his hand like a crossing guard waving to stop traffic.

"I see how he stares at you," Sonya interjects. "Watch out, Nick."

She elbows Douglass playfully, and he laughs so hard that he pulls her close to his hip. She chews at the end of her straw and winks at Nick. The shy kid from Kenilworth only shakes his head and tries to play along with a weak grin.

"Wish I could stay, but I do have to go," I say, stopping the joke. "Eighty should be enough, right?" I set the cash beside Angela's empty glass. No matter what I think about Miss Proper, I trust the money with her.

"Where are you off to?" Douglass persists in a more serious tone. All heads turn, staring at me with anticipation. The tote feels heavy in my grip. I hesitate. Any minute, they are going to ask about the bag. I wait. Nothing. Douglass is cocking his head waiting for my response –

So, I'm honest.

"I have a man waiting in my bathtub." I sling the grocery bag over my shoulder.

"Kinky," Sonya says, rubbing my arm. "Girl gets it."

But I don't.

Mr. Walter

When I first started, it all made sense. Simple. Clean. But now, I can't seem to control myself. I feel a quenchless thirst. Yet I have bills to pay. So at least I earn a living and make money while ridding the world of men like Mr. Walter.

By the time I make it to my building, the autumn sun has set. The entire way home, I run possible scenarios in my head. Leaving bodies like this, even when it's for only a day or so, doesn't bode well with paranoia. My imagination can be toxic. Paranoia is a terminal illness that spreads unsettling outcomes. But in truth, I'm doing just fine. Really. I will be fine. I'll be fine when there isn't a rotting corpse in my bathtub.

My high-rise stands like a glass titan reaching to the dark blue sky. Not exactly luxurious, but it beats living in a crusty townhome on the edge of the city. Newer buildings have bigger closet space, sometimes two, and tubs that fit more than one person. My perception of city-living changed when I started to earn money on my own. Not the teacher's salary of course, which justifies killing in itself, but my nightly engagements. Chicago is small enough to live comfortably without paying outrageous prices, but large enough to keep your anonymity. I maintain anonymity as long as I retain the job of the kind, young elementary school teacher.

My neighbors' shouts bellow in my ears as I exit the elevator on the thirteenth floor. I pause for a moment outside my door, listening. Someday, I think to myself. They're a young couple, around my age, and enjoy partying late with friends, keeping the noise level just as loud when they're alone. Their consistent disregard for remembering their unit number pokes needles in my spine. Every time they order online, the package ends up at my door. 1303. Not 1302. Each time I deliver a package they scoff and accuse me of stealing. Or they accuse me of simply opening and resealing the box. Last time I nearly got caught. I had arrived home to find a box at my door. Sure enough, it was addressed to Roger Stevens. Without thinking, my foot slid to the side of the box to kick it across the carpet, but I hesitated. The sender intrigued me: Xtreme Restraints.

I kicked it inside my apartment. The box contained an array of BDSM harnesses and sex gear. It made me curious how anyone could find it pleasurable to clap what looked like electric cables around their nipples. The handcuffs I could get around, so I kept those and re-taped the box to appear untouched. When I walked it over to Roger and Kate, she answered the door. I wanted to ask her about the nipple clamps. Maybe they were for him? I couldn't be sure. But one look and she accused me of opening the box. I of course denied it like I always did, but somehow this time she could tell.

"I swear, if something's missing," she began, but stopped. Who confessed to buying bondage gear online? I wanted her to notice. I wanted someone to knock on my door yelling for the whole floor to hear that I stole their sex handcuffs. Please, I begged internally, please find out.

They've never secured the nerve to come by and demand the handcuffs. Tonight, they must be enjoying the gear for the first time, because Kate keeps asking Roger if it's tight enough, and the subtle crack of a whip echoes in my ear like a clap at the end of a tunnel. I look forward to when Roger mans up enough for the strap-on. About forty minutes later I find out he can only handle a few strokes before screaming.

Mr. Walter waits for me in the tub, tightly wrapped in black trash bags. Tape connects the bag at his ankles and a knot at the top secures his head. The candles and oil diffusers I left on had done their job. I step into the bathroom, greeted by the scent of lavender, vanilla, and death. I had stuffed ice packs inside the trash bag, fastened over his lungs and heart and along his arms and legs; a trick from Uncle Jones.

I take my own shower before giving Mr. Walter his lye bath. Luckily, my place has a separate tub and walk-in shower. After drying off, I apply body cream butter over my pale skin, wrap my hair in a towel, and drape myself in a bathrobe. I pull out red nail polish and set it on the sink. Then I fill the tub with the sodium hydroxide and warm water. This stuff is used in store-bought drain cleaners, how bad can it be? As a fuming steam starts to rise from the basin, I plop myself on the edge of the closed toilet seat, light an American spirit, and coat my toes in a new bright red.

"It's a nice color," I say out loud. "Don't you agree, Mr. Walter?"

I continue to brush paint over my toenails. Then I fan the wet polish because blowing it fails to dry the new scarlet coat. "What is it with some men that make them so dull? Have you ever seen such a poor spirit in a man? So quiet. So boring." I am sure Mr. Walter listens from somewhere.

As I sit there, I think back to the previous night. The night I killed him. Waiting under the Lasalle Street bridge, the titian city lights barely poking through the evening fog. How cold it was waiting for his limo, my fingers aching on the tip of my dying cigarette. He had taken me to his 'other' residence as he put it. A pretentious bungalow in Logan Square decorated with photos of him with his young female orchestra students, classical instruments, and a grand sterling piano. It could have been beautiful. Except I knew why he came to a place like that. He had a sock drawer, all women's and petite, some of them used. The smell from some had lingered. But I wasn't like them. He had made me slip on a pair of the metatarsal negligee while he changed into a robe.

I continue painting the cardinal red over my toenails as Mr. Walter begins to slowly dissolve. So slowly. Not that I can see him melt, but the steam tells me so. As does the smell. My cigarette only cuts it so much. A swift breeze of acetone and fumes from the bath invades my nostrils. I can't help but enjoy the light-headed feeling that comes with it.

I leave the body to its own dissolution and close my bathroom door. I step into my living room. Still clad in my robe, I walk on my heels so the new polish doesn't smudge. Feeling a little hungry, I move into the kitchen to make a snack before my nightly routine. Usually on Friday nights I get a hit or two online. They directly message me through my exclusive escort site. All I have to do is accept and message back agreeing to the location, after they provide me with their basic information. I avoid double dipping while I still have a body to manage, so I hesitate after opening my laptop, leaving it on my couch. I slip on a record, allowing the classical tunes of Beethoven's seventh symphony to serenade Mr. Walter's final departure.

I keep my vintage records neatly stacked in alphabetical order on a black shelf beside the record player. Mozart, Bach, Tchaikovsky, but my favorite is Beethoven. The record spins on a McIntosh turntable, slick, black with chrome accents and vintage green bulbs along the side. The speakers are the same, bolstering a pure, even tone with a harmonic balance that makes the music flow through me, running into my veins down to the tips of my fingers and toes; a fresh current of euphoria in the bloodstream. Good music is a drug. Great music with great sound practically gives me an orgasm. The tender violin strokes tickle my nerves and rub me in a way that Kitty used to do when she'd dance her dainty fingers across my skin, encroaching closer and closer to the treasure of pleasure that awaited the perfect touch. The brisk intros would guide her hands down my stomach and along the edge of my waist, teasing as the scherzo passed, traveling the inside of my thigh, yes, then back up and finally making her landing upon the rollicking finale; she would-

A knock on my door interrupts my ceremony. I jolt to shut my computer, leaving it on the cushion next to me as I rush to the bathroom.

There's another knock.

The steam fills the entire bathroom, seeping into the vent on the upper wall. Of course, it connects to Roger and Kate's vent.

Another knock.

I rush for the window. Damnit, why hadn't I opened it before?

Knock. "I'm coming, you fucks," I mutter.

When I open the door, Kate stands with her arms crossed in my doorway. Roger remains a safe distance behind her right shoulder. Her robe sits perfectly on her broad shoulders, draping over her bare, golden skin. The thin fabric highlights her subtle curves. I like the heat coming from her stare – the gaze of authority that dominates with soul bending eyes. Roger appeals to me far less, with his receding hairline, and gray shirt, tight enough to show the seeping layer of extra meat that clings to his love handles. Under his gym shorts, he's no doubt going commando. His man tent is only halfway deflated between his legs, which explains the distance behind Kate.

"What the hell are you cooking in there? We smell something awful in our place." They are a *we* couple. "What the hell is that smell?"

"You guys smell it too?"

"What's that?" She leans to get a glimpse inside my apartment. "Why is there so much steam?"

"I left the water on. Was gonna take a shower. I think there must be a gas leak or something."

Kate doesn't budge. Roger reminds me of the kid on the playground who follows around the bully, casting ugly looks from behind her. I can't help but notice Kate's arms. Toned like copper armor. Her skin, though artificially tanned, seems firm and smooth. A sharp, pencil-thin line outlines her jaw. Roger scratches the loose strands of curly chest hair protruding from his shirt's neckline. He tucks his chin, a bulb of excess weight around his neck as he narrows his eyes at me. I've seen the inside of their apartment. Roger keeps several old photos and trophies from his college sports days. It's like he's held onto the memory of his old life but has abandoned the lifestyle all together.

"You look pale, Roger." I say to him, knowing full well why.

"I'm going to let the building know first thing in the morning. This is the second time this month. The smell is unbearable." Kate works as a lawyer based in the north loop of Chicago but reminds me more of a New York lawyer. More east coast cutthroat than Midwest nice. She pushes back an intruding strand of her raven hair. Straight and shiny, but not greasy, resting over her shoulders and cascading her chest. She gives me a look of disgust as she turns to leave. My mind changes from wanting to go down on her to cutting her face off and wearing it to school for Halloween.

Mr. Walter proves to be a messy cleanup once his body completely melts by Sunday afternoon. The smell remains strong most of the weekend. When I order food on Sunday evening, the delivery man scrunches his nose and rolls his eyes yet tries to catch a glimpse of what could have given off such an odor. By late Sunday night, the shower drain sucks down Mr. Walter's final remains. With the help of some grout cleaner and KABOOM, he leaves behind nothing but the lingering smell of his dissolved parts. I figure far worse sediment falls off a living body, so the bathtub drain could handle it. If it absorbs what falls out of my hair, some melted gut juice is easy.

Danny Hilton

"So, do you know why I asked you to stay after class?"

He sits inaudible at a chair I've pulled out from the front row. I'm sure Danny Hilton thinks he's in trouble. That's usually the case when a teacher requests you stay past the bell. But that's not why. No, it's much worse.

I tried avoiding the sight of it as best I could throughout the day. Scratching my arms, occasionally staring out the window like I'm an addict going through withdrawal. I caught myself forgetting my place in the lesson, distracted by the sight. I avoided looking at my entire class, hoping that by gluing my eyes to the board or the teacher guidebook, I'd be able to focus. But it stared at me, even when I tried refusing to look. Every time I turned my head, it stared back. Not a period went by that it didn't catch my eye.

It's mainly blue, with specks of purple, like spots on a dog's fur, uneven and blotchy, as if paint had dripped onto Danny's face. The black eye stares back at me from 7:45 am until 2:50 pm. It reminds me of a growing lie. A guilt aching revenant of a crime that I haven't felt personally, since I hardly feel remorse for anything I've done, but when something follows in the back of my conscience. A shadow of a memory. A distant voice that only clings to the loose tissue of my mind but is still somehow incredibly unavoidable.

I'm not sure if fear or concern pushes me to ask him to stay once the bell rings. His hands hug his book bag and his eyes wander, as if prolonged eye contact is threatening. Not a far reach. I've killed people for staring too long. It makes me uneasy too.

After a few minutes, I catch myself involuntarily mimicking his own anti-social strategies. Unlike the way I imitate Angela while sitting in the teacher's lounge or at faculty meetings, this is effortless. Natural. I don't try imitating him to appear normal. It just is normal. The avoiding eye contact, bouncing his leg, the fidgeting of his hands. It's like a mirror.

"So, do you know why I asked you to stick around?" I repeat.

He shakes his head, wearing his apprehension like a crown of thorns. I don't want to make him feel uncomfortable, I'm struggling with how to give him a sense of safety.

"I know Mrs. Greene took your notebook last week," I say, pulling the black composition book from the drawer and placing it in front of him. He doesn't touch it. His eyes raise and lower. "Go ahead."

The notebook shoots into his bag faster than a rabbit sprinting to its hole after seeing a hawk. He buries it between his folders and books, zipping the backpack shut the way I had pulled the black bag tightly around Mr. Walter's lifeless feet.

"Your entries are really coming along." That gives him a small spurt of life. His head rises and his eyes widen. No smile just yet. "You know, writing can help get things out. Emotions, feelings, the past." I don't really want to talk about the notebook. All I can do is bite my tongue, eager to question him about his eye.

"You want me to write more about the past?"

"If it's helpful. Or write about the present."

"I'm only eleven."

"Well then maybe just how you feel." I pull my chair. "These notebooks are meant to be private. You can say anything you want and no one can read it. Think of it as top secret."

Sometimes I wonder why you can't split open a skull to learn someone's thoughts. I want to know why he's always alone and how things like his black eye might have occurred. I don't consider it manipulation. I don't care for the kid, but I see a sparkle of myself in his jaded green eyes.

"What if Mrs. Greene takes it again?" he asks.

"You know what happens to people who pry into top secret information?" He responds with a puzzled look on his face.

I widen my eyes and stretch out my neck, wiping my index finger across my throat. "I'm pretty good at making people disappear."

He responds with a meek laugh, and I see his teeth for the first time. A few baby ones still cling to his gums and one of his canines on the bottom shelf is still growing in. I offer a smirk, and finally signal he can leave.

"Thanks Ms. B," he mumbles.

"You can tell me, you know." I point to my own eye and give a subtle grin. "You can trust me."

"It's nothing," he says back, lowering his head. He looks up, biting his bottom lip before speaking again. "Can I go?"

Our eyes meet for a prolonged moment as I give him a delicate nod of permission. An invisible ghost of emotion breathes between us as I lose myself in his pupils. They are like little black pearls in an emerald cloud. Usually, I can't keep eye contact. It makes me feel awkward, unsafe. This is an exception. I can tell a similarity exists, a personal parallel one only finds with a handful of people throughout a lifetime. Why? I need to know why.

He stands up slowly, fastening his bag around his shoulder and easing the chair back to its original place before making his getaway.

"Was it your parents?" I finally blurt. The sting of my own father's hand feels as fresh on my face as the last time he struck me. It was nearly fifteen years ago now, but it feels new. Danny freezes at the door, paralyzed. I've only met his mother briefly in passing. My guess is they are divorced. Danny never mentions his father – or his mother, really – but she picks him up early whenever he has headaches, which he gets often. She strolls in, complaining that he forced her to leave in the middle of work to pick him up. Once, I swear I overheard her telling him to stop faking migraines.

"It's nothing. You aren't going to call them, are you?" he asks, speaking to me, but looking at the floor.

"Danny, it's ok to tell me. Are you worried about tattling? We don't have to call it that. I just want to help." I hate how much I sound like a teacher.

"My parents wouldn't hit me." He inches for the door. In an instant, he disappears amongst the flow of students rushing in the steel lined school hallway.

I intend to follow Danny. Not sure what called my interest, but an obscure curiosity tugs me. After grabbing my things, I lock my door. But before I can pursue, Amir ambushes me.

"Mary Ann Bonny." When he uses my full name, he always says it the same way. He prolongs the long A in Mary, half singing my name and half calling me out like a scolding parent. He enjoys giving everyone a quirky nickname. He calls Sonya, J, because no one can pronounce her last name. Douglass is Big D. Angela, well, Angela doesn't really have one. Always Mrs. Greene—an emphasis on the Mrs.—or Mrs. Angela Greene, never just Angela.

Amir stands in the hallway, beckoning me to go with him. He lacks the usual buttery smile as his foot taps against the tile. I don't give any excuse to escape, nor do I have one. Plus, I fear I know what he wants.

I follow Amir to his office. We pass Sonya's room, where I catch her eyes before she averts them towards her purse. My mind rushes to conclusions. She told Amir I stole chemicals from the science lab. Her science lab. Had she seen me? Had they known the whole time as we laughed at happy hour that I had contraband from the school's science lab in my bag? How could they have? How could she?

No, I think to myself. No, I'm being paranoid. I'm being crazy, I am not crazy, there is no way they know about the chemicals. No way they know about Mr. Walter and his many sins that forced me to remove him from this earth. He made that choice to hire a prostitute online. He deserved death and I issued it. That's all. I just carried out the sentence he made for himself, a punishment worthy of its recipient. If anything, those chemicals were given real purpose. A pure purpose. It was an act of justice, actually. One I do not regret.

In his office, Amir catches his breath, hesitating to speak for a few moments. He scratches his head and shifts in his chair, far from the usual calm and collected principal.

"So," he finally begins. "Tell me, Bonny, what is your position on stealing?"

He is very still, and I am very uneasy. My foot taps first, then my leg follows the anxious strain and thumps, faster and faster until it bounces rapidly.

"I - I don't know what you mean?"

"Stealing," he says, a direct drop in his tone. "What do you think about it?"

"It's wrong."

"Good answer, that makes this easy." His head rolls back. Is he stretching his neck or searching for the proper way to deliver my sentence?

"So why," he stares just past me, his eyes absent and avoiding my own, staring out into the lobby of his office. "Why do people steal when they know it's wrong?"

"I can't say. People do things. Things they wish they didn't do… but are necessary."

"Necessary? This crime is hardly necessary."

"I'm sorry, sir, I'm not following."

"My pens."

"Your pens?"

"Yes, my pens. Every morning, I set my pens at my desk, lining them up like so," I watch as he arranges four pens laid out between a small Moleskine notebook and his computer keyboard. "You see, one, two, three, four." He straightens each pen as he counts. "Three black, one blue. Now, for the past few weeks, Mrs. Baxterly has repeatedly come into my office and taken one of my pens. Today, I saw her from this very desk using one of my pens while she was on the phone to scratch her head."

"Mr. Salem, if they are just pens, then -"

"They aren't just pens! They are MY pens! They are expensive, they are not a secretary's pens, they are an administrator's pens. I have given Mrs. Baxterly pens, but she loses them. They are probably caught up in her big Wisconsin hairdo!" The more flustered he becomes, the more he rises, until he's fully standing, pressing hard on top of the wooden desk. "I don't know. I gave her money last week to go buy some of her own. Do you know what she came back with? Take a guess."

"Not pens?"

"Pencils."

"What's wrong with pencils?"

"They make a mess, plus I don't want to hear her sharpening them every 25 minutes. That would make someone go insane, Miss Bonny, insane! Think about it, I could be on the phone with a big-time donor or hysterical parent, and in the background is the buzzing of a pencil sharpener! That can't be! It's unacceptable. I already have to listen to her making phone calls. She talks and talks and goes on and on. She noses into my personal life, too, asking about my family and if I got a dog yet. Amir falls into his seat. The sweat smells as it seeps from the nervous pores along his skin. The whole glass encased room feels humid and close.

"Mr. Salem." He masks his face with his palm.

"Yes?"

"Are you sure everything is alright? It seems like this is more than just about pens?"

"Yes… I mean, well, look." Another sigh as he runs his hands through his hair, returning the unruly strands to their place. His dormant computer screen serves as a vanity mirror. "It's a lot of responsibility, being a principal. You have the students and the parents, but the faculty…ugh, what a mess. They are the real challenge. Squabbles and drama. This school especially – I have never seen such a rabble of horny bunnies. It's like every week I have someone in here to sign a new sexual nondisclosure or some papers to avoid being sued. Anyway, I'm rambling. I need someone. I need someone to lighten the load. And you've probably noticed since you arrived that I abstain from having a vice principal."

"Until now?"

"Yes. The job is too big. I need someone to hold back the storm of teachers and keep junk off my desk. I don't want to deal with teachers bitching about not having enough supplies or claiming they had something stolen from their rooms or what not." He gathers himself. "Sometimes, I'm not gonna lie, I feel like their babysitter. Look, my priority is to make this place the best for our students and the parents. I wanted to let you know that I am considering you... as a potential candidate... for the vice principal position." As he points at me, I notice the uneven teeth marks on his fingernails.

"You want me to be your VP?"

He sits back in his chair, recovering from his performance. He seems far away, much farther than before. Another sigh, more comfortable as he nestles into the leather like a baby blanket.

"I am considering you as a candidate, yes."

"But why? I don't have administrative experience."

"No, but let's face it, the other teachers seem to like you, and your students all love you. I called the references you gave me from that school you used to teach at, what was it? Somewhere in Ohio?"

"Minnesota."

He sits up again, taking a moment to shift to a more 'professional' looking position.

"Minnesota, right. Well, yes, I called– well I had Mrs. Baxterly call, but she couldn't get ahold of anyone...figures, she probably dialed the wrong number again. She said I should give it a try, but then I figured why make the call behind your back. I know you well enough now, so I want to be straightforward. You've been here for only a quarter, I know, but I'm a good read on character and ability. And I've never had a problem with you. Plus,

I think it's best to evaluate a person on their present work, don't you?"

"Absolutely."

"So, you will consider?"

"Am I being offered the job?"

"God, no, I am letting you know you are a candidate." A crack sounds as he opens a can of Diet Coke. I guess from the ring stain on his desk that it had been sitting there for a few hours waiting to be opened.

"Who else is being considered?" My eyes remain stuck on the stain. Doesn't he have coasters? Nope. It's strange that someone so neurotic about his own pens ruins his desk so inadvertently. Perhaps he hasn't noticed yet, or the pens preoccupied his mind so much that he's failing to register it. He is probably cursing himself inside for ruining a perfectly good desk but refuses to let it be known that he had made any sort of mistake or neglected the sweating soda can.

"Well, Angela Greene, for one. She would be a good fit, don't you think?"

"Angela is quite… authoritative." Please, no.

"She would make the other teachers fall in line no doubt."

Just as he finally notices the ring stain, uselessly wiping at it, the door opens behind me.

"Mr. Salem?" Mrs. Baxterly's voice. "Phone call." Her pine scented perfume lights up the room, homemade of course, probably from some cabin or waterfall resort town that she and her husband visit twice a year. She loves to brag about her timeshare on Lake Michigan and always shows us photos of her nieces and nephews on their big family trips to the Wisconsin Dells. My guess is she's been at Pearcey long before Amir Salem arrived. I doubt he has the stomach to fire someone who yes, steals his pens, but also fills every candy bowl in the office with seasonal favorites, who never forgets a birthday, and who has so many pictures of young and newborn family members from her big midwestern tribe that he can't look her in the eyes and say, "You're fired." She's a lifer. A secretary who will live long past the reign of principals and administrators, maybe even board members, and especially parents. She knows too much to be fired and released onto the rumor factory of Chicago suburbs. Teachers are indispensable, but a good secretary is an ace in the hole, and a bad one can be your worst nightmare.

She waddles into the room. I wonder how much of our exchange she has been able to hear from the other side of the thin glass walls— how much of every exchange she listens in on.

"I'm not sure if I would be a good fit as vice principal," I say as he struggles to connect to the phone call, rushing me out.

"Look, take a day or two and let me know. I plan on making my decision by the first parent teacher conference. It's a few weeks anyways, so there is plenty of time to convince me."

"Convince you of what?"

"Of what makes you a good candidate."

"And if I don't want to be considered?"

"Up to you. But then you'll report to Angela Greene." I shudder at the thought.

Teachers and students still linger on school grounds by the time I walk outside. From the top of the steps, I scan the pick-up line and the clusters of kids and parents while I try to gather myself. The thought of working for Angela Greene is, well… unsettling, to say the least. I don't consider her an enemy, although I worry about her intentions whenever she asks about my old teaching job or background. It's always an interrogation with her. If she becomes vice principal, would I be out? Would she dig deep enough to find out about me? Would she uncover the truth?

I notice Danny Hilton trot towards the end of the sidewalk to a bike rack. He stops, dropping his bag from his shoulder and kneeling in front of his tire.

I move closer, tugged by the curiosity that purges reason from my mind. Why do I care about this kid? Sure, I'm his teacher, and I invest in my students. But I care more about doing a good job so that I can teach. So that I go unnoticed. So that I blend in.

Even though it offers some consolation of accomplishment, I worry. Every year brings new faces, new personalities, and new problems, or at least it seems like that. Every year I connect with my class just to see them move on and forget about me the next year, even though they'll be just down the hall. After a while, they eventually blend together. They become the same kid, the same year. I won't be teaching twenty or so individuals or molding the identity of two dozen children to be unique humans, empowered to express themselves. I will stand before one massive nucleus. One blanket identity interlocking each body from the front row all the way to the back. Each class will be one homologous repetition. And so I will grow old routinely grading, attending meetings, disciplining behavior, riding a carousel of mundanity - going around and around, growing more insane each year while the children all stay the same. Will I end up a lifer like Mrs. Baxterly? Or worse, turn into a version of Angela Greene?

Danny seems to break that worry. He's different. I suppose that difference is why students do things to him like punch him in the eye and slash his bike tires. Difference is what molded me into me. Danny jams the machine and halts its cyclical routine.

"Got a flat?" I ask him.

Danny is still on his knees, staring at the pavement and sulking before his bike as if in front of a tombstone. The front tire presses on the deflated rubber, and shred marks line the black rim along the sides. Not a natural flat. The tire has a puncture wound. A few actually. I guess whoever did this had a few laughs while slamming the knife or fork or whatever weapon of choice used to deflate Danny's day.

Lowering myself beside Danny, I survey the parking lot and school entrance as kids rush into their parents' cars, line up for the school buses, and congregate into cliques for a final chatter or playdate scheming session before heading home. Staring into the sea of pubescence, I try catching a glimpse of someone smiling amongst their gang of fellow mischievous runts, slapping hands or pumping fists as they triumph over poor Danny. It's probably a good thing I don't see anyone suspicious. I might hand Danny off only to get his ass kicked again, because I would surely suggest that he take his revenge. I am trying to think of a more diplomatic method.

Nope, nothing.

Danny's sniffle draws my attention from my recon. He wipes a stray tear from his eyes and hides his face in his shoulder. Not sure if he's more upset about how he will get home or about the damage to his bike.

Poor kid.

I offer to walk him home. He isn't much of a talker, so the stroll is composed of silence and a metronome of our shoes clicking against the sidewalk. The bike gives out rusty metal groans as we walk it between us. The surrounding city life plays over a musical soundtrack of car engines, humming sewers, and distant trains. Most kids commute from the suburbs to Pearcey Elementary, but a handful, like Danny, live in the city. There is something about the kids who live downtown. They're more independent, a little more savvy. They've seen things, lived a certain lifestyle that only people who were born and raised in the leviathan of high rises can understand.

Danny doesn't ride his bike to school every day, so I'm right about his parents. One must drive him on certain days. His mom probably lives in Evanston or a Northern suburb. I figure our destination is his father's place as we walk down Rush Street into Gold Coast. We pass by the designer streets and high-end restaurants of Viagra Triangle where wealthy men show off their $2,000 per hour escort one night, and then bring their wife the next. A hundred-dollar bill keeps the maître d's in this town quiet. I never come here with a man. There are too many eyes. Too many who might see a photo of me and put me at the scene. I'm careful. Viagra Triangle is the last place I agree to let clients take me.

Danny stops in front of a building with red awnings and a gothic exterior. A spire points from the top and gargoyles stare like a sentry of ghouls from above the pointed arches. We don't reach the front doorway yet, but Danny stops, just before stepping onto the stretching new driveway that loops to the main entrance.

"Is this it?" I ask. The building surely receives an interior renovation each year or so but retains its old-school wealthy flair, the doorman to welcome residents, the golden mailbox wall where they are greeted by another staff member, in what I guess is a dark green uniform with gold trimming and a name plate. Then they'll buzz the person to their floor, in a rackety metal, cage elevator. A comfort lies in the ways of old. Especially for the wealthy.

The door attendant notices us. He lights up when he sees Danny.

"Yes," Danny says, looking at me. "Thanks for walking me home."

"Is your dad here?"

"No. He gets home late. Thanks again, Miss B."

"Outside of school, you can call me Ann."

He nods and starts towards the door, walking his bike at his side. The doorman rushes to Danny's aid, his dark skin glowing against his uniform. Green and gold as I predicted. He gives Danny a pleasant smile and a, "How are you today, young sir?"

Danny of course does not answer.

"Wait, Danny." I rush over to him. The doorman walks away with the bike, and gives me a quick studying glance, probing my face like a robot. I don't like it. The way his eyes scan over me, collecting data for a hard drive of humans he stores in his mind. Danny shuffles towards me, stuffing his hands into the pockets of his zip-up hoodie. I open up my bag and pull out a book. The Count of Montecristo.

He takes the novel in his hands, pausing with interest.

"Is this for class?"

"No, Danny. I think it might be something you will enjoy. Don't mention it to any of the other kids in class though; I don't want them to know I'm playing favorites."

He looks up to me for a second, his eyes widening and his small dimple slightly showing.

I bend down to meet his level. "If you ever need to talk, I'm around, ok? But if you can't say it out loud, then write it in your journal. But this book here, this might give you something to think about next time someone treats you badly, ok?"

"OK, but what do you mean?"
"The bully always gets what is coming to him." Always.

Mr. Big

He'll be here any minute.

It's Wednesday night and I stand outside of a motel with a cigarette between my fingers, waiting for my newest client.

I'm wearing a pair of bright red Louboutin pumps and a snug pink wig that reaches my jawline. After hours in front of my mirror, I've achieved the appearance of a twenty-one-year-old. I'm playing a college junior at DePaul University trying to pay my way through my fall quarter, saving up for that once in a lifetime opportunity to study abroad in Rome: artistic, kinky, and down for anything. My fake profile also mentions I allow men to eat candy out of my pussy. Needless to say, I keep a hidden switchblade masked as lipstick in my clutch, just in case he brings his own M&M's.

Every drag helps ease the nerves, soothes the excitement. I'm not anxious, but I boil with anticipation, waiting for that curtain call.

I'm not the only one who subtly enjoys the ruse. Clients like "Mr. Big" love being serviced by working girls in college. It gives them a sense of power, like they are single handedly putting me through school with four generous strokes of their hips and a small white puddle of their dignity sprayed on my chest. The less sick ones prefer girls over twenty, but I've come across a few men who get off making a minor cry. Admittedly, most twenty-one-year-olds don't have vintage Porsches that they can drive to Rogers Park to meet a man for sex.

I guess I'm the exception.

When a black Lincoln SUV pulls up to the lot, I know he's arrived. I toss my cigarette onto the ground and smush it into a flat heap of ash with the toe of my shoe. He climbs out from the back seat. He looks well into his forties, despite his nice build. He has a tight face and salt and pepper hair neatly trimmed with a taper on the sides. A small gray stubble coats his sharp jaw and runs over his chin and around his mouth, seasoning his strong face with experience. He reminds me of Uncle Jones. The casual proper look. No tie, jeans and sport coat. Even with his addictions and abuse, Uncle Jones kept his low-key, I-don't-give-a-shit-but-I take-care-of-business look. With the drugs he had done, his cheeks should've been swallowed in his skull and his eyelids soft, tired half-moons. But his forehead never creased, his eyes didn't crack, and his hair, minus his receding hairline, never shed. I guess that's the difference between cocaine and heroin. Regardless, Mr. Big has the look. It intrigues me when men clearly handsome enough to earn sex lower themselves to buying it.

Ordering an escort is as easy as ordering a pizza. People sit at their computer, log into a site that promises something they can't go find themselves, and in a few clicks, their humanity dies.

Most of these sites have the girls create certain attributes that portray the ideal escort for a man looking to purchase a human for a few short hours. I provide an optional backstory, my age, height, and all that fun stuff like cup size. It also asks what type of "activities" I enjoy most: positions, meeting spots, fantasies, kinks, and secret desires. I become a fleshy checklist for whatever sicko clicks my profile. I never include that I'm a talker. Some men enjoy just sitting at the end of a bed and venting. Prostitutes double as therapists, providing a physical or emotional release for men too scared or too incapable to do it any other way. The clients are, for the most part, monsters. But every now and then I'll get a man in real pain. Mr. Big, however, is the former.

When I see him, I know I made the right choice when I listed "looking for a man who likes being tied up" on the profile. He wears his suit like a rhino draped in linen. He walks over to me and his arm swallows me as he wraps it around my shoulder, guiding me to the motel room.

The room has a double bed, a nightstand with a blindingly orange lamp, and a television coated with scuff marks along the sides. The bathroom sink doesn't have any soap, and the shower is half the size of my bathtub at my apartment. Anything about this sound romantic? But that isn't what guys like Mr. Big want or offer. They want to show they are in charge. They want to slam a girl down and pin her face into the mattress until her nose bleeds and her head goes black with cloudy consciousness while he rams her from behind. Not me, though. I take charge.

I had set up the room before we went inside, tying a belt to the head posts and sailing rope for his feet at the end of the bed. I'm no novice. At this point, it's routine for me.

"So, you're Mr. Big?" I chew on my pinky finger and rub my tongue along the edge of my bottom lip. I remove his jacket and let it fall on the floor. "Is that what you want me to call you?"

"Yes," he says. His hands are sandpaper rubbing along my waist and up my shoulder blades. His large fingers tighten as he makes his way to the back of my neck.

"You can call me Chastity." The names are not all winners, but these guys seldom give a shit what I want to be called as long as I refer to them by whatever ego boosting or chauvinistic alias they bestow on themselves.

"Call me Mr. Big." His hand wraps around my neck and his thumb anchors like a hook in the side of my mouth. "Say it."

"Mr. Big," I use a voice I mimic from Natalie Portman. I can't remember the movie, but she inspired my look for the evening so I figure I might as well give her a shout.

"Say it again," his head cocks back, his chin nearly smacking my face. This time I play around, inching the words out and hissing on the "s" in mister.

My mouth hangs open, playing with him as I run my tongue along the wall of my bottom teeth and then my upper lip. I rub the edge of his pants, caressing my way between his legs where I realize he is anything but "Big."

I won't lie. I enjoy sex. I usually make a decision within the first few minutes to wait until before or after they come to finish the job. Sometimes I figure they actually know what they are doing and get off twice in a night. Other times I take pity and don't let them die with blue balls. Sixty-forty, I guess.

Once I nearly brought a man to climax right before I ended him. I had him blind folded while going down on him. Just as he announced his brewing orgasm, I slit his throat. But then he blasted on my face with his final breath. Sweet release indeed.

"You want to get more comfortable?" I nod to my set-up on the bed. He pays no attention. At first, I wonder if he ignores the notion, or hasn't heard me. He dives headfirst, wrapping his arms around me from behind and squeezing everything he can get his hands on, heaving me against the TV dresser. My knee cracks against one of the drawer knobs. I wince, but he keeps going, pressing me up on the wooden furniture set. He starts kissing the back of my neck and works my skirt, yanking the seam until it rolls along my waist. I cringe from the loud snap as he tears my panties.

At first, I play along, rubbing the back of his head as he removes his belt. "Let me tie you down," I say, clinging to the remains of my sexy voice.

But he's assiduously horney, devouring me in an eager attempt at forced entry.

"Hey, hey," I turn to him, catching a whiff of salty breath as he pants, his forehead pressing against mine. He looks about to burst, adorned with swollen neck veins and a sweating forehead. "Slow down, alright? Now tell me, what do you want me to do for you?" I caress his cheeks, rocking my hips in a circular motion.

"I want you to stop talking so much. Shut up, will ya? I'm paying you to be pretty, not speak." He snatches my shoulders and propels me against the dresser. I catch myself and prop upright in front of the TV. In the black mirror of the television, I see the tiny-dicked monster who calls himself Mr. Big behind me. He pins me down with one hand while he shuffles his pants off. Not the type to remove his shirt during sex. I reach for the TV and pull it from the dresser, allowing myself to fall forward as I throw the television screen back. My face plummets into the edge of the wood. Everything turns black.

I wake to a throbbing headache and gray specks dancing in my vision. After a second or two, I can see straight again. Beside me lies Mr. Big, unconscious. The television's pieces are scattered across the floor, and a few fragments of glass stuck in his head.

No, I think. No, he can't be. I check his pulse. Good, still alive. I want this one to be awake for his end.

I manage to lift Mr. Big from the floor and roll his body onto the mattress. Luckily, the frame is lower to the ground than most motel beds. I leave him pantless and strap him down by the wrists and the ankles as I had originally planned. With Mr. Big secure, and still knocked out, I slip out of the room to the Porsche where I keep another set of clothes, a trash bag— the extra-large kind that doesn't tear —and a bow saw.

The thing is, without me, this man would still be at large. Without me, he would still be assaulting minors and getting away with it. Without me, he would continue buying young prostitutes, shoving them against dressers and nightstands, until one day he'd push too hard and she'd hit her head and die. Someone will end up like Kitty. Without me, this man won't be stopped.

Killing him saves others from this man. It's up to me.

I'm careful. Sharp as a cocked revolver. I'm meticulous, dismembering the body so neatly, chopping the corpse limb for limb. I start with his arms. First the left. Then the right, sawing through where the shoulder meets the collarbone, making sure no blood will be left for someone to even notice he was murdered. To them, he'll have simply vanished.

His legs follow. I saw them into two pieces, once at the knees and then again where the thigh meets the hip. The duct tape muffles the screams for the most part. It only lasts a few minutes. Once he runs out of enough blood, the pleas and shaking lessen to a mere twitch in his feet (which end once I chop them off). I leave his head for last. Once I completely dismember him, I stuff the separate pieces into the trash bag and head for the car.

The night has gone quiet. Peaceful. The lights on Lakeshore Drive whiz by like angels flashing past my windows as I cruise back into downtown. On one side sits Lake Michigan, calm, serene and black under the overcasting night sky. The city on my right stands electric, quiet at 3 am, but I get a buzz just by looking at the vibration of the pulsating heart of the city. It has a soul of its own, pumping a million lights that glitter against the skyline like diamonds.

I have to go through the alley to get to my building's freight elevator. The parking garage has cameras, and the desk attendant, Amanda, a heavy-set woman who knows every face and remembers every name, will surely have questions seeing me drag a mammoth-sized trash bag through the lobby. She will notice, and worse, remember. And that's all I need, another large person to make disappear.

I pull around to the alley between my apartment complex and an equally high office building. A few restaurants use the bottom floors, tossing their trash late at night into hefty dumpsters lining each building in the alley. It isn't incriminating to be seen dragging a large black bag through the steamy narrow alley where cat-sized rats inhabit every corner.

The freight elevator ordinarily processes oversized deliveries and movers. Luckily for me, it comes in handy quite often. It operates as the direct line for transporting death. When I get to the elevator, I check the bag to make sure it doesn't tear or leave behind a trail of blood. My throat heaves when I reach the elevator and press the button. My arms between my shoulder and my elbow are tense like a stretched rubber band and my hands ache like they'd been left out in a frozen winter chill. I plan to bring him into my apartment and keep him in an ice-bath until I can get more chemicals from school. His limbs will keep just fine and I can fit a few pieces of him in my freezer. I don't use it for anything except ice cream anyways. The elevator stops on floor thirteen. Finally. When I flick on my lights, I see a slip of paper at my feet in the doorway. It has the word MANAGEMENT on the top left corner.

Dear Residents,
We aim to provide a healthy, comfortable living situation for all our tenants and appreciate when improvements or issues are brought to the management's attention. Please be informed that we will be conducting a precautionary gas leak inspection of all units from 8 am until 3 pm tomorrow, Thursday, September 30th.
Thank you
Management Team

Shit.

Teacher Coffee

This isn't the plan.

My knuckles whiten around the steering wheel as I peer at Pearcey's empty campus. It looks more like an asylum than an elementary school at four in the morning.

If Mr. Big hadn't put up such a struggle, I would be clearer of mind. The bump on my head still aches, my arms are sore, and the clock on my dash ticks closer to the start of the school day while the corpse parts in my trunk begin to smell. There's growing pains in any fresh enterprise. But I'm calculating. Let me assure you this: I'm not rash. I'm not impulsive. Nothing about this has ever been impulsive. It's always been perfectly planned.

At least in my head.

I should've just burned him on the border of Wisconsin. Not enough time. I'm not going to let "Mr. Small"—as I begin mocking him in my head—ruin my streak. No, he's got to go. I just need the right way to send him off.

I could leave him in the car? Not an option. I want the Porsche safe and limb free in the underground garage as soon as possible.

4:42 am, still not a teacher in sight. The first of them don't usually arrive until closer to six. If they see my car, there will be more questions than if I walk into the police station right now and announce I have the severed limbs of a small-dicked man who called himself Mr. Big in my trunk.

The September morning air stings like a bee swirling in my nose. I haven't looked in a mirror yet, but when I step out of the car, I immediately feel the cool breeze against the drying blood on my forehead.

Morning brings a certain serenity. Especially after a kill. The sun barely sheds through the cloudy sky. I take a moment to admire the leaves that have started to fall. They remind me of orange and red ash descending from a burning mantel. October nears, and the air's pleasant chill will soon turn into a frigid gust.

I'm not sure how it happened, but Mr. Big gained weight overnight. At least that's how it feels dragging his remains out of my trunk and into the school hallway. The creak of rusty hinges lags like a faint scream from the empty rows of lockers. No students. No teachers. I saunter, alone, through the forest of dark classroom doors. The still drying floor lets out an exhaust of dried bleach from the late-night mop. The tiles squeak as I inch across with the minced corpse that ruffles behind.

The empty halls lack the beat of lockers closing underneath a melody of backpack zippers and high-pitched laughs. I relish the silence that lulls before the manic school day morning.

Life is really just one school morning. A symphony of noise and confusion while people take part in the same melodramatic cycle. They try to customize themselves with pictures on their lockers, colored backpacks, and new shoes. Adults are no different. They buy something like a car to make them feel special. Something that aligns with their taste or produces an image of their individuality. But to no avail, they end up in traffic. Waiting in line with the rest of those 'unique' people going from their same starting point to their same ending point. The object of their individuality does nothing but send them straight to the noose of conformity. They are hamsters spinning in a nonsensical circle. They go from home to work, from work to home in a current amidst the others trying to stand out, yearning to be accepted, yet ultimately just blending in with the uniformity. Until one day they die. A meaningless, tiresome sequence filled with people who want so desperately to stand out, that they are blind to the mundane purgatory they exist in until death.

Danny comes back into my mind as I reach the outside of my classroom, fumbling with my keys to open the door and hide the bag. He seems to be the only kid I've encountered who might possibly avoid that cycle. If it's true, the black eye is the least of his worries.

Once in my classroom, I lock the door and stuff the bag into a bolted closet where I keep a few extra supplies for in and out of school. I struggle, considering his weight equals a wild boar. I slump onto the floor, my back resting against the closet. A warm stream trickles from the top of my eye. Shit, my head has reopened from lifting and pressing that damn bag. I dip my fingers in the fresh blood on my forehead, wiping it on my black track pants. The ticking clock across the room reminds me I don't have time to rest.

I rush out of my classroom, locking both it and the closet, and sprint through the hallway to get the Porsche home safely and maybe if time allows, clean my head before getting back to school by 6:30 am.

I reach my apartment by 6:01 am. I luck out. Not a drop of blood had spilled in my trunk. I would rather clean up an entire motel room than have to scrub the back of that Porsche, again. Once I get to my room, I undress and check on my face. Not too bad, just a small sliver on the tender flesh above my right eye.

Blood trickles from my face, collecting around the drain on the shower floor. The water warms my skin and wakes me up like a recharged battery. Once dried off, I take out a bottle of hydrogen peroxide, a few gauze strips, and cotton balls from my medicine cabinet. I dunk the cotton in the hydrogen peroxide and neatly wipe the cut. The chemical stings, but the face I see in the mirror doesn't flinch. My heartbeat's steady, and my mind clear. Or just empty. With the excess blood gone and the cut clean, it's barely a quarter inch long. If I worked anywhere else, I'd slip on a pair of big sunglasses and blame it on tequila, but I don't have that option as an elementary teacher. I press the gauze strips neatly on the cut to keep it from reopening and pause as I revisit my reflection in the mirror to put on my modest make-up.

Every time I paint my face in mascara and blush, I see someone else; building a costume to disguise a person that is just not me. I don't recognize the idea of what 'me' even is. There is no me. Only what I portray. The sex worker. The elementary teacher. Those aren't who I am. If not them, who am I? The killer? I like the sound of that, since my desire for blood and violence seems to be the only thing I long to quench. But it's a thirst I cannot control. An appetite I cannot satiate. It seems to be the only antiseptic for my insane, chaotic mind. I'm a lost ship, struggling to balance a storm. Is killing the only thing keeping me afloat? If I stop, I worry I'll sink.

Maybe I want to.

"Hi class, today we are going to go over the difference between an adverb and an adjective." I give a big smile in the mirror. "What's that Rebecca? Correct. Quick is an adjective. Do you know what the adverb form would be?" I do my best to sound light, to sound innocent and bubbly, the way a young fifth grade teacher is supposed to sound. "Quickly. Good job." Then my face falls off. Replaced with my pale complexion that governs my true self. "Don't you dare raise your hand until I'm finished speaking!" Now the soft, smiling Ann, the bright Miss B, returns. "That is quite alright, Jonathan. You will get it next time... Jessica! Sit up straight!" I glare at myself, tightroping some sort of sanity and madness. I can stand here all day. Silent, only myself. Myself, and whoever stares back at me.

I still have Kitty's old pills in the medicine cabinet. The clear orange bottles with her name, her real name, typed in black next to the words either Ativan or Haldol, along the prescribed dose that she rarely followed to hold back her anxiety. Though she refused to take them, I find them often helpful. I have this recurring pain in my head. A chirp in the back of my skull.

Kitty had told me that the pills aren't for every day. She had instructed that they were only for when the breathing exercises she learned from an unlicensed therapist lost the battle between her soothed disposition and what I referred to as 'the shakes'. I have the shakes far more than she used to, so she would make me take her pills. I can't tell if I enjoy them or not. I never shake more than when I do take them. But as I stand before the bathroom mirror, thinking of Mr. Big's body in my classroom, Kate and her ill-timed call to the building management, Angela Greene and her snooping, and my hand, fidgeting as I attempt to grip the rim of the sink; my mouth waters to crunch down on a few of them.

After chewing down a modest bunch, I gargle with the faucet water and swallow to rinse down the remaining shards of pills. I never swallow them whole. I turn from the mirror and quickly slip into the outfit I had left on my bed, folded at the end of the neatly pressed comforter; a white button down and black pants with a trench coat to cover up.

My phone says 6:45 am as I step up to the front entrance of Pearcey. The parking lot already spurs with life. The school buses spit out kids one by one. The congregating cliques and friend groups savor the few minutes of freedom before class. The drop-off is already congested as parents, lined up in their cars, dump their kids to the trusted care of un-qualified educators.

Since I had no time earlier, I go to the teachers' lounge for a caffeinated pick me up. There are two types of teachers. Those who drink tea and those who drink coffee. I don't like being in either group. I don't joke around in the morning holding some themed mug with cat ears or a mustache on the lip. Nor do I feel the need to show my co-workers that I have been to Los Angeles and had the coffee mug to prove it. I don't care about the quality beans or the tea leaves from India that invigorate your soul and cleanse your insides. The only thing I know that can clean a human's insides is a drill. Straight up the nose and into the brain. Done. No clean up, everything wiped like an erased hard drive.

I never want to be a teacher with a "thing" at Pearcey. Mr. Richardson is the "tie guy," always wearing a new one with a subtle dry joke on it or a goofy pattern or holiday (all holidays) themed print. He's still single, of course. Sonya's the flirt, Douglass the rogue (and the plug), Nick the soft spoken, handsome guy, Angela the bossy bitch. Mrs. Bridenbaugh is the "dinosaur" (which no one called her to her face), Mr. Henry is the one who always gets sick, and so on and so on.

It has started to be a "thing," however, that I'm the one never around. A "thing" I do not intend on keeping. I try to stay clear of the teachers' lounge. I avert empty conversation about what talk show host is banging his secretary or whatever social media has created a fluster about this week. I don't notice when women get a new hairstyle, and I'm not about to compliment a man's tie.

I first expected the teachers' lounge to be a hub of educational debate, or at least some type of watering hole to discuss students and curriculum, but it ended up being nothing more than a shrink's waiting room, filled with people eager to vent about how shitty the school or their lives had become.

The middle school teachers always arrive first. Hard workers, driven, and passionate. The elementary next, fresh, and praying for a calm day. The high school teachers come in their own wave, last of course. Their earthy toned colors, scruffy beards to make them feel like college professors. 'If I wanted to teach at the university I would.' So they claim. They spend the least amount of time in the lounge, lingering in their respective classrooms from sunup to sundown. Their caves. Their "office".

When I walk in, Sonya and Douglass are sitting together. Angela sits across from them but not "with" them. She hacks at a stack of quizzes with a red pen, her favorite object in the world. She never lets anyone borrow it, not even to write a quick note. They always have gatherings before work. Reminiscing about the bar they went to the previous night or gossiping about students. It's 'this kid this' and 'this student that' and 'Oh my god did you know her mother is so and so?' Today Douglass doesn't even try to hide his early morning jawing. He grazes his bottom lip with his teeth, then grounds his rear molars together, shaking his bottom jaw like he needs a reminder it was still connected to his skull.

"Ann Bonny is in the lounge everyone!" Sonya calls out. She waves, beckoning me to join them. I offer a nod back, keeping my presence as little known as I can.

I try masking my coffee with chocolate milk. The bitter taste still lingers. More sugar? Still bad.

I search through the cabinets. The off-putting cream color looks like mustard compared to the blue countertops. The whole lounge smells of popcorn and coffee grounds. Excess mugs sit in the sink. Spilled beans on the edge of the counter collect small bugs that line the sharp edges of the cabinets to feast on the fallen sugar swatted onto the floor instead of wiped with a paper towel. These are the habits of the people teaching your children, I think to myself. Gossiping sociopaths who leave the microwave dirty and their dishes unrinsed in the sink.

I empty the remains of a sugar can, the store-bought kind made from some cardboard-like material. I don't want to be seen as the last person using it, so I keep it close to my chest, shuffle over to the trash can and drop it inside.

"Mary Ann Bonny." Ann, you fuck.

Amir stands in the teachers' lounge doorway. If anyone despises the lounge more than me, it's our fearless leader Amir Salem. He knows these teachers treat their lounge like a frat house instead of a respectable employee communal area, so he keeps in his office, where he has his own lounge.

Amir's usually dark, jolly complexion has whitened. Is he upset or heartbroken? He remains in the doorway, making sure not to take a single step inside the lounge, as if the floor would contaminate him on impact.

"Come with me," he says, signaling with a wave. Amir never really raises his voice. He's the "friend first" kind of principal. You know, the type of friend who says they love you but never comes to your house. Not unless there's a fire at his."You need to see this," he says, closing the door behind me. His hand touches my lower back, the way a friend guides someone to show them their dog was just hit by a car or that they found something of great importance. It's neither of those things.

I know something has gone wrong when we walk down the hall and there's a group of students congregating around my door. They circle, staring at the ground as if they'd found a diamond hidden in a sandbox. But it's not a diamond. It's a trail of blood, seeping from under my classroom door.

"Any idea what this is?"

Sugar and Dust

"Ok kids nothing to see here," Amir says, shoving through.

All I can think is that it's over. It's all over. How can I be so careful and let this happen? This isn't like me. I'm smarter than this. Well then, I can get out of it. I just need a reason. Sure, an honest excuse. Just as long as Amir doesn't open the closet.

I can get out of this.

On the other side of the four-foot-high crowd, the janitor waits on command with his mop and bucket ready.

Shit. The fucking bag. It must have ripped. God damnit that fucking bitch of a bag.

Amir wedges himself between the circle of kids and the puddle, trying to block them from seeing it. Why do they need to be sheltered from even the sight of blood? Most of these kids see their fair share in movies and definitely pretend to kill people in video games. Why is the real thing any worse?

"Miss Bonny," he repeats.

I keep a straight face, as if it's natural to have the Nile River of blood flowing from your classroom door.

"I hit a deer," I finally say.

"What?"

"A deer." Still no change in my tone. "I was driving home last night, and it ran right in front of me."

"Go to your lockers," he orders the students, looking around for any faculty back up. He turns back to me. "I'm not sure I get what you're saying."

"You don't get what a deer is?"

He points to my classroom, signaling me to go inside. I unlock the door and open it wide enough for only Amir and me to fit through. He follows, stepping over the blood and into the classroom. Now we might have a problem. I lock the door again once both of us enter.

"What the hell is wrong with you, Ann?" He walks towards my closet, following the trail of blood.

No, stop. Don't open the closet.

"Just let me clean it." He freezes. "I didn't know what to do," I say. "I panicked. I hit the thing. My phone died so I had to flag down a tow truck and then he told me I should hang onto it for insurance."

"Really?" he says, turning his head around. "You couldn't just take a few photos? You had to bring it here? This is going to be a disaster if parents find out?" He waves his arms, shaking his head. "Why'd you bring it here?" He steps again– right for the closet. Right for Mr. Big.

"My place is getting fumigated." There, a little dash of truth might help the recipe.

"I want to see it."

All I can think of is what happens if he opens that closet door. There's no window big enough for me to climb through. No escape. Will I have to kill him? I grab a freshly sharpened pencil from my desk… just in case.

"It's really gross. Please don't make me take it out. I felt so bad for the thing. I couldn't just leave him."

"I'll get Ernie. He can get rid of it. Ugh what a terrible smell."

It really is an awful smell. Amir plugs his nose as he closes in, an arm's distance from the closet door. I step closer to him. The pencil is ready. Please don't. The kids. He extends, wrapping his fingers around the knob.

"No," I lunge at him, slipping between his reach and the closet. "I'll get rid of it."

"I can't risk more students seeing this!"

"They won't, I promise – it'll be gone before they get here."

He crosses his arms, biting his top lip and exhaling a long sigh as he stares at his feet. Now's my moment. Maybe my only chance. He takes hold of my shoulders, and he steps close.

"Look," he says with a sprinkle of 'I give a shit' to his calming voice. "Ann, when things like this happen, you can come to me for help. This can't be a thing, OK? I don't wanna make a big deal about it but what happens when these kids go home and their parents ask about their day and their answer is, 'there was a pile of blood in Miss B's class'."

"Might be funny."

"It's not."

I nod, the ever-so understanding female teacher. My grip on the pencil lightens.

"You have until the first period… or I'm sorry, my dear, but you'll be out of here along with your deer, if you catch my drift."

"Do people still say, 'if you catch my drift'?"

"You have until 7:30."

His finger in my face silently says, 'you better not fuck up' and he plugs his nose again as he heads back for the hallway. As I let him out, he corrals the on-looking students away.

Ernie leaves me his mop and bucket. The school janitor is more like the secret service. He subtly appears in times of crisis as though it's his job to see and know all. The thin blood trail, really just a single vein of running red, smears as I mop. But after a few swift strokes, it's all but disappeared.

I peek out my classroom window to make sure the students aren't still looking in. 7:05 am, twenty-five minutes until class begins. The first few usually shuffle in around ten minutes before. The smell from Mr. Big has started to break through the bag (which is also supposed to trap the smells inside) hitting me like a piece of rotten meat when I open the closet. The kids would catch it in a second. I hadn't planned this far in advance. I still have no idea how I'm going to get rid of him. Especially before first period.

The air around me thins. Something begs me to jump in the closet, close the door, and just live out my days in darkness. It's not like anyone will miss or notice my absence. The clock on the wall spins wildly, both hands rotating at blitz speed.

Doing my best to gather myself, I hold my elbow over my mouth, looking for the tear in the bag. There! Fuck. I figure it must have ripped when I stuffed it into the closet. The hole tears more every time I try moving it, exposing one of Mr. Big's severed legs. It's lost all color, like a white fence post snapped from its base.

With the bag out of commission I need an exit strategy for the body. I swap glances from the trash bag to the left and the mop bucket to my right. I look up at the clock.

7:08 am.

No one has knocked on the door yet. I still have time. I tear open the trash bag and pull the mop bucket closer. Then, like Santa pulling gifts from his sack to place under the tree, I remove each severed piece of Mr. Big and dunk him in the bucket. Piece by piece. A few drops of water spill out, but I don't care. He fits. I top the edge of the bucket with solutions and cleaning chemicals from my closet, making a bubbly foam to mask the human limbs, torso, and severed head.

With the body parts submerged and hidden below the layer of soapy foam, I make my way out into the hall.

I have to improvise this time, heading to the teachers' lounge. I leave the mop bucket at the door for only a moment. I slip inside and rush for the trashcan.

The empty sugar container will be the perfect size. The rest of the teachers haven't noticed me in the lounge just yet. I wipe an empty Ziploc and a banana peel and skip back to the door. Nearly out of the lounge and safely back to the mop cart-

"You can't take that." Angela's voice behind me. Even though she's shorter than me, at around five foot four inches, she seems like a giant in the room. Her white blouse nearly blinding me as she props her hands on her hips and sneers.

"I forgot my coffee in my room. I'll bring it right back, Angela." She draws a clipboard from under her arm. She has a six-inch thick stack of other folders and some books she somehow manages to lug around all day, even though she barely weighs a hundred pounds.

"You need to fill out the sign out sheet if you borrow something from the lounge." She holds the clipboard in front of my face.

"A sign out sheet?"

"It's one of the new initiatives I want to enact as vice principal." How courageous of her. If anyone wants such a job, it's Angela Greene. No one is more suited for that role. Such a nag about rules, just enough of the faculty hates her, and the others love her. She'd be perfect to throw her little authority around like a new puppy on a leash.

"So, you got the job?" I say, writing my name in the 'sugar' slot listed in the 'lounge items' column of her spreadsheet.

"Not yet, but I think I know what Mr. Salem wants."

"And you're going to give it to him?"

"Did he ask you if you wanted the job?" She rolls her eyes, speaking with a soft, yet degrading tone. "Why would someone so good at teaching sacrifice her talent for being vice principal?"

Out of the corner of my eye, I notice a few students heading down the hall, straight for the mop bucket.

"That's a great point, Angela." I inch backwards for the door. Two boys and a girl, yards away. At any moment, they'll reach the bucket, stop, and see a hand sticking out from the bubbles. This is not happening. My throat goes dry and the hallway begins to shrink.

"Hey, I never asked," (I want to throw her out of the way and yell STOP) "what did Mr. Salem want today?"

"I'm sorry, what?"

"Must've been important for him to come to the teachers' lounge to get you." She stamps a certain emphasis on the word 'teacher'. I had just gone to happy hour with her last week. Now she inserts the idea that she's the boss. My boss. I don't have to tell her anything. I can just turn and walk away.

My attention goes back to the kids. They are approaching the bucket. My throat closes. My teeth could smooth iron, they grind so hard. The kids are no more than two feet from the bucket. The girl on the far left of the squad clicks away with her thumbs on her iPhone, half-laughing at whatever the boy in the middle is saying. The other boy on the far right has earphones in, staring down at his phone.

"Oh, it was nothing. I hit a deer last night."

"A deer?" She puts her hand on her chest pretending to run short of breath. "Are you ok?"

"Yes, I'm fine." I point to my forehead. "Small scrape. Mr. Salem just had a good car guy to fix me up with." The kids get closer with every second. Closer. No. Stop.

"How generous of him."

I nod, unaware of what she is alluding to. I take a full step away, watching with awe as the kids walk past the bucket without even giving it a moment of attention. Never looking up from their phones.

What a world.

After escaping from Angela, I roll down the hallway towards the art room. It will be the safest place. No art classes until 11:30 am. The art room is on the other side of the school. At this point, I don't mind being a few minutes late for class. At least they won't show up to a faulty trash bag filled with body parts instead of their teacher.

The wheels of the bucket shriek as I push through the middle school wing. Most of the students file into their respective homerooms for first period. A few stragglers, the kids who arrive five minutes before the bell, gather their books and shove their bags into their lockers with haste as if they are going to miss the moon landing.

Then I see Nick. He walks through the hallway drinking from a thermos he brings from home, a few books stuck under his arm. I get a waft of coffee and mint from his breath as I rush past him without even a glance or hello.

"Ann?"

I feel him turn as I keep going down the hall, pushing the bucket in front of me.

"Ann," he calls again. His footsteps click like a firing squad as he walks after me. I quicken my pace. Hurry, Ann. Hurry. I make it around the corner and through the first door on the left. I slam the door behind me and charge with the bucket to the pottery kiln that sits in the back corner of the classroom. I wipe each limb dry with a hand towel before tossing them inside. One by one, like slipping logs into a fireplace. With each piece loaded, I latch the kiln shut and flip the switch to FIRE. I let out a long breath. A cooling chill of relief rushes over me. It will take a while to hit the right temperature for a body, so I head for the door.

Nick is waiting outside when I pop out with the empty bucket, save the remaining water and suds. His arms are crossed, and his weight thrown to his right leg while the left gives a slight bend.

"Nick," I say. "Hi." I do my best to keep my voice as casual– mellow –as I can.

"What are you doing with a mop bucket?" He has a giggle to his voice, like he finds me amusing. "And my gosh," he says, holding his hand up to my face, "what happened?"

"I hit a deer." Plain. Straightforward.

His eyes widen with surprise. Then his face softens, offering silent condolences to my pain.

"Are you feeling alright? I have some ointment if you need some."

"I really have to get going. I'll be late for class."

"Right. That fifth grade first period." His hand wants to grasp my shoulder; I can feel it. "Maybe I'll see you later today."

"Maybe." Maybe. What a great word.

I check on Mr. Big at 10:45 am. No one has touched the kiln since. Amir has a fondness for the art program and works with the city to get a bump on funds for arts and music by agreeing to take out-of-county students. A whole diversity program that I don't pay much attention to but enjoy the fact that we are able to get a brand-new kiln worth over four grand. Perfect for pottery, and the occasional body.

I hum to myself in the empty art room as I check the temperature. 1600 degrees Fahrenheit. I give it a few more minutes, waiting until 11:00. The kids have their first recess until 11:20.

When I lift the latch, I'm filled with a small spark of joy. All that remains of Mr. Big is a pile of white dust. I scrape the ashes into the sugar container and leave the art room. Domino Sugar, now Mr. Big's final resting place.

I walk through the empty halls holding the sugar container filled with Mr. Big's vestiges the way a nun carries a candle in front of her chest. Though he's gone, all I can think about is the relief that I didn't get caught.

"Ann." I stop.

What's with these people?

Angela waits in the hallway in front of the teacher's lounge. I haven't figured out what to do with the sugar container yet. I think of keeping it safe in my desk drawer. I'm not one to keep trophies of my prey. The trash would do the job. If a search has gone out for Mr. Big, a school's thrown out sugar container is the last place they'll look. "Don't think I know what you're doing?"

Does she know? My grip tightens on the container.

"You think you can just steal the lounge sugar?"

"What?"

"That belongs to all the teachers." There she goes again emphasizing teachers. "You can't take it out from the lounge

again." She holds her hand out like a child requesting a
sample at the supermarket.

"I wasn't stealing it."

"Give it here."

I hand it over. Once she has the container in her small
hands, her face lightens, and she grins.

"I know we are friends..."

Are we?

"...but I can't treat you differently from the other teachers."
Then I get a wink. "If Mr. Salem notices I have favorites, then
I might not get the promotion. And c'mon, the last thing any
of us want is some outside person coming in here as vice
principal. Now c'mon, we have a faculty meeting."

"We do?"

"Didn't you read my email?"

"The kids have been a handful today."

Angela takes my hand and walks me to the lounge.
Calling meetings already. How ambitious. Soon she'll be
taking everyone's addresses, emergency contacts, checking
backgrounds...

I want to break that doll-sized hand of hers as she tugs
me through the hall.

"Is everyone here?" Angela begins the meeting, passing
it off to Amir with everyone accounted for save the lucky
few who are monitoring recess. One of those is Nick, thank
God. The rest of the elementary and middle school
teachers gather for Amir's announcement of the two big
events everyone has to mark on their calendar.

Amir stands at the front, uneasy while addressing the
congregated teachers. Behind him, the walls are adorned
with posters for CPR, the food pyramid, book clubs, and

food drive proposals. A newer looking sign is an ad for the first event.

The middle school fall dance– which starting this year the fifth graders are allowed to attend. Angela, Amir's hound on what she considers, "crucial school policies," makes note to correct the term 'dance' with 'nighttime social', because a dance gives the impression that there will be dates and she doesn't want the kids fooling around, primarily the seventh and eighth grade pubescent adventurers. She also mentions, "dances are toxic for social stability within a school's adolescent environment because they promote certain kids being asked to the dance and others not."

Angela also 'suggests' to the committee in charge of coordinating the dance, which consists of a few teachers and a handful of parent volunteers, to send reminders prohibiting dates and 'close' dancing.

When I ask Angela later on why she doesn't just organize the dance herself, she simply replies, "Oh no, dear, I don't do the social events, that's for regular teachers and bored parents to organize. It's just impossible for them to achieve anything efficiently. I encourage them to meet and plan. But I end up doing most of the work anyway."

Amir makes sure to remind the teachers to "keep things PG this year." He plans to have a faculty meeting the following morning. "Mandatory," as he puts it, pointing his nail bitten fingernails at the lot of 'horney bunnies' as he has also put it.

"So, the morning after the dance, I will see you all at 8 am here. It's not the parent teacher conference. I know you have your rituals, which I have been mighty liberal on over the years. Which brings me to the second big event. Conferences this fall."

And the groans heard round the teachers' lounge.

Still a new teacher, I have yet to complete a real parent conference. I will be on my own. I don't worry. As long as no one brings up me having the body of a "deer" in the classroom, I will be just fine.

"Get ready," Douglass whispers from behind. He reeks of coffee and cigarettes. "This is your first PTC, which means you'll be properly initiated."

"Initiated? PTC?"

"Parent teacher conference," Sonya says from the chair to my right. "We have a tradition. Don't worry, it will be a fucking blast. Also, what the hell girl? If you need an animal disposed of just call me next time, I pretty much do that for a living."

"It was a deer," I say. "A little bigger than frogs and pigeons."

Douglass chuckles. Angela stares us down from the front of the room, standing to Amir's right, assimilating her potential position as his number two. She doesn't say anything, just stares, intense and firm. Sonya must have noticed, because she shuts up and returns to pretending to listen to Amir's speech about transparency with our parents and how they are our primary focus. I always thought the children are the focus, but I refrain from challenging him. That will only make the meeting longer, and I have done enough today to question my own 'readiness' for vice principal.

When Amir releases his "team of excellent educators," most of the teachers book it while others linger in the lounge, enjoying the few minutes before the bell rings and a flush of students, dirty and sweaty from recess, come rushing back into the halls.

I want to slip out as fast as I can, but I don't want to leave the sugar container in the cupboard where Angela returned it.

But I'm too late. By the time I get past Sonya, who talks my ear off about every accident she's ever had, including one where she compared me hitting a deer to her accidently knocking into a woman in a wheelchair when backing out of a Jewel parking lot, the sugar container is already in use again—

In Angela's hand.

A heat wave washes over me. I push through the mingling teachers, trying to reach Angela and her coffee. She talks by the kitchenette to a few of the middle school teachers. Ones I have never even met before.

"Been waiting all morning for this," she says as she shakes the sugar container. "Can you imagine drinking coffee black?" She always uses the same mug; white ceramic with AG in big monogram red letters on the side, and an apple and small cursive phrase that says, "an apple a day".

No one touches her mug.

My heartbeat stops as I watch her. I want to lunge forward and swipe the mug from her hand. The coffee will spill all over her shirt. Hot coffee. She'll be burned. She'll be mad. Her mug will most likely fall and shatter against the lounge carpet— the cheap, hard as rock kind of carpet. No doubt the mug will break. No doubt she will be burned. I'd like to see that.

But I like my job more. I need my job.

On her first sip she doesn't budge. In fact, she adds more, probably assuming she hasn't put enough in. Whether out of pride or stupidity, she doesn't budge on her second sip either.

"Ann." Stern, her eyes on me.

"Angela."

"Do you know what this is?"

I don't dare answer her.

"Well, I'll tell you. It's the worst coffee I have had in my entire life. Do you know who made it this morning?"

"I – I um…"

"Sonya," she yaps. "Who made the coffee?"

"It's Dunkin," Douglass says walking over. "Good shit, too. I think Mr. Richardson brought it in. Some doughnuts too, but those were gone before the meeting even began."

"I don't eat doughnuts."

"Well, then I guess next time he will bring a croissant, just for you, Angela."

"No," she says. Her voice is as flat as her body. A pure wooden plank of a human being. "First of all, if people are going to bring in sweets, then they should get the OK before doing so. Someone could have had an allergy."

"If they have an allergy, then wouldn't they know not to eat them?" He has size, probably around 6 '1 and broad, too, but stands with a drunk's hunch and his eyes drool purple circles. She reaches nowhere close to 5 '4, but while they stand off, I swear she seems stronger, taller, and more powerful in every way. "I'm guessing you have an allergy?"

"Don't have any allergies, Mr. Douglass, I am just gluten free."

"Well, maybe you put less junk in your coffee and you'd actually taste it."

A silence brews. Angela stands before Douglass– a stare down –boiling hotter than anyone's coffee in that room. I am sure she preferred pouring it on his head instead of his papers and books. But she chooses wisely, I guess. She pours out the whole mug. Every last drop. He jumps back, but not far enough to get out of the coffee's range. His papers are soaked, and his pants have a pee area stain from trying to pull away, which causes his own coffee to spill.

"What the hell is wrong with you?"

"I am sorry," she says. "It just slipped from all the extra stuff I had in it. I guess now we will never know."

And with that, she places her mug into the sink and walks over to the tables carrying a stack of quizzes and papers.

"Starbucks, people. Or brew it yourselves with the coffee maker we have here," she says in an announcing voice to the remaining teachers. I watch with a look of awe, hidden from her fulsome posture as she slams the stack down and sits, presuming her daily routine of slashing quizzes with her red pen. I can only describe it as vicious. Each mark she makes is like drawing blood.

Douglass slouches as he strolls past me on his way out of the room. He wastes no time patting his sport coat for cigarettes, or a THC pen, I'm not sure which he needs more but I've seen him use both. As he walks out, his pants stained and his papers ruined, he leans at me and whispers, "I bring my own coffee every day. Never trust the teacher coffee. How long until she poisons us all?"

After what I consider the longest day as a teacher, the bell finally rings and 2:45 smiles on the digital red clock at the end of the room. I stay, waiting for the students to filter out of the classroom before packing up, wanting to shoot home as fast as I can, but I want to avoid walking by anyone. And I mean anyone.

The children step out in their typical end of the day haste, somehow invigorated with energy from the triumphant rings of the bell as if they have yet again, bested the system and survived another day. Though I'm not in a rush to leave, I still hope that I'll get off easy and avoid the verbal dealings with my fellow teachers or students. Wrong on both accounts.

Rebecca dances up to the front of my desk. Her pigtails wave like golden ropes. Her hands plant themselves on my desk and she attacks me with a smile from the two feet distance between us.

"Miss B."

(here we go)

"Yes," I say with my famous PR smile. "What is it, Rebecca?"

"Is it true that you hurt a poor deer?"

"I'm sorry?"

"Well, I got a text from Jessica, who said William from sixth grade said that he saw Mr. Salem outside of your classroom and that there was blood everywhere and a deer--."

"Let me stop you there, Rebecca." My head fills with a proceed with caution amount of disgust for her. Not her curiosity, but because in all of this, her eyes, the way they peer at me like drawn arrows, seems to concentrate on me as an enemy. My hand clenches around my kneecap, hidden under my desk as she speaks. Her fake little smile with her perfectly orthodontist-altered rows of white teeth. I focus on just getting her out of my classroom.

"Look," I say. "You should try and only believe things you see for yourself."

"So, there wasn't blood?"

"No, there was."

"You know, I know about periods Miss B." what the fuck "you can tell me," she winks.

She gave me a wink. A wink. Can you imagine? This girl just winked at me, trying to bond over periods. She has no idea what she wants out of this. And neither do I. She's attempting to either out me for a murderous liar or trying to walk out of here and brag to her girlfriends that she is on such a higher level with the teacher that we discuss menstruation.

"It was a deer," I finally say, barely keeping myself composed. "Poor thing ran into my car. I did everything I could to keep it alive though."

"That poor animal." She makes the same motion Angela Greene had made earlier that day. Her hand on her upper chest, as if she has suddenly lost the ability to breath. I can't help but see Angela in Rebecca's eyes. In her face. In her hand motions. It suddenly becomes clear; she is just a miniature version. A tadpole of Angela Greene who feasts on the knowledge of people's business. One day she'll grow into a full-sized fledgling. Species genome: Bitch.

For a split moment, I can't tell who's standing in front of me. Rebecca or Angela? She appears for an instant, crossing her arms after tightening the flap lapels of her white sweater. Her eyes narrow and she flashes a smile to mimic my own. Where do you think I learned it from? Rebecca bobs in front of me again, her pigtails swinging as she fiddles with the end of one of her braids. I nod, agreeing that the animal I killed was in fact the victim— though we all know the opposite to be true. "I can keep my mouth shut, don't worry." She gives me another wink and leaves, skipping into the hall to join a posse of girls waiting for her.

Then I notice Danny still in his seat. His face bowed; his eyes glued to his lap. He sits like a statue, his bag packed, his body frozen in his seat.

"Did you hear the bell, Danny?" His view remains glued to a book— my book, the one I had lent him. I stand behind him, surprised by his devotion to (if that's what it was) The Count of Montecristo. I hear my mother's voice, looking over his shoulder trying to zoom in on the words. "How do you like it so far?"

He lifts his head up for only a moment. "It's good." He savors the second of breath then lowers himself back down in a concentrated slouch.

"Are you getting picked up today?" He turns the page. "How's your eye?" I hadn't noticed it yet today, but the blue moon has faded to a faint bruise just under his eyelid. "Looks good."

"My dad put some ice on it," he said as he turned back to the story of more importance. "He was upset."

"Did you tell him what happened?"

The book closes. He slides it into his backpack and zips the bag shut. Then he lifts himself off his chair and heads for the door.

"I told him I would handle it," he says, turning around. "I said that my vengeance would be slow coming, but I think then it is all the more complete." Holy shit. He's read into the story more than I anticipated. "I won't wait as long as Dantes does in the story though, don't worry Miss B."

"You know I didn't give you that so you would take revenge."

"You told me that all bullies get what they deserve in time."

"And this was done by a bully?" I point again to my eye. I want to know, why him? Why do they choose Danny as their target? He's different indeed. He dresses differently, he keeps to himself, and he doesn't seem to care for the social expectations placed on a child of eleven. The cliques, the text chains, and parent-planned play dates. To him they are meaningless, or at least that's how it seems from my view. Reminds me of myself at that age.

"It doesn't matter."

"Yes, it does." My tone hardens.

"Why do you care? Why did you even give me this book in the first place?" I pause. I don't care. Whether or not they punch him in the eye again makes no difference to me. It's an experiment if anything. He sparks a curiosity that I cannot understand. And I need an explanation of my interest. His face begs for a response, his back hangs forward from the weight of his backpack and his mouth gapes open, as if he could catch my answer with his slack jaw.

"Sit down for a second, Danny." It takes him a moment to consider, but eventually the bag slips from his shoulder, and he perches himself in the desk chair closest to the door. I sit on the desk and cross my legs, trying to break out a smile to let him know I'm on his side.

"You know, I knew this girl once. She was a friend of mine I guess you could say. She was in a pretty similar situation as Dantes."

"Her boyfriend was with someone else?"

"No, not exactly. I mean more like earlier in the story, when Dantes is in prison. She was in a prison of sorts. Not jail or anything like that, but imprisoned, nonetheless. And with that comes a sense of powerlessness. Especially when she tried escaping from the prison and the person keeping her there, well, he did some bad things to her."

"Like what?"

"Bad things."

Danny slumps, still listening but I gather he feels a little cheated from the lack of action in my story.

"Anyways," I continue. "Everyone told her to get rid of Uncle– the bully who was doing the bad things. Even the people closest to her. The ones who actually loved her." I drift for a moment, pausing and leaving Danny's eyes. She pops into my head for a split second, but I shut myself from allowing her to fully appear.

"Miss Bonny."

"Yes, sorry. So everyone was saying, get rid of the bully, just walk away. But they didn't realize that it was impossible and that she had to wait. She had to wait until it was the right timing. And then when she was ready, she struck."

Danny lights up as if his skin's been pulled back from the jet stream of a roller coaster.

"Did she get away?"

I nod. "Yes, she did. But listen, after retaliating the way she did, she was never the same."

"How come?"

"Because she got a taste of what it was like to hurt someone... even though that someone deserved it. Getting revenge stuck with her, like an addiction. What my point is, Danny, is that you should ask for help before retaliating. Never let someone push you around, but remember, once you stoop to their level, you will never be the same." He gives a stiff nod, closing his eyes to seem understanding. He looks at the door and I give him permission to leave nodding with a closed eye grin. Before he steps out of the classroom, he turns back to me.

"Miss, Bonny, the girl in your story, what happened to her?"

"Oh- I'm not sure. I haven't seen her in a long time."

That's My Girl

I've never been big on visitors since I moved into my new place. Even when I lived with Kitty, we rarely entertained or had friends over. She was really my only friend, though she had several of her own and kept a social life. I think I learned too late the life hack of maintaining some social presence in order to appear normal.

Having Kate over tonight after getting rid of Mr. Big makes me feel transported back to those days. The nights I shared with Kitty. We would sit in silence, listen to music together or she would watch TV shows I didn't understand or enjoy, but I'd still laugh whenever she gave me a 'isn't that hilarious' look or nudged me and began to laugh – I would always join in. I didn't care. I would fake laugh for Kitty. I would do a lot of things for her. I did. Even kill. In the end, I did it for her own good.

Kate had invited herself over. When she knocked, I had been busy trying to figure out the fastest method to grade 35 multiplication and division timed tests. News flash, there is only one way.

One

At

A

Time.

Grueling isn't a strong enough word. To be honest, I don't have one that fits. I felt a sense of drowning. Maybe this is how it feels to be suffocated. Not under water, but under piles of papers with 25x2 and 3x6 and 64÷4 and 8x9 and on and on and on until she knocked, armed with a bottle of Zinfandel.

According to Kate, it's from New Zealand, which makes me think immediately of Kangaroos and rugby players retiring from the Kiwi to the vineyards – I don't know why but it seems an odd place for wine. But I also consider myself a novice when it comes to liquid under 40% alcohol.

"No, no," she says, after making me rummage through my drawers for a corkscrew. "You need to try. It's the best, really. So many great restaurants have reds from New Zealand now. That's where I first had it." As if all great restaurants in the city of Chicago are lumped into a single joint that exists to serve Kate new wine trends.

I apologize, saying I deem myself a whiskey girl, and that my ex drank only white wine, which makes her laugh for some reason. I have yet to open a bottle of wine in my new place. I have enough red stains to deal with on occasion. Nevertheless, I make an exception for Kate.

We sit in silence for a bit. I'm insecure about how I should sit, what I should do with my hands. I know I must look insane, skeptical of my ability to appear normal when she's so distracting. She slips off her tennies and lets her toes (freshly painted blue) wiggle freely as she perches with her knees slanted towards me on the opposite end of the sectional. The sofa really takes up most of the room. It's nice, the silence, her with her wine and me with my glass of whiskey as I study her cute toes and the way her

University of Michigan t-shirt rests over her post-work, braless top half.

The question of why she's here keeps bobbing in my head. She isn't usually so friendly, so outwardly comfortable with me. Maybe that's changed. Or maybe she's trying to manipulate me. Does she want the sex cuffs back? This could just be an elaborate scheme to get me to crack. She's a lawyer, I remind myself. And a good one. I try to hold my barrier, stay as impenetrable to vulnerability as I can. But how can I when her legs are perfectly smooth, and her eyes - she is staring at me without blinking. What is this tease?

I guess her shorts had once belonged to Roger. I want to slide them up her legs. I want to see more of her and what type of panties she's wearing. If any at all.

The shorts make his presence linger. A most unwelcome guest. Did she come over to fuck? No, that would be far too easy. If she had, she wouldn't be wearing pants at all, or at least something else so as not to bring the weight of a boyfriend and her bottle of Zinfandel from New Zealand into my apartment and onto my couch. But then again, we aren't friends, at least not yet. For fuck's sake she bitched me out this week about my apartment's smell. Now she sits on my couch, drinking wine in a very see-through shirt with no bra underneath.

Please don't notice I'm sweating. Her perking nipples push on her shirt, holding up the word Michigan like tacks on a bulletin board.

Thank God for whiskey. Thank God for wine.

"So, you're pretty old school, huh?" she says, breaking the silence.

"How so?" I wonder back to the bra. I still have mine on. Usually, I clip it off right when I walk in the door. I enjoy wearing a robe at home and grading topless sometimes. I often kill topless; that seems to bring a sense of freedom to the deed. A sense of power. Tonight, I was so flustered when I arrived home, thinking of the school dance, still thinking of Amir finding the body – was I out of the race for vice principal? Wondering, will I end up working for Angela Greene? I won't last a month.

If I hadn't been so rattled, Kate would have knocked, and I would have opened the door half naked, and we wouldn't have to do this silly game of will we won't we. We will, I think to myself. I promise myself. It irks me that I have not joined Kate in her nipple freed tease, if it's a tease at all. I want to at least play along.

"The music." She looks at the ceiling, even though it comes from a shelf behind me. "It's always classical."

"Always?"

"I mean, the walls in this apartment are pretty thin. Three grand a month and you can still hear your neighbors."

"Does my music bother you?"

"No, no… it's kinda hip to be honest."

I can tell you one thing. My music and I are anything but hip.

She lifts herself from the couch the way people rustle through the sheets and roll from the bed after sex. My eyes glue to the crevices of her body as she skips along with Saint-Saen's melody. It isn't graceful, but every move she makes still seems sexy.

"You're so unassuming, Ann." She says, filing through my records. "My dad has like, this same shit, I mean, music. It's like an art collection. I have been thinking about investing in some prints. Roger doesn't get art. This system must've been a fortune, girl." I stare as she fingers my record collection with her firm, yet dainty hands. How they dance… I bite my lip.

"It was a gift," I say, shrugging. "My uncle. And most of those were his too." Lies. Paid for by me. Collected by me. Uncle Jones didn't possess this elevated taste. The collection is mine.

Kitty had lied about liking my music at first too. It was her way of fake laughing.

Kate turns back to me. "You are so, I don't know, intellectual. Like a renaissance girl or something."

"I don't know about that." Or what the hell she means by it. "What about you? You are a lawyer. Much more intellectual than I am."

"Yeah, yeah, blah, blah. Being an immigration attorney associate is a bore." She slinks on the back of the sofa, rolling onto the cushions. Throughout the whole acrobatic move, her wine glass remains in her hand, its contents refusing the spill as they shift closer to the edge of the rim. She takes a lengthy sip and has the bottle in her hand to pour a new one before the glass has emptied.

I take note how close she sits. Closer than before. I can smell her.

"I honestly deal with paperwork all day. That's why I need my red friend here after a long week. And someone to enjoy it with."

Is that a wink she just gave me?

"Me?"

"Well, that's why I am here silly. Neighbors can be friends too." This truly jams my mainframe. Why does this girl want to be my friend? Is it something else? I still have her sex-cuffs. I want to go pull them out and chain her to the leg of the sofa or the post of my bed. Or to me, that will work just as well… she could never escape then.

"What about Roger?" I ask.

"What about Roger?"

"He doesn't seem to like me."

"Well, fuck Roger. He's out with his friends getting high and trying to get into clubs he can't afford and stare up girls' skirts he'd never dare touch. We can have girls' nights. Just us." Just us. I like that.

"So, do you not like your job?" I ask, hoping my conversation skills are up to par.

"I wanna do criminal law." I tire of the back and forth 'tell me this' and 'tell me that' pleasantries. I want to know more her as she props her head up, seeming so very interested in me, and her hair dangles. I play along with the barbershop level exchange. "You're a secretary, right?"

"School teacher," and down goes my third glass of whiskey.

"That's actually really impressive. What grade?"

"Fifth. But I was asked if I wanted to be vice principal." Fuck me for trying to impress her with that.

"Shut up, girl!" She gives a loving slap on my arm. I want her to do it again. "That's so insane."

"Is it really any better?"

"Fuck, yes, it is. Do you know how many teacher strikes happen in this city? They cut pay all the time and teachers get laid off constantly. VP and you'll have like, an actual career, plus no teacher can tell you what to do. You can be the bad bitch on campus. Plus, don't you get tired of dealing with so many kids?"

My mind runs to Angela Green as VP again. If she gets the job, she'll be the bad bitch on campus. Then who knows how long I can keep my secret?

Kate pours herself another glass. Her mouth is purple with a layer of wine over her injected lips.

"I guess I'll go for it," I concede.

"That's my girl."

Her girl? I wish.

Believe me, it takes every ounce of resolve to keep me from trying something on Kate. I slide closer to her on the couch as the night goes on. Close in fact to where my knee touches hers.

Once I finish talking about the vice principal, she tells me all about her relationship, complains more about her job, shares her experiences in law school, she even tells me she kissed a girl once. We look at each other for a few silent moments before she submits to going home. She uses the excuse that her dog needs to be taken out. When she does leave, I feel used, manipulated once again, and left alone. How did she know that a drink and a braless shirt would work to dissolve me into an open canvas for her to paint her life's problems across free of charge?

I'm insulted, yes. She toyed with me, drew me like an ice bath along a teasing circuit of pointless banter until she got what she wanted, the reassurance that someone else's life is just as boring and just as confusing as her own. I'm not a friend. She used me as an emotional sponge.

But I do learn her relationship is weak, but resilient. You can't just leave someone when you live together. You just go weeks without fucking and then days when neither of you get out of bed. She explained it as a cycle of hot and cold – a washing machine relationship.

I wait until the middle of the night to sneak into her apartment. Sometimes I just like smelling her things. Studying her dresses. Corporate and sexy.

Roger is sprawled out on the couch, fuming with that post-club stench of sweat and sticky Grey Goose and cranberry. She had kicked him out of the bedroom for barging home at 3:41 am and wanting sex, which she denied.

The walls *are* thin.

Smiley Face French Fries

Did I kill Angela Greene?

Death is the only thing I can think of when she isn't at school on Friday. I ignore the "deer" incident the best I can and instead focus on my strategy to approach Amir. It's the perfect day to make the move because Angela has called off sick. Not dead, unfortunately. But I have Amir all to myself.

"I heard food poisoning," Sonya tells me in line with my class during lunch period. To be honest, I'm a little bummed. "It must be bad because she has literally never taken a day off. I would've guessed the lunch here caused it, but she packs her own." Angela Greene usually brings the same lunch every day: baby carrots – no ranch – chickpeas, and canned tuna.

I know the culprit must have been the "sugar" she had put in her coffee. I want to ask Sonya if it can kill you, but I figure I'll wait and google it later. It would deplete most of my problems and certainly my worries if Angela disappeared altogether. I can't just murder her though. As her only competition for the same job, I'd be suspect number one, teacher or not.

"I wonder if something else is going on," Sonya says.

"You think Angela Greene has secrets?" An ally against Angela is well received in Sonya.

"Honey, I think everyone has secrets... by the way, some advice, don't eat the food here. Douglass might order some delivery. Shoot me a text if you want to add to the order, okay? Gotta jam."

She leaves me in the cafeteria amidst a mass of four-foot hungry 5th graders. They line up for their lunch as if they had one chance to collect food before an apocalypse. When lunchtime arrives, all the sweet, charming respect they show in the classroom goes out the window. Kids crawl over one another, fighting like piranhas to get a tray and collect their small-portioned meal. Their whole day surrounds this moment. The epic battle to be first in line. To be the first to sit down. They claim sections in the cafeteria like kings conquering an empty pasture. They claw, yell, cry, and fight over who gets there first. Efforts from faculty are futile. We have no real power here. For legal reasons, at least two teachers at a time are required to serve.

Everyone wants to be the first to claim their seat, even though the majority sit in the exact same spot every day. No one wants to be the kid who heads right to the lunch tables because they have a packed lunch. I've learned that kids with packed lunches are of a different status. Not in our skewed adult views of status that separates people based on social prejudice or wealth. But in the cruel world of Kid-Dom, bringing a packed lunch is a social sin equivalent to having a roller backpack, or showing up to your first day with an exposed love note from your parents.

Social suicide.

I decide to test the waters of the cafeteria, sacrificing my stomach's balance. A mystery meat sandwich? Or a hotdog wrapped in fried bread? Perhaps the square shaped pizza-esque slices. Or if I'm lucky, fried chicken. I feel that if I have to endure the cafeteria surrounded by suffering children who have no choice but to be fueled by the failed system known as the public-school lunch, I might as well join them by partaking in their mephitic cuisine.

The menu today consists of a meager pencil-thin "meat" patty between pre-packaged white bread buns and a sheet of plastic wrapped cheese. On the side, Jello and French fries in the shape of smiley faces. I wait until all the children have lined up and then take the final spot in line. The kitchen aroma greets me with a gust of spattering grease and day-old cooking oil. The sizzle of burger patties and the beeping of ovens play a tune over the children's begging for more fries or requesting cookies instead of Jello.

I watch a student in front of me. Not one of mine. He wears a striped shirt and dark jeans. It's obvious when a student is a younger sibling. They wear hand-me-downs. This poor boy clearly dons pants his brother had outgrown, but he has yet to fill in. His heels step over the bottom of his pants making them dirty and slightly torn in the back. He drags his tray along the counter, quietly accepting the meal that will sit at the bottom of his stomach for the next few hours before tearing through his intestines like a sack of boulders wedging through a golf hole. Meanwhile his teacher will be left wondering the whole of fifth period why he can't stay awake.

As the patty sandwich flops onto his plate, my stomach falls out of my body onto the floor. I place my tray down on the counter, greeted by the woman across with a less than cheerful stare. She wears a clear plastic apron over her clothes and a net on her head. Dark circles painted under her eyes could be makeup or lack of sleep. I'm not sure. Her skin is cracked and wrinkled like the very meat she serves.

"Miss Bonny," she says with a hunk of snot in her throat.

"I'll just have the fries."

I pair the fried potato smiley faces with a carton of chocolate milk. I walk past the register, nodding to the woman operating the final checkout where the kids give their last name, meander through the kitchen area, and exit into the freedom of the open dining hall. I eat without a payment plan. Oh, the perks of being a schoolteacher.

I look for a safe seat, embraced by the chaotic chorus of chatter and laughs. The madness and hectic din infiltrate my mind. I stand frozen, unable to connect my brain to command my body. Suddenly I transport back to happy hour, invaded by noise and uncertain social interaction. The groups all seated together, girls in their closely chosen friendship circles while boys scheme, narrowing down their next victim on the playground.

Snap out of it.

Then I see him, sitting alone at the far-left side of the cafeteria hall. His head is bent low. Beside his tray sits his composition notebook, held open with the tray holding down one end and his elbow with his pen clicking on the opposite fold. His free hand hides under the table, tucked close to his lap and out of view.

I have a pet peeve for when people plop down next to you without invitation; impossible to avoid living in a city like Chicago. The bus or trains, park benches, any public building, it's inescapable. People fester everywhere, socially inept and intrusive. However, given the rambunctious lot taking up most of the cafeteria, and spotting Nick on the other side, sitting beside Danny is really my only option for a somewhat peaceful lunch.

He looks up for a brief second as I set my tray down, the way a poker player peeks up from a freshly dealt hand. I pop the carton of milk and take a long sip, wiping my face of the excess that clings to my top lip. I hesitate on eating the fries, but with enough ketchup, I snuff out the lingering previously frozen flavor.

Danny remains silent for a while. If he wants to sit alone, then why bother? It's not like he misses out on anything pretending to be cool with the rest of his prepubescent peers. I take a bite of one of my fries, just enough to remove part of the smiley face. Then dab it with the blood-red ketchup. It seems like a bullet has carved a hole in its head. I slide the wounded fry across the table to Danny. He looks at it for a moment, giggles, and I give him a playful dead man face.

"You aren't eating?" The Jello still has its slightly solid gelatin shape that wobbles along with Danny's nervously thumping foot. His meat patty sandwich remains in the same un-centered position from the inaccurate spatula placement, and the fries are all smiling, unthreatened by Danny's short appetite.

"You can have it." Danny pushes the tray closer to me. I don't think a few inches could make it smell worse, but I'm wrong. My nose curls, as if it's trying to run off from my face to save itself from the cruel stench of the cafeteria food.

"What are you working on?" I ask. He shields the notebook with the same arm he uses to pin it down.

No answer.

What is he holding that was so secretive in his palm? I bend sideways and peek under the table. He's so engrossed in whatever he's writing in the notebook that he's too slow to notice my intrusion. I steal a swift glance before straightening my back and tossing a French fry into my mouth. He glares up at me, frozen.

"You wanna talk?" I hope he says no. I let out a gust through my nostrils when he shakes his head. My gaze lingers, matching his own attempt to avoid eye contact. He knows I saw it. The plastic knife tightly wedged between his hand and thigh, the serrated plastic edge digging into his palm. A small splotch of blood dried on his pants, his hands are grimy from pen ink tattooed under his nails, and red has stained his fingers from cut flesh.

I remember hearing a quote from Ernest Hemingway— "There is nothing to writing. All you do is sit down at a typewriter and bleed." Danny is taking it quite literally.

I notice browning stains lining the crisp paper on some of the tips of the thin notebook pages, no doubt from the blood on his hands. What does that notebook contain that forces him to carve into his tender hand while writing it down? From the look on his face, he's not in pain, not a flinch of emotion washes over him. But when I look closer into his eyes, those little dark beads, so deep brown they're almost black, I sense a slight wisdom of loneliness. I've seen it before in my own opaque reflection. His eyes scream a lifeless cry of yearning, of misery, and of accepted solitude in his misinterpreted sanity. Danny dares to be separate, refusing to ride the carousel of social systematic torture. But not by his choosing.

"Did you finish the book?" I know he'll never explain his self-torture. Should I bring it to the attention of other adults? The ones who claim to care for him? The ones who would rather send him away?

"Almost," he says. He closes his notebook and stares at the untouched tray.

"You have it with you?"

The slight sigh of exhaled breath from his clenched teeth tells me otherwise.

"I left it."

"Left it where?"

"My dad's." For a moment, I think he's lost it. I sense a real strain on his sense of comfort. He hesitates to speak as if a wasp sat on the tip of his tongue. "I promise I will give it back to you! I'm staying with him this weekend."

"Danny," I say, tempted to rest my hand on his. But of course, this school has a no-touch policy. "It's totally fine. I want you to keep the book. I gave it to you." He leans back with another sigh. This time as if he has just escaped a guillotine. "It's good, right?"

"I didn't like how it took so long for Dantes to get his revenge."

"Here's Dantes' issue," I say, working to open the impossible paper flaps of my second chocolate milk. They really seal these things. You'd think having nails would help. "He believes that he represents God's divine justice. But what we forget is that we make up what we think justice is. God has nothing to do with it. It is simply an excuse we give ourselves, refusing to accept that maybe, we just want to spill a little blood." I lean close. "And sometimes, that's ok." He nods, as if for the first time I've connected with him. "All this," I say, waving my hand around. "This is just noise. It's fake. You're a step ahead."

"Ahead of who?"

"The other kids. Some teachers even."

"They aren't nice to me."

"Fuck them." His eyes widen. I bet he never thought he'd hear that word from his fifth-grade teacher. "You think you're ever not gonna get bullied? Forget that. You will always be bullied. Because you're different. But guess what."

"What?"

"Being different," the side of my mouth perks up into a half grin. Mischievous and relishing. "Is awesome."

I raise my carton of milk, saluting Danny. He grins, a full one, and lifts his milk to mine. A plastic clink and a silent 'cheers'.

We drink to it. Being different. Being insane.

While the students have recess, I make my move to Amir's office. Mrs. Baxterly eyes me as I enter. Sure enough, she's using one of Amir's pens. She doesn't write with it, just holds it, staring at her computer and tapping the pen on the keyboard.

"He's not in," she says.

"Do you know when he'll be back?"

"He is having lunch with a few school board folks today, so it could be a while. Last time he didn't come back for the rest of the day. I can take a message for you if you'd like?"

"I'll come back."

"Did you hear Mrs. Angela Greene is sick today?"

"I did."

"Food poisoning."

"Shame."

"You know, it is the first day she has ever missed."

"You don't say."

"It's incredible. I keep all the records for Mr. Salem. For the faculty and students. Absences, meetings, job history and background."

"You have records of the entire faculty's history?"

"Well, there are a few without any history or background. Weird, isn't it?"

Whose side is she on? Her usual jolly persona has diminished into a passive, midwestern ice stare.

"Very weird." I inch for the door. "I'll just come back to see him after school."

"You do that, Ann. It is Ann, right?"

I nearly sprint back to my classroom. The whole time I feel eyes on me in the halls. A paranoia grows like a shadow cast across the narrow corridors of lockers and classrooms. I shrink, sweating, and panting. I rush to my room, only to nearly collapse from what greets me when I step inside.

A set of horns almost pierce my face.

They're attached to a life-sized deer. A statue? A target? Holes adorn the sides from what I guess were arrows. I remember a story Douglass had told me about how he goes hunting every year with his cousin in Montana and uses a deer dummy as practice.

What the hell, I think, my heart finding a more temperate pace once I start to relax.

The plush beast has a sticky note pasted on its forehead:
DON'T HIT ME! LOL
-D

D for Douglass. I'm not sure if they are taunting me or not. Do they suspect I lied? No, I try chuckling. This is merely a prank. A fun prank which means I'm part of the group. Right? That's what pranks mean. That we're friends.

I move the deer to the far end of the room. I cover it with a sheet, but when my students return it's quickly unveiled again.

Prank or not, the thing stares at me... taunting me. Whispering, "I know... I know. I know."

With some time left in recess, I decide to visit Dr. Tina Marcus: School Counselor.

I've always been skeptical of therapy. Especially when it comes to children. Kitty had seen them all. Psychologists, therapists, psychics, Buddhists, even a hypnotist. It was exhausting, all the times she tried to make me go. She never let it down; "you really should see someone," she'd say. I refrained from any mental chiropractors who prefer their patients spin in loops of self-discovery, puzzling over the most minute revelations just to keep up with an ever-recurring session fee.

Her office is cold. One window with the shades down and a floor fan spinning back and forth. There's a smell of must, as if she's been held up in this oaky wardrobe for years with no one but the moths for company.

Despite the rather 'state-funded' appearance of the office, Dr. Tina herself exudes a certain level of class, quite rare in public faculty members. She is a regal woman. Dark skin, beautiful ears with dangly gold hoops and bulging eyes. They're the kind that scour each centimeter of you, searching without a single blink. As I sit across from her in silence, I find myself steering from her gaze. Her eye contact is troubling, unbreaking. It's difficult to express how I can feel cold in such a humid room. But I'm somewhere between sweating and cold to the very bone.

The silence is thick, tangible as the moisture in the room. As she stares at me, she taps her long, colored nails against her chin. Her stoicism makes me like her despite the discomfort. There's a certain amiability to those able to endure silence. A respect to at least appearing to be a listener. She clearly wants me to make the first move. I'm fighting it. I'm not here for me. I'm just checking up on Danny.

"So, how's he doing?" I finally blurt. My hand grips my knee cap. I'm trying to keep my leg still. To look confident. Don't give her anything. She's a tyrannosaur, able to smell fear.

She doesn't respond. She's good. Instead, she digs into a file, sifting through pages and notes out of my line of sight.

"I asked him to draw some pictures," she says. Her voice is an eloquent baritone. Each syllable long, drawn and quartered with unmistakable intention. "He's such a quiet boy. Sullen, like yourself. Children usually evoke more freely when permitted to create something artistic."

I toy with the cup of colored pencils she has on the desk. She sees this, blinking for the first time. Then she pulls out a pad and writes something down.

"You want me to draw something?" I ask.

"Do what you want. You came to me."

"For Danny."

"Right." She hides his work from me after spending a few seconds, I guess, pondering whether to show me. I can imagine they are similar to the contents of his notebook. "Dr. Salem mentioned Danny's been bullied, yet he's made no reports and there's some fellow students who claim he's lashed out. Even hurt himself."

"Sometimes the bully gets what's coming."

"You tell him that?" I shake my head slowly. "Children often repress some type of trauma and allow it to manifest in other aspects of their lives. Sometimes, if not treated, you threaten that trauma to bleed into adulthood." She cocks her head, leaning forward. "Miss Bonny, are you aware of repetition compulsion?"

I squint, pretending to appear like I might have any idea what she means. Though somewhere I feel like we aren't just talking about Danny.

Why won't she blink?

"Instead of confronting his problem," she continues, "he's recreating traumatic events in other ways. It's all in the pictures." She pauses. "However, if done improperly this can lead to further psychological destruction and extreme emotional distress."

"Such as?" My legs are turned onto rapid fire.

"Disassociation, paranoia, hallucinations, self-harm-"

"Violence?"

"Often."

I grow absent, drifting a little. For a moment, I feel as if someone else is in the room with us. Giggling and listening behind the bookshelf.

"What if it feels so good, though?"

"Excuse me?"

"May I see his art?" She stares at me. No doubt the gears in her therapist's mind are rotating. If she wasn't a member of the school faculty, I'd worry about being charged for this. "What happens if someone who recreates or whatever you said, recreates events-"

"Repetition compulsion-"

"-what if they suddenly stop. What happens?"

"Well, that's impossible to speculate. Given the severity," I'm on the edge of her very uncomfortable seat, "there lies the potential for a spiral to occur. It could be mild. Or catastrophic."

Catastrophic.

I storm out of her office. Like all therapists, she's been no help.

Somehow, I manage the chaos in my brain until last period. On a wooden rocking chair, with my class folded in front of me, pretending to listen while I read from The Adventures of Alice and Wonderland, I can hardly concentrate. The plastic stag looms in the back corner, but I do my best to draw the kids' attention from it. I've told them it can be our class mascot, as long as they don't touch it. A couple girls had said I was trying to replace something I had killed. Ridiculous.

While the others sit on the floor, Danny remains at his desk, scribbling in his notebook as if the rest of us are nonexistent. He looks up for a split second, offering a light smile as our eyes meet. I drift to the deer, then back to Danny, then to the deer.

"Miss B, what's the matter?" Rebecca rattles my attention back to the book. "I thought you told us not to let the deer become a distraction."

"Thank you for reminding me, Rebecca."

I shrug her off and return to the page, keeping my eyes focused on the book until the bell rings, relieving me from my students.

What a day.

The Count

If I had a world of my own, everything would be nonsense.

My thoughts entice me to believe that with the new position, once I become VP, I might start over entirely. No one will challenge my job history or qualifications. Maybe the itch to kill will fade.

Maybe.

Though I'm not sure I want it to. Even so, I know more will have to die in order to get there.

I walk home, carrying Alice in my head. The buildings transform from steel and concrete into blossoming giant mushrooms that glow purple and green. The L train resembles an elevated stream of watery glass, a suspended sparkling rainbow bridge. The sidewalk sprouts soft grass that squishes with every step, and the people dance into butterflies and forest creatures, scurrying into holes and trees. It's a good indication to lay off the Ativan I've been popping throughout the day.

The city breeze caresses my ears and neck. The cotton candy sky that wraps the buildings in pink and blue is anything but what an autumn sunset should look like. And yet, it holds a bright tapestry of color, as if the sky itself is happy to be alive.

Douglass said that Chicago is one big, small town. It's disheartening; I came to a city for anonymity but turns out its intrusive hamlet is just masquerading with skyscrapers and elevated train systems. You think when moving to a big city that life will turn into the magical montage of success and enjoyment. Of bike rides along an empty bridge. Of endless nights with friends. A never-ending summer in your twenty-somethings. It doesn't register; the pain, the loneliness, the horror that living in a big city brings. 'That's just today, tomorrow will be different' I've lied, trying to console the deep tissues of my sanity that scream GET OUT, leave this place. But I will stay. I kind of enjoy the torture. It gives me a sense of strength.

I can't help but notice how cyclical everything has become. I feel like I have gone down a rabbit hole, one that leads to the same place every time. Again, and again, I travel it. The same scene repeats itself in a sick, agonizing fashion that plays with my mind. I start predicting how things will play out. The school days blend. I come home to the same annoyance next door… a package meant for Roger and Kate in front of my unit… the cries of sex or an argument shattering my eardrums.

Sometimes I press my ear to their door, listening. Just listening. A few times Roger has stormed out, nearly knocking me over as he stampedes to the elevator. She always chases after him. I don't know why.

Whether it's pleasure or pain, there exists a root of resentment in the sheer echo of their voices. I contemplate killing them, avoiding it, and continuing my night. I choose instead to prepare for a client or continue to master my portrayal of the innocent young teacher through TV shows and movies. I'll often sit and imitate Samantha Jones as she works her nets, ensnaring the most recent sexual victim. My nightly activities present my only stimulation. My bloody hobby that, sadly, has started to dwell in my mind as a worrisome addiction. It will only result in my untimely demise, or it too, will sadly take its place riding along this spiraling nightmare of consistency. I'm worried. Worried that it too, will sink.

Nothing would be what it is. And everything would be what it isn't.

I make it home, welcomed by hateful chants and accusatory volleys from next door. "Are you fucking kidding me, Kate?... I can't believe what a bitch you are. Don't you see what you make me into?... Look at me? Do you like what you see? You did this! You make me into someone awful." Kate's response to Roger is shrill screams, condemning him for a battery of crimes to their relationship and the inability to keep a job. He blames her for it all, of course. "Eat my dick! Eat my dick, you fucking bitch!"

I try to shut them out of my brain, but it makes me feel lethal.

He slams the door on his way out, so heated he barely notices me standing there as he storms down the hall. When he does, he flips me off while passing to the elevator. I don't do or say anything. His time will come.

Once inside my own apartment, I pause for a moment, scanning a place I hardly recognize as my own. The white sofa in front of a glass coffee table. A black TV stand and an ornate Persian rug, white with some bone and I think what constitutes charcoal (or is it gray) patterns. My walls are mostly bare. Besides my coveted music, I'm most proud of my bookshelf; it's an antique, black ebony wood that holds over three hundred books. I step close to the bookshelf, able to smell the pages along with the fumes of the wood's stain. Glancing across the collection, I dance over the leather-bound spines with my finger. Each a thing of beauty, gold inner bead detail along the edges, with a deep bloody maroon or espresso finish. I stole most of them. Uncle Jones had an extensive art collection that included vintage American classic novels. It pains me that our school requires reading the dumb-downed version of books like Alice's Adventures in Wonderland to my class. Amir claims it's what the curriculum requires. There it is. My hand freezes as I find the unabridged version, printed in the first half of the 19th century. Not just a print-out of the 1951 animated film manuscript. I flip through the pages. The spine creaks. The pages are stiff from years of neglect. I turn to the chapter with the Queen of Hearts.

"Off with her head!"

"Off with her head!"

When Lewis Carol says, 'if I had a world of my own, everything would be nonsense,' he went about making his whole world, his way.

Why is my method any different?

I remove myself from literary reminiscing, called by an empty stomach that labors over the handful of half-cooked French fries from lunch. I attempt to eliminate their lingering flavor infecting my throat and lips. Multiple pieces of gum and a few cigarettes throughout the day have helped. But now that I stand near my kitchen, my stomach growls. I journey to the fridge, pulling out a glass container. I only buy Belgian chocolate milk. Yes, the store sells it for nine dollars a half gallon, but I'm worth it. I pour a healthy amount into a glass and enjoy, pondering over what I'll cook for dinner. The cold milk's refreshing, chocolatey sensation chills my gums with a sweet rinse, eradicating the stale fried potato.

I drink the milk in a nearly ritualistic manner, sipping it gently, allowing the milk to graze the edge of my lips before entering my mouth, savoring each drop. The perfect preparation. Mix that with a shot of whiskey and I'm ready for a night of pure ultra-violent delight.

I'm interrupted by a buzz from my laptop indicating new messages from escort boards. Each time I fulfill my bloody needs, I create a new profile, deleting the past to remove the possibility of prior messages with my victims resurging. If authorities actually ever find the bodies or look into records for last contact, it will lead to Chastity, who lives in some apartment that doesn't exist, an IP address that has no real name and a fake bank account attached to it. The server doesn't belong to anyone, so I don't need to worry there. Completely anonymous. You don't need an email, a social security number, or even a credit card. Payments are cash, and identities are always fake. It's easier to sign up as an escort and sell yourself than to open a legitimate business. Just three clicks and they are purchasing you as their one time, pay by the hour, skin bag. Cyber prostitution is not a new concept. There are review boards, blog posts, and lists of girls on hundreds of sites monitored by third parties, private escorts, and pimps.

Past clients post about experiences, rating the girls as if they are objects for sale on Amazon or Craigslist. Of course, there are never any reviews about me. No one I service lasts long enough, and I never play the same girl twice. My system allows me to indulge my rowdier pleasures. I know most of the girls involved in this racket are abused, working against their will to appease evil men or to simply make ends meet. I do not intend to exploit a life filled with such a nightmare. It's not like I need this, not anymore at least. Or do I? And I'll really make an effort if all goes well with Amir's proposition. I promise myself.

But I can't help it. They think they purchase someone, something. Their egos want control of a woman. But I prove them wrong. I prove them wrong with the flick of my wrist when I slice their throats. Click. Click. Click, they write their own death sentence. They get what they deserve.

This is why I have to do what I do. If not me, who? For Kitty.

My new character's name is Mercedes Valentina. Not the typical hooker name. One reserved for a classier girl. My profile portrays me as enjoying wearing a tight black dress, not too revealing, something with a spark of danger, but a flavor of sophistication. I'm reserved, shy, but beneath my resolve sleeps a wild tigress of passion waiting to be let out of her cage. My hair is black, easy to dye from my natural brunette, or a wig will suffice, and I don't go overboard on my make-up. Why hide something naturally beautiful? Mercedes's profile has several hits within the first hour or so.

I lay across my couch, my hair drying with the black dye against my roots. I wear a robe over my naked, previously showered flesh. I can't help but smile as I run my hand along my smooth, shaven legs, admiring my toenails' red nail polish.

The profile page, a modest black background with red trimmings like the frayed edges of a Victorian dress, shows a message window: THE COUNT.

(Like Dantes?)

When a potential client messages that they are interested, a link pops up to a profile they have made for themselves.

I click the link. A new window pops up with a confidentiality assurance at the bottom. The Count doesn't give his name; usually men use fake tag names like

TOMCAT007 or BIGDICKBOI69. It's the same type of alias that Mr. Big had used. No different from my own false identity creation. Fantasy land.

For most escorts, payment works through secure wire or money transfer online. Which is a great way for pimps to track what their girls make so they can steal from them. But my pages always have a disclaimer that says, "CASH ONLY." So, they bring the cash, of course not paying until the job is done and they've had their fun. But it's on them, nonetheless. Usually, I charge around $500 per hour. Most nights, especially dates, can go longer than three if they are the talking type. They don't care about what I say or even how quick they are in bed. They just want someone to listen and nod while you sip the rest of your cocktail and act as a voiceless audience. That's all they usually want - someone to sit quietly and listen with no care in the world. And also, someone they can bend over.

The Count's page seems promising, and soon I'll learn more. Enough to bury his fate. It says he prefers casual dates, a good sense of humor, and no sick sexual perversions. Sure, there are a few times a man's profile claims he doesn't have any fetishes or kinks, but I've discovered that all of us have something, whether we act on it or not, that is perversely amusing to our darkest selves.

Anyways. I indulge The Count.

Accept.

A new window pops up that allows him to message me through the secure website database. It doesn't take more than three minutes for him to reach out.

"Hello there…"

No smiley faces or emojis… a good start.

I respond with a subtle – "Hi you". Online messaging isn't my thing.

"Do you go by Mercedes?"

My fingers rattle on the keyboard. Pause. Backspace backspace backspace. Then a quick rapid fire like a semi-auto machine gun.

"Call me Val. And you are the Cunt?"

(fuck me, shit)

"COUNT***"

"Hahahaha. I like you so far."

"So far?"

"Can't wait to meet in person."

"What did you have in mind?"

"Sunday night, 8 o'clock. Wicker Park."

Sunday. Discrete and usually less crowded. This guy doesn't want to be seen. At least not with me. My first thought … he's married… or lying about his age.

Most apartments in Chicago, at least newer ones downtown, use garbage shoots to get rid of trash. There's a shoot on every floor in the apartment building. Mine is only a few yards down from my door, so I can zip in and out, not worrying about having to put shoes on every time I need to toss a bag down the shoot.

I limit the human excess I throw down the shoot, realizing that if anyone finds a body in the garbage, the authorities' first reaction will be knocking on the tenants' doors, mine included. Not that I don't always have an alibi. I do; or at least no connection to whoever they find bloody and cut up in a pile of garbage.

My bare feet slide across the patterned carpet as I step through the hallway, trash bag in hand. The walls are a dark gray, ribbed with a textured wallpaper. The carpet has one of those unending diamond patterns. The kind that each shape connects to the tip of another, eternally sprouting across the hallway floor.

I heave the trash over my shoulder as I pull the latch that leads to the gaping black, seemingly endless shoot. The bag slides down with ease, I watch, staring and waiting for the thud as the trash bag collapses down the steel abyss. Starting strong and falling to a distant whisper like a muffled cloud of applause.

How whispers always grow, I think to myself.

"Ann, Ann, Ann" a whisper sparks. Dim. Like a dove. "Ann."

I'm not crazy. There aren't any voices in my head. I can promise you. At this moment, I think of other things. Of things that happened throughout my day. Of students raising their hands, their high-pitched voices saying "Miss Bonny! Miss Bonny! Miss B, Miss Bonny!" waving at me with questions, with answers, with comments… "Miss B!" Their voices ride like screams of gusting winds. The hazy voices grow. "Hey Miss B, twenty bucks Nick asks you out again,"–Douglass–"New hairdo sweetie?"–Sonya–"You look fucking dynamite."

"Are you wearing my wigs again?"–Kitty. No. Stay away. Get out of my head. You aren't allowed here, because you're gone. No, you're gone. Go away. "Ann, I'm not mad it's just that-."

No!

What's scratching me?

It's on my ankles first. Then my toes. A painless scratch. Then a panting, a tongue slung out and a slight yelp, not a bark, a yelp, more of a purr, but it isn't a cat. It's a tiny dog. White, fluffy, and fucking irritating.

The dog meets my stare as it claws at me if you can call them claws. I know it belongs to Kate and Roger. I recognize the shrilling yap as it begs for my attention, beckoning me to clap my hands and speak in a high-pitched voice.

The yapping persists. Pricking my brain like tiny needles.

"Pickles, hush." Kate's voice is direct, but still carries that same tone of sensuality that seems to slip from her tongue with every word. She's one of those girls who drops her lip after she speaks and bites the bottom as she listens to you or stares at you, and sometimes licks the top row of her teeth and the rim of her mouth while making long eye-contact. The perfect instructor, without even knowing it. "Hey, neighbor!"

No way she forgot my name, again.

"Kate, hi," I say with a slight tickle in my stomach. Her hair is up in a bun. Sport shorts, the kind you can see through the loops and barely make out the beginning of her crotch and the round curves of her perfect butt when she bends over. And her shirt a gray tee, no bra underneath, again with the tease. I see it all, tastefully perking up like two perfect mountains. I catch myself looking for only a second, but she must have noticed because she picks up that damn dog and holds it in her arms, covering her pointing nipples with the ball of white yapping fluff.

"Was Pickles bothering you?" Now she talks to the dog. "How did you get out? Huh? Roger must have forgotten to close the door. We will deal with him later." (I would be happy to deal with him for you) I want to say it. God, I want to say it. I would do it for her in a second. Then it would just be us. No, I appeal to myself. Time. Time will do its work. It has to. "Sorry about that," she starts. "Are you not wearing shoes?"

"What?" I look down at my bare feet. "I was just taking out the trash."

"That is so gross." Her feet are snug in a pair of black ankle socks.

"I just ran over to the shoot—."

"Pickles loves bare feet, don't you, Pickles?" Back to me. "You shouldn't be in the hall barefoot." Her eyes scan, switching from narrow to wide as she touches her hair. "Did you dye your hair?"

"It's just some coloring. I found a new stylist and wanted to try it out."

"Well, it suits you." It suits me? As if my hair color somehow automatically makes me not me. I nod with an attempt at a thank you.

I stand and watch as she skips back to her apartment, disappearing behind the gray slab of wood with the metal numbers 1302. I observe every inch from her ankles along her thin, but defined, calves up her thighs to her waistline, sailing along her curving torso along her back to her head. I feel a need. Not a romantic spark that I had felt for Kitty. But a call to navigate every centimeter of her perfectly sculpted figure, "Have a good night."

After my encounter with Kate in the hall, I return to my room, open my laptop and scan through pages on Facebook, studying photos of Kate online. She's into fashion, posting on both Facebook and Instagram regularly. Seldom are there photos of her and Roger, but every now and then there's a post with the caption, "So happy to have you in my life." Or "Happy Birthday to my best friend." I want to vomit. I like the posts where she's intentionally showing off her cleavage for a few hundred extra likes. She tags the designers and retailers in a few posts. I choose one that will be perfect for my date with the Count.

<u>Showtime</u>

I walk to a small bar in Wicker Park to meet The Count. I can't help but think I should've taken a cab. Sometimes though, I like the way the chill in the air crisps my focus. The cold hones my desire to kill.

The 30-degree evening coupled with the wind chill makes me curse my outfit: a leather jacket over a black skintight "Kate-tagged" dress. "Escort" or not, I'm not about to wear open-toe heels in October. My YSL boots crunch over the fallen leaves that have begun piling up on the sidewalk. Every so often, I kick the air trying to remove a stray brown leaf stuck between the soul and heel. One hand firmly grips a cigarette, while the other clenches the collar of my jacket. I left my phone at my place, and I don't carry a bag tonight. The less to carry the better.

It's far more practical to keep my ID and a few folded twenties between my left boob and the breast line of my dress. The neck of the dress lines my throat, with a slit in the fabric around the top of my chest. It has sleeves, but exposed shoulders, perfect for that initial touch where he'll glide his warm finger across my skin for the first time. The zipper, which took fifteen minutes to pull up, holds everything together in the back. The culprit of my tardiness.

I stop ten or so paces before the bar. A bouncer waits outside with his tally counter, clicking away like a struggling playwright on a typewriter. I stomp out my cigarette and pull the single strand of gum from my jacket pocket. Cinnamon Big Red. Mint flavor is for schoolgirls. I ignore my instinct to drop the wrapper on the sidewalk and, instead, shove it into my pocket, simultaneously feeling for the switchblade I have hidden away.

"ID," the bouncer says as I walk up. He stands three feet taller and two feet wider than me. A bead piercing decorates his bottom lip and a few rings dangle from his left ear. What little hair he has on his head he makes up for with a bushel red beard along his chin and mouth.

I offer my ID into his tattooed hands for inspection. He glances at the card – Mercedes Valentina. Born in 1992 (I always give my real age) and resides in Evanston, Illinois. I have every detail memorized in case he interrogates me. As the bouncer reads every inch of the ID, I shift, impatiently, wondering what awaits me inside. What The Count will be like. I don't like meeting 'clients' like this. It's a little too real in public settings. At least it's not the Viagra Triangle.

I can work with a vacant bar.

The bouncer takes forever with the ID. I shiver in the cold. My guess is he needs to do the mental math while figuring out the legal drinking age. I think about Mr. Big, Uncle Jones, Mr. Walter, now, The Count. I'm certain he'll be just like the rest. Despite a few traits here and there, what I've learned most through my bloody exploits is that they're usually all the same. A blended form of the same monster.

Industriously putting together the beast I'm about to meet in my mind, I neglect the bouncer as he repeats, "here you go ma'am," holding my ID for me to take.

Inside, I spot The Count the moment I walk in the door. Easily the most handsome man inside. He has dark hair, neat and freshly cut. His lips kiss the rim of his glass as he sips from his whiskey, his sharp jaw line even to the tilted crystal glass. He wears a suit though most of the clientele sport jean jackets and flannels. No tie though. A freshly poured drink waits with his smile as I approach the bar. Whiskey, neat (how does he know?)

He rises.

"You must be Val?" He says as he shakes my hand. Big. Honest. "You look bangarang."

"That's a compliment?"

"In my vocabulary."

I grin. The pleasant embers of his cologne wash away the peanuts and spilled rum aroma from when I first stepped up to the bar.

"I know your profile claimed you were a martini girl," he pulls the chair for me at a table in the corner. The smooth blues music fades. The crack of pool balls ricochets off the walls every few minutes. He rolls my jacket from my back. I sit, the glass in front of me smiling with a golden shimmer. Most men have the need to stay at the bar, to show off, or they move their chair and set it down, corner sitting. "But then," he continues, "when are internet profiles ever a proper depiction of someone?" His voice is neither sensual nor degrading... it's just – well – his voice. It's Clooney-esque with a peppered, cigar rasp. A confident ease, but not cocky.

This is all wrong.

"You know, there's nothing less sexy than a man whose first impression is 'I'm sorry'." I bring the glass to my lips, keeping my eyes on him while tilting it to my mouth. A warmth sweeps over me. I savor it while closing my eyes, swallowing and slowly placing the glass back down. "But lucky for you, you were correct. I actually despise martinis."

He rolls his shoulders and taps his finger nervously against the oak tabletop. He bites his lip, nodding his head ever so slightly—almost awkwardly—to the rhythmic tunes that string above us. Surely, he's old enough to have been on a few dates, even married before, or still is. But he fumes with those itching first date nerves. It's a first for me. A first that a man who's hired me acts so cautious, so careful. But there's confidence in his boyish anticipation. A certain eager, yet straightforward lack of pretension.

He clears his throat.

"So, tell me something that isn't on your profile." He finishes a sip, grinning as he sets the near-empty glass down and peers off to find the waiter. He doesn't wave him down or call out, instead he waits, sitting back in his chair, getting comfortable and studying me with his warm green eyes. "Tell me something true."

"I'm not sure you could handle that."

"You aren't from here. Moved to the city alone, most likely." What was this, his version of twenty questions? His eye contact is hypnotizing. "And your name can't be Val. Not sure it suits a girl like you."

"You're right. But what does "The Count" want with a girl like me?" He leans in. Enjoying this.

"Depends on what kind of girl you really are."

"You read my profile."

"And we've already established profiles are inaccurate."

"Why so interested?"

"Am I being too forward?"

"It doesn't usually go this way. This has to be your first time-."

"-that obvious?"

"But you could also be stricken with a sense of misplaced confidence. A common trend in impotent men. I've had too many who blame the whiskey, or claim, this happens all the time." I do a little mimic act which makes him laugh. I like his laugh. It's one that happens seldom, but when it does, it's warm and inviting.

"Maybe it's you."

"Don't be foolish."

"So now that we've established we're both skilled in bed," he says, crossing his arms. "Let's dig deeper."

Deeper?

The word makes me draw blank. My mind's a firing squad out of ammo. I had him. Didn't I? I need to refocus.

"What way does this usually go?"

"I mean I am a prost-."

"Let's not use that word while you're here." I'm not sure what to say. Is he ashamed of buying an escort, or does he genuinely want to treat me like a human being? He's far too handsome to be single, and so far, not terrible when it comes to being a gentleman. So why? Is it paranoia? Why does he need to pay me for company? There has to be something. A reason. There always is. Soon I will find this 'Count' guilty of something.

Soon.

I keep quiet for a moment, allowing a lull of silence to kill the conversation. It has started pleasant, now taking a dip as I ruined it with my wall of insecurity. So what if I tell him my life story? It isn't like he'll last the night.

"Can I get you another round?" The waiter swings in, breaking the silence. The Count snaps back to life.

"Yes," he says as he arches his back and rubs his hands together. He keeps his eyes on me while he orders. I guess I'm a better view than the nutmeg seller look that the staff wears. "Val, would you like another?"

(He's asking?)

I want to ask if he works for the police.

With a cough to kick the frog from my throat, "Yes, please. Another whiskey."

"I'll have the same." That grin returns in the corner of his inviting mouth. "Thank you."

"My pleasure," the waiter says, writing down our order. "May I offer any appetizers or small bites? Our kitchen will be open for another thirty minutes."

"Did you want food, Ann?"

(Ann?)

Suddenly I'm no longer sitting with the Count. I'm in a smaller bar, busier and hip. The music blaring.

"Ann?" I look over the table and Kitty sits across from me with a concerned smile. She's diddling a loose strand of hair from the blonde side. The pink is tucked behind her little ear, the one with piercings in the cartilage. "Ann, do you want anything to eat, babe?" I scratch my arm, shaking my head with a mute reply of "NO! Stop talking to me." Get out of my head. You're supposed to be dead. "Ann... Ann...." Did I take the last Haldol? A harsh lance of ringing pierces through my brain.

"Miss Val?"

The Count is sitting across from me. My racing thoughts become calm.

"Yes?"

"Are you hungry at all?"

"I'm fine."

I retreat to the bathroom to 'freshen-up'. To re-engage. The walls are marked up with "Will and Lara were here" and other random little cliche bathroom messages. Polaroids of dicks and boobs. The mirror even has scattered syllables that as I stare longer, rearrange themselves… "Off with his head. Off with his head."

In the adjacent stall, a few finance bros do coke. Ducklings lost in Wicker Park on a night out. In the opposite stall I can hear a girl moaning. Belts jingling and heaving gusts. The deep breathing of a young man trying to hold on. I wonder if the guy she just met is what she hoped for tonight. The stall walls shake. They are struggling to get that perfect position on top of a bar toilet. She's not the first to be used like that under a foggy crimson light in a bar bathroom smelling of cigarette butts, piss, and wet towels. It's anything but pleasurable. Unless he's got a killer dick I suppose. Tomorrow she'll be sore. Her knees bruised from the sticky tile when he makes her go down on him because she refuses to let him finish inside her. Her skin and outfit she spent hours deciding on graffitied, like the bathroom walls, with his squirted manhood. And he'll have a sick story for his friends. Maybe they're the ones in the coke stall.

I need to get back to The Count.

The mirror takes hold of me. I stare at my reflection. Lost in some crystal universe where I'm not in this grimy sex and drugs dungeon but instead backstage somewhere. The light bulbs lining the perimeter of the vanity. My stage set. My makeup is fresh and the audience drools with anticipation for my performance. I can hear the applause. Five minutes to curtain. Soon I'll get that order:

"Showtime."

"How about a game of pool?" He says when I return. My posture straightens. I'm doing my best to stay on target, confused if this is some charming ploy to force me into vulnerability.

"I am more of a darts girl."

"Oh c'mon," he says charmingly. "We can make it interesting."

"I'm listening."

"If you win, you don't have to sleep with me tonight."

"Excuse me?"

"That's the deal," he chuckles slightly. More drinks come and I don't let mine touch the table before I pick it up. There's a far too normal silence drifting. A specter of comfort.

God, his eye contact burns.

"So, let me get this straight," I say.

"You win, you don't have to um…"

"Put out? Earn my dollar?"

"I wasn't going to say that, but-."

"You're not – ," I point downward, "You know, your down there isn't, should I say, sad?"

"I can assure you that's not the case."

"Well then what is this?"

"I promise, there are no motives." But there's always a motive.

"But what if I want to?"

"That I can't control."

"Wrong," I say to him, teasingly as I run my tongue along the rim whiskey glass. I was told as a child to never play with my food. But it made things fun in these situations. "That is entirely in your control. Men don't seem to get that." I want to make him need to have me. If we don't end up in a more private setting, how else can I kill him?

"So, you agree?"

"What if you win?" I ask. "You gonna make me do some freaky sex shit?" Suddenly Kate and Roger sift through my mind. Is the Count a customer of Xtreme Restraints? Is this all a trap to get me into a harness or a belt strap? Come to think of it, I don't think I would mind going reverse with him. He seems like he can handle that.

"If I win," he rubs his chin, performing contemplation. "How about this," he says. "If I win, you agree on a second date with me."

"Date?"

"Outing. Whatever you want to call it."

"Bit of warning, I just got out of a relationship. Can make a person unstable."

"So we have that in common."

"You just got out of a relationship?"

"No."

I'm thrown. What does he want me for twice if not to fuck the first time and then find a new body to fill? He's so different from the usual type I encounter.

"So, what will it be?" He wants a second date. All he needs to do is return to my profile page, request a new appointment and pay for it. But the Count wants me to know that he's coming for seconds.

He not only wants me to know, he wants me to agree to it, no strings or payments attached. Equal price for an equal date. Of course, the night will eventually end, and everything will be gone. Even me. Mercedes Valentine will vanish. Her profile will disappear and the Count, well, the Count will be dead.

So, I indulge him.

"Am I supposed to refer to you as The Count all night?"

He softens, letting out a stoic breath before introducing himself simply as, "John."

We only get one game in, which I lose, before the squad of ducklings waddle in two by two across the bar. Their leader guides, his attempt at a strut alone helps build back my lethal edge.

"Check these guys out," the Count says as the gaggle whistles at the bartender. He must have noticed me staring at them. He leans against the pool table with me. Our shoulders graze as he chuckles. "I worked with guys like that for years when I was in finance. Used to fucking be one of them."

"You used to be a duckling?" I say.

I can't imagine him wearing the typical light blue collared button down, walking around smelling like old spice and cheap after shave. Not anything like now. I can name his perfume. Tom Ford. Tuscan Leather. A perfect balance of smoothness, with a dash of musk to cling to his manhood. Not too much. That perfect amount that invites you to sniff the air around him because you want that scent, his scent, rushing through your body. The inkling creeps in my mind to check his jacket label. I'm not one that judges on name brands, but if a man wears a suit, where it's from tells a lot about him.

"A duckling?"

"It's just—" I shake my head, biting my tongue. "Never mind."

"No, I want to know. C'mon, I won't judge." His tender voice calms the anxiety from spilling my inside joke.

"It's just what I call guys like that."

"Explain." His voice is playful. Interested, like I have an embarrassing vacation story to tell and I'm holding out on him.

"No, forget it."

"Oh c'mon, you can't say something like that and not expect to explain it." His smile breaks me. It reminds me of how Kitty smiled at me once. When she'd wake up in the middle of the night and see I was there. Or when we'd drive together, and I'd look at her from behind the wheel. The type of smile that two people share when the rest of the world around them vanishes.

"You see them all over the city, corporate gaggles, walking around in little lines like baby ducks trying to follow their mother. They're all the same. Just following the other in line. I don't know, it's kinda stupid, I guess. Just a name to make fun of them."

He laughs. Not one of those closed-mouth fake ones that boyfriends do to make girls think they're funny. Genuine. His teeth show and his head shoots back with a laugh that gives up trying to appear attractive. Real laughter drops the barrier of vulnerability. An intoxicating joy that highlights someone's true self.

"You know what," he say. "I bet you they all order the same drink." I can't help but smile. This might be harder than I thought. No, I think, stay in character a little while longer. We will finish him soon.

What happens next is a blur. One second we are in the street, the next I arrive at his apartment, stepping out of a cab in a neighborhood I recognize. I observe from a distance, taking in my surroundings and seeing the events transpire, but I stand outside of my body, out of whatever cockpit of control my brain usually holds over me.

I see myself, walking alongside the Count–John–whoever, up to a building I have seen before. The red awnings, the gothic exterior and high-rise balcony apartments. Gold Coast. So what? Most classy, wealthy bachelors live around here. Then I see the doorman. A dark-skinned man I swear I've met before. He nods at us, his eyes glaring at me as I step out from the cold October night into the warm building.

"Welcome back," he says as he tips his hat. Very old fashioned. Yet his eyes are focused on me the whole time, not welcoming John, but me, ME, back to this building. His eyes remain glued to mine as the door closes behind us.

John fingers me in the elevator while I rub the outside of his pants. I don't see which button he presses. I moan louder than the clanking metal of the antique ascending cage. My eyes are hazy, my vision and hearing blur with confusion and lust.

"I never wanted this to feel like it was about this," he says, pulling an envelope from his jacket pocket once the door to his apartment shuts. Inside is dark. There's an outline of silhouettes from his furniture from the moon peeking through the curtains. He places the envelope on a small table next to the doorway. "For whenever you're ready," he says. "This is yours for tonight. You are free to leave whenever you like. I included enough in there for the whole night."

He leads me to his room.

We start to make out beside the bed. I can't help but feel something is wrong. Like this entire thing is wrong.

My dress is off, and his shirt unbuttoned, he kisses me like he's known me for years. Most men who hire prostitutes refuse to kiss at all.

"Is this real?" He says, unlatching from my lips and kissing my neck.

"What?"

"I did win pool," he says, his hands rub me, gentle, but passionate. "But I had no intention of making you sleep with me tonight. Tell me one thing, tell me that you will do this because you want to, and not because you are being paid."

"When do people do anything they want to without being paid?" I say, unbuttoning his pants. "We just get paid in different ways."

"Fair point, but just say it. This is something you want. I could feel it when I touched you."

"You talk too much." His pants and boxers hit the floor. Mr. Big would be a better alias for John.

I stroke him, hoping it will make him quiet.

"Please, just tell me." His breath is short. "Tell me that you came back with me for me, and not an envelope of cash."

That's when I realize it. That beneath all this man. All this class. Lives a child. A child too far gone to exist in a world that doesn't say yes; I want to be pleased, to be part of you. His desperation makes me dry up, but I'm in too deep. I know in order to do what I came here to do I have to sleep with him first.

"Yes," I say, as I kiss his bare chest, making my way along his neck and chewing his earlobe. "I want you."

Afterwards, we lay in silence. Our heavy post-battle breathing tells me he's still awake. I feel like I owe him at the very least a chance to catch his breath, to relax and to maybe fall asleep. I need to get to my jacket, which I left in the entryway.

He rolls over, his arm resting across my naked chest. It holds me down like a prison bar. I try prying him off, waiting until his breathing has slowed, and he drifts into a peaceful slumber.

I slip out from under his arm and sit upright on the edge of the bed. He's asleep. Heavy sleeper, good to know. All I need to do is grab my knife, straddle him in the bed and slit his throat. Judith and Holofernes style.

What about clean up?

Honestly, the sheets are so soft I consider taking them with me. They are the kind that don't crinkle or scratch against my skin. They're cool, but also warm without being suffocating. What a tragedy they'll be ruined, smothered in his blood.

Sheets can always be cleaned. Any girl who has had her period knows her way around a few bloodstains.

I slip my panties back on. No way I'm stuffing back into my dress. I grab his shirt from the ground and wrap myself in the white cotton button down. The sleeves hang a few inches past my fingers and the end droops to my mid-thigh. I don't bother buttoning the shirt as I gently step towards the door. It's still ajar, releasing a cricket's chirp as I nudge it open just enough so I can slip through.

The hallway floorboards chill my bare feet as I tiptoe across to the living room, trying to keep their creak to a minimum. A haunting chill creeps along my spine as I work my way through the dark apartment. I pass another closed door. A second bedroom? Why? I let the cool marble countertop of the kitchen island guide me in the darkness as I make my way into the kitchen.

Once my eyes acclimate, I see he has taste in more than just clothes. The unit must be on a very top floor. I see the whole city through his curtains, humming with a brilliant glow.

"Ann?" A voice says behind me. I turned my head so violently as though I have springs in my neck. The kitchen is still dark, a tarp of shadow hangs over the countertops and sink. It's only me. "Ann" the voice repeats, not completely behind me, but inside of my head.

I ease through the kitchen, inching with my hands extended, feeling for a light switch. As I cross the counter, a wooden knife block catches my eye. The black handles of the knives call me, their inviting slick ebony hilts pleading. I graze my fingers over the ends of the handles.

This will work. Do it quickly.

Now. Or you might never leave.

The knife blade sings with a gliding soprano whisper as the steel slides from its nook. With the chef's knife in my hand, I step over to the light switch.

Flick.

A girl sprawls across the kitchen floor, her blonde hair mangled with crisping dried blood sticking the yellow strands of her locks together. A pool of blood, seeping out from holes in her throat, belly, and torso, spill onto the floor and flood the kitchen tile. The deep, scarlet pond rises to my ankles. Her skin beneath the layers of rose petal-colored stains, crawls with flesh-eating parasites devouring her from the inside out.

I flick the light off. Closing my eyes, I follow the darkness. I know she's not real.

Flick.

The lights are back on. I open my eyes. The kitchen tile sparkles, clean and dry as it was before. The girl has vanished. Kitty is gone. But something else catches my eye. A framed photo on John's counter shows me something far more horrifying than the ghost of Kitty's corpse.

Run While You Can

John stands on a beach somewhere. It's a typical father-son vacation photo. The kind that divorced men like John probably use to remember from time to time that they are still in fact parents. I recognize the child. Faces are things I hardly forget, especially the faces I see every day.

Standing next to the man I'm about to kill is Danny Hilton.

Beside the frame sits a book, the page side points my way and is turned on its face, but I immediately recognize it. The Count of Montecristo.

Suddenly I feel very naked. Exposed on some cold stage before an audience of shadows. I'm just dreaming, I tell myself. Wake up! No. I am awake, my throat constricts. Am I suffocating? I'm drowning, filled with cement as I fight to move. But my feet are useless. My body is motionless. How can this be? This man. The man who has hired me to sleep with him. It's me in danger. Me who is suddenly trapped. And I intend to slaughter him in his bedroom with his own kitchen knife.

My arms grow heavy, my spine turns into mush, barely strong enough to support my body. My head spins, winding while my skin crawls from my bone; bloody flesh to rot against the truth that shuts me down.

I take a step back, slipping out of the kitchen, away from the bedroom where a man I have to kill still lays unaware and asleep. I need to kill him. That's the job. I must kill him. But before I know it, my feet are sprinting beneath me.

I panic and run.

My head screams. My mind straight jacketed from sense. I need to kill him. He's one of them. But I can't.

All I can do is run.

I dart down the hall. My feet thunder across the green and gold trimmed carpet. I still only wear his shirt, and still clench the kitchen knife. All the signs of a person fleeing a murder-scene; a racing heart, an anxious head, and a weapon in the fist of the runaway offender. The only thing missing is a dead body.

I gallop down to the elevator, smashing the down arrow button.

Fuck, my stuff.

I can't go back for it. What if he hears me? What am I supposed to do? Is that extra bedroom Danny's?

All at once, I remember walking him home that day. The doorman, his subtle judgmental stare; and Danny, disappearing with his backpack and novel, gifted by me, snug under his arm.

The elevator arrives with a loud ding. A 90's horror film ding. I practically punch the 'L' button into the wall. The elevator rattles as the doors close, finally descending with a gentle shake towards the lobby.

I rest against the side of the elevator, breathing heavily, trying to remember why I ran, trying to remember what I left in the apartment. I try to gather myself. I'm safe, temporarily. Safe enough to realize I stole a kitchen knife. Will he notice? Will he look at my ID that is still wrapped in my black dress at the foot of his bed? He'll have the wrong name, wrong

address, no way he can track me. The address isn't real.
He'll hunt me down and see there is no 118 North Cherry
Lane, Evanston, IL. I doubt he'll hold it against me, being
a prostitute and all. He'll probably respect the effort I've
made to be anonymous.

Then the elevator doors open. I forget the shirt is still
undone, and quickly fasten the buttons, somewhat
covering myself.

It has to be around 2 am when I edge out from the
security of the elevator and into the main lobby. The
doorman is off duty, but there's a desk attendant nosing
off. An older gentleman, peppered and frail, snores with
his chin tucked into his chest and nearly drools into his
folded arms. I tiptoe across the lobby floor. I hide the knife
on the opposite side in my right hand, the steel tight
against my forearm so if he does wake, he won't see it. A
few jackets dangle on a coat rack behind the slumbering
desk hand. I sneak to the side, trying to keep as much
distance as I can while still managing to reach the rack.

I snag the closest jacket I can reach, slipping it from the
hanger and around my shoulders. I dash out of the
building, through the double doors that are typically
controlled by my friend the doorman.

Now I brace for the bitter night. Barefoot. Freezing. A
knife in my hand and a jacket clasped around my shivering
chest.

Ghost Town to Old Town

My teeth chatter like rat claws prancing across the hard street. I wrap myself in the stolen trench coat, my head nuzzled in my neck. My lips vibrate over my quivering mouth, and my fingers shake even under the cover of the thick wool. The wind invades my body, covering my skin with an icy chill. I'm certain I might freeze to death before reaching home.

A fresh, deadly awe to the city emerges at the pass of the witching hour, drifting across the conscious skyscape like a forgotten dream. The fabrication of the city remains, but the tissues and cells turn dark, and a new energy ignites. One of danger and of caution. Of course, it isn't fear I feel while struggling to maintain my balance. A heavy canvas of weariness rests on my shoulders. I trip over my feet, which start to bleed on the concrete, trying to stay warm while keeping my head up, keeping my wits. I take Wells Street all the way into River North from Gold Coast. It's the faster way but might not be fast enough. I'm already breathing short and losing feeling in my toes, face, and fingers. If I go down Wabash or Rush, I'll be around more people, passing the bar scene, illuminated with and protected by lights, crowds, and everything else I hate. A girl half-dressed walking with a knife wouldn't be that foreign a sight, but I'm too cold to take the long, safer route. A seemingly undeveloped part of the city stretches along Wells in between Gold Coast and River North. A street without identity. No train stops for the L line, no major restaurants, and scattered government housing and foreclosed storefronts. Just a lull in the downtown atmosphere of cluttered, chaotic excitement. A Ghost Town to Old Town. That's what makes it so dangerous. An arsenal of low lives and thugs patrol these streets.

I hobble along, a quick pace, but not one that arouses suspicion. I left my ID at John's. I don't even remember why I even ran out now. The cold air fries the working circuits in my head.

My steps drag, my head grows heavy. My lips, which I cannot feel, tremble and the inside of my nose stings. I glance over my shoulder. Maybe John woke up and realized I left. He won't think anything of it, I hope, until he notices his shirt and kitchen knife missing. And that I left my clothes and belongings. He'll try to return them. Will he? Or will he hold on to them? Smelling the inner workings of my dress while he touches himself at night, wishing I'm there again, climbing over him and rubbing against his skin. He expects a second date. What will happen if he realizes I'm his son's teacher? I cannot let that happen.

A rumbling hum from behind me halts my scattered thoughts. The frozen sheet that stiffens my body shatters, leaving me covered in a heat of alerted panic. Something is following me.

Whatever it is gives off a low whine as it draws closer. I don't dare look back. That will make me look suspicious. Instead, I walk faster, doing my best to stay balanced over the sporadic patches of ice.

But it follows... rattling and mechanically grunting behind me. A blinding light shines, and I look back involuntarily.

When I see what it is, I run.

The car roars from behind me. Without streetlights I can hardly tell the make and model. Squad car? If it's a cop, I can make up some story about getting mugged and running for my life. Although I don't know how I'll explain the kitchen knife.

It follows.

Keep going.

Is it John?

Run!

The car picks up. I'm so frozen my legs can barely go forward. No turns, no crossing the street. I sprint through a crosswalk. The light's red, but the car doesn't stop. Shit. I reach the other side, but my foot catches on the curb–

Next thing I know I'm sprawled out on the frozen leaf-filled sidewalk.

She helps me to my feet. It's a tall, dark woman in a turtleneck, wearing a puffy jacket. Before I can register anything, I'm sitting beside this woman in the front seat of her car.

"You're lucky," she says. "You probably would have frozen to death. Wanna share?" I give her a puzzled look, still unsure where I am. "Why are you half naked running around in the cold? You do know this is Chicago, don't you?" I enjoy the warmth of the seat heater, waiting to speak. I need to savor the slight comfort I'm feeling.

"You do this often? Pick up and interrogate random strangers in the middle of the night?"

The knife? John! What happened? Did she take it? No, I must have dropped it in the leaves. She scans me from head

to toe. She has clean, black skin and a sturdy frame. She's
fit, and seems to have a young, kind disposition.

"You seemed a little out of sorts. Felt like you needed a
hand. I have an eye for the bad ones. Don't worry. You're
safe. Where are you headed?"

"River North. Just down Wells." The car stops at a
light.

"You warm enough? You're still shaking" I nod.

She puts her hand on my knee. It's soft, warm on my
skin. I don't want it to return to the wheel. Our eyes meet
for a moment, but I turn away, staring out the window.

"Bad date, I take it? Unless you're fleeing a crime
scene." She cackles.

"Are you laughing at me?"

"No, no. I'm sorry, you just – you're just not what I
expected to see when I turned you over on the sidewalk.
Not the typical nighttime wanderer."

"And how does your typical night wanderer look?" The
light goes green and the Corolla takes a minute to get
going again.

"They are never as pretty as you. I'm guessing this isn't
common for either of us."

"No? And what does a usual night for you look like?
Huh?"

"I drive around all night, trying to find a pretty ass and
when I do, I pick her up."

"Quite the stalker."

We both laugh. She is quite pretty. Stern, but
something soft deep down. She gazes down the road
ahead, one hand on the wheel. "No... most nights are
spent alone. You?"

"Alone."

She takes her eyes off the road for a moment and we lock for a sprint of a gaze.

"That's a shame."

"Let's just say it was somewhat of a first for me tonight. It didn't go how I planned."

"He was that bad, huh?"

"What do you mean?"

"Honey, I can tell." She gives me a slight grin. I like her face. "After my ex, I tried men for a while, too."

"You're very intuitive. And forward."

"Here's the deal. It didn't take. I don't know if it's something I can control or not, but at the end of the day, I don't care. I know what makes me happy. You can't control what or who makes you happy. Sometimes it's just an urge, you know what I mean? You ever have those urges?"

"I think so."

There's a lull of silence under the monotone clicking of her turn signal. I try studying her car for any signs of a job or identity. Unsuccessful, I plant my head on the window, blowing air on the glass and drawing a little upside-down smiley face in the fog.

"You ever go to the Navy Pier?" I ask, a bit distant. "There's a carousel there. Spins all day, then at night, it is so still it makes you think it could never move in the first place."

"The pier is too touristy for me."

"Not at night. At night it's like, gorgeous and desolate. The first night I came to this city I slept on that carousel." She chuckles a little. I can sense her unease. "I can't sleep sometimes... just still spinning."

"You can call me Blake by the way."

"Blake?"

"Everyone at work calls me that. I've gotten used to it by now."

"Chloe."

I'm wondering if she's going to make a move. Should I? Some people say friends are all you need. At times I think all I need is meaningless sex. I find it funny, whether you love someone or not, sex is often anything but meaningless. And in hindsight, it abolishes logic and premonition. I need more blood, or sex, to get the thoughts of John Hilton out of my head.

I'm slipping. I can feel it. No matter how hard I promise to hold on.

A teacher, I remind myself, I still have that. For now. Seems teaching is the only thing that keeps me from going totally lethal. But now with him—with John Hilton—out there in the world, how do I function? Without the promotion to VP yet, how can I stay sane much longer?

<u>Hooky</u>

How can I possibly be expected to handle school on a day like this?

I pace in my living room in my underwear with a cigarette in one hand and my cell in the other. My body is sore from my marathon of a night. I've taken too much of a physical and mental beating to brace a school day. The ringtone of Pearcey's office phone hums through my speaker. I take a long drag and hold the smoke in my mouth until the voice on the other line forces me to spit out a quick exhale.

"Pearcey K-12 principal's office."

"Hi Mrs. Baxterly, it's Miss Bonny, any chance Mr. Salem is in?" I cough, waving the smoke from my face and setting the cigarette between my teeth.

"Good morning, Miss Bonny," she replies, bubbly as always. "Happy Monday." I imagine her on the other line, bouncing at her desk as she speaks. Every week she arrives with her hair freshly done from the weekend; a curly puff like a bird's nest. "How are you doing today? Shouldn't you be here by now?"

My alarm clock says 7:11 am. It's a miniature merry-go-round, spinning round and round. I want to smash it, quite honestly. Make it stop spinning. I set the cigarette in a glass tray.

"Can I speak to Amir?"

"Unfortunately, Mr. Salem is not in right now." Her Midwestern accent flows just as clear through the phone as it does in person. "Of course, Mrs. Greene is here, would you like to speak with her?"

You gotta be kidding.

"Do you know when Amir–Mr. Salem–will be in? I won't be able to come into school today."

"You feeling a little under the weather dear?" I tap my foot and stare at the ceiling. "You know I have a great recipe for a chicken soup that clears those sinuses right up. Everyone's got those sinus issues this time of year. My sister's son is sick. He had to stay home all last week. Can you believe that?" Then she blows her nose. Yes, she actually blows her nose while we are on the phone. "Do you want the recipe sweetie? I can forward it to you on my electronic mail if you like –?"

"My uncle died."

Fuck. It just comes out.

"Oh, sweetheart, I am so sorry." I can't know for sure, but it sounds like she's tearing up on the other line. Who knows, it might just be post nose blowing sniffles. "Is there anything I can do?"

"Can you just let him know? And please, ask him to keep this quiet."

"You can count on me, Miss Bonny. I will let him know right when he walks through that door. You know, death is natural, dear. Just know that your uncle is in a better place now. Oh you poor thing, I hope you are –."

I hang up.

A slight sigh comes from between my grinding teeth. I have in an instant lost my one good excuse.

Amir will certainly confide in Angela about my uncle. I imagine how it will go. All she has to do is look at him. Those stern, razor blade eyes. She has a vulture look to her. She'll approach him, after planting a few initial rumors in the teachers' lounge, rooting her system of parasitic teacher talk, and walk up to Amir. She won't ask directly. God no. Angela Greene is a passive aggressive mastermind. She will say something like, "So, I'm handing out assignments for all the teachers to clean one area of the lounge before the weekend." Showing her dutiful initiative as potential vice-principal, Amir will nod, not really paying attention to her. "I was just heading to Bonny's classroom. I think she would do a great job wiping down the counters."

She'll match his gaze with that grin of hers, relishing his capture in the prison of her manipulative talons. Then he'll tell her, asking of course, to keep it quiet and that "Miss Bonny's privacy should be respected."

I'm ruined.

In about an hour, they'll all know. Movies get it all wrong. Sure, kids gossip, but in my experience their attention is so limited and so rapid that one second they're talking about one thing and the next totally fixated on something else new and exciting. But teachers, please. They treat new gossip like a Christmas bonus.

My uncle dying will open the gates to Nick. Now I don't have an excuse for him; but I can't focus on that. Nick isn't really the man on my mind.

All I can think of is John Hilton. His scent still lingers between my legs.

I sit in the shower deleting all concepts of time. Staying under the boiling water pressure forever sounds nice. I might even nod off for a little.

Suddenly more alert, I try scrubbing off John's remnants. But I can still smell him. His touch has tattooed itself into the fibers of my nerves. Images of the night rush through my head. I need something, anything. Danny, my student, is his son.

Alive, John poses a threat. That's enough reason to end his life.

Beethoven's humming symphony keeps me company, spinning on my record player while I try to plan how to expel John Hilton, for good.

I'm not nervous; I am not mad. When I get nervous, I sweat. No. I'm only shaking. Not shaking. Shivering—fuck it's cold in here. The autumn wind smacks against the glass of my windows. The closed curtains don't shield the cool air from outside. John won't know where to look. He can't find me. There's no way he can find me. My address is fake. My name is fake. I'm not in the system. No, I'm not mad. I pull at my hair. Goddamn pills sound good right now. My teeth rake across my bottom lip. No, I'm not mad. I just need to kill someone.

The sofa cushion crunches beneath me as I plop down with my laptop on my thighs. I pin up my hair and wear a pair of black shorts and a gray t-shirt with no bra. The computer's engine warms the flesh on my thighs as it dings. Just a few clicks and I delete the profile of Mercedes Valentina. Quit the site. Erase all software memory.

What if he's out there looking for me right now? Maybe he's over it? Took the free sex, since I forgot the cash, and went on with his life. Maybe he's already looking for a new prostitute for the weekend. You are overthinking it, Ann. Ann, you are overthinking it.

"Ann." Kitty is that you? What are you doing in my head? Get out! Get the fuck out!

My fingers drill into the laptop keyboard.

JOJHNN HITLON.

Jesus Christ my fingers don't even work. Connect with my brain, God damnit. Backspace, backspace, backspace.

John Hilton.

There he is.

His face pops up, along with links and articles. I can't help but fantasize about how he woke up this morning. He's probably an early riser, requiring no alarm, designed through habit and routine by now. He'll notice the bed empty beside him, wondering where the girl has gone from the night before. Sure, he hired her so why bother with breakfast for the sex-worker. Does he really expect her to stick around until morning? No. He'll be fine with that. What he won't be fine with is her leaving her things, stealing his shirt, and taking his kitchen knife.

I follow the webpages. Senior Partner at Hafford and Associates Law Firm. Impressive. I click the link for the firm.

96th Wacker Drive, Chicago IL.

I need more. Let's see, articles, twitter, Instagram, Daily Mail…

Nothing.

Fuck.

I slap my laptop closed and set it on the coffee table beside a stack of books. A hardcover collection of short stories by Edgar Allen Poe. I notice a few magazines I also have sprawled over the glass now look like a deck of cards shuffled by a toddler. Most of the magazines are women's titles. The most up to date blogs and articles on sex, work, healthy living, and fashion, all to create a character that people see as nothing out of the ordinary. That I'm just like one of them: a guzzler of cosmopolitan and journalized vanity. As far as personal entertainment goes, I much prefer the Poe stories.

I'm not aware of my decision to move, but suddenly I'm up from the couch and spring to my bedroom. I pull my t-shirt over my head and let it fly on top of my bed. I strap on a bra and rummage through my drawers for a pair of pants. I need something simple. Something I can wear to blend in.

C'mon c'mon. Why am I rushing?

Ok, Ann, relax. Just breathe.

That therapist keeps circling in my head. That word: "Catastrophic." No. What does she know? She's a school counselor, not a psychologist. She did introduce herself as a doctor though. She might - no. I'm in control. I'm in control.

Black bottoms, white button-down blouse. Long camel trench raincoat will work on top. I wrap a scarf across my neck and stand before a mirror. No good, I think. I roll off the scarf and unbutton the blouse, throwing them both onto the bed. I slip into a black turtleneck.

I fluff my hair, draw some mascara over my eyes to cover the tired, sleepless night that still lingers on my face. Once I finish, I stand in the bathroom before the mirror, motionless, just staring at myself, or at least whatever the image is looking back at me. Moments pass, losing the blast of urgency that originally propelled me into such a frantic dressing session.

My reflection gazes back with a disapproving smirk. I shake it off, smiling in the mirror, then close my mouth again, this time displaying my angry face. I do this quite often, practicing an array of emotions for every occasion. Happy. Sad. Now, give me light empathetic. A mental coach instructs from inside my head like a film director. No that's not it. I said empathetic damnit. Smile, not too much though, now, how do they do it in that movie? Drop it down a little where your eyes aren't as wide and your bottom lip starts to inch farther than the top. Eh, we'll get there. Keep at it. Every day. Every night, until I look the part of everyone else.

"I think you look beautiful," a voice says from behind. Over my shoulder, I see her. Kitty. Standing clear in the mirror.

"You aren't here."

"Then why do you notice me?" Why do I? I've had only a handful of sights or thoughts of Kitty since the day I... since she well... "So, you want to see him again?"

"No." I turn. She isn't there. No one's there. It's just me. No, I think to myself. I'm not mad. I am not. I can't be. A mad person wouldn't look like I do.

Look at yourself.

I'm beautiful. Aren't I?

"I think you are." There she is again. Closer now. Standing behind my shoulder like a devil perched on the collarbone of my conscience.

"Go away," I say, lowering my head, staring at the white porcelain of the sink. I squeeze my eyes. Tighter. Tighter. "Go away," I repeat.

Off with her head!

"Go away!" I look up.

She's still Kitty, but now bleeding. Filled with bloody holes like a punctured voodoo doll. Bleeding from her chest, neck, and stomach. Still conscious. Still walking closer and closer to me, holding the knife from John's kitchen.

My knife. Her knife. Aloft over her head.

"Go away!" A soaring pain runs along the roof of my lungs as I violently plea to the mirror.

And with that she vanishes. I shiver, like I just woke from a bad dream. Like I have said, I am not mad. Only mad people see ghosts.

Not me. Only mad people talk to dead people.

Not ME.

A dream is not reality. But who is to say which is which?

I leave my apartment slamming the door hard on my way out.

96th Wacker. 96th Wacker. I repeat in my head.

I take the train to the Loop. It's a gorgeously dreary Chicago day. The sky is an oil painting gray with streaks of blended white and charcoal smudges. I still wear sunglasses. By the time I step out from the underground train stop nearing Hilton's building, the sun begins to break. It's always wise to bring an umbrella and sunglasses wherever you go in Chicago. Most days I use both.

When I arrive at John's building, It's complete glass, but I'm cement, just a petrified fixture on the sidewalk. Stationary, I command myself to go inside. But I can't seem to make the first step, terrified he'll be the first face I see when entering. I'm walking into a trap; I just know it. But what choice do I have?

96th and Wacker

There are too many people. I can't do this.

I have to.

Wavering, slightly shaking, I stand outside of the building, Hafford and Associates Law Firm, staring up at the gothic bones of the brilliant external workings. Wacker Drive stretches along the river that flows through the middle of downtown. Some of the best hotels, restaurants, and views are on this street.

There are SO many people.

What am I doing here? I think to myself. I can't just kill him in public. Maybe I can. It depends on his office. Maybe I can follow him into the bathroom. Or wait, follow him on his way home and sneak behind him. No. John Hilton doesn't walk home to Gold Coast.

Beethoven is playing, as I listen to my headphones to drown the chaos of the city around me.

Let's just call it recon then. Unless of course, the situation presents itself. I get a little pleasure thinking it just may. And then, I can make my move.

Marble plates every inch inside the building: the walls, floor tiles, even the front desk. It's sterling white, like an early morning after a heavy snow.

I pass a handful of men clad in black suits. Two walk together, the older one runs me up and down with beady eyes. I match his stare, walking directly towards him. When he notices, he ducks away, burying his chin into his neck.

I waltz myself to the front desk guarding entry to the elevators. Behind sits "Lawrence," which I derive from his big gold tab name tag. He's a busy man, peering down from under his wide framed black glasses. He fills out a mad libs page with phallic terms in each blank. A curly head of hair dangles like flaming orange pubes over his forehead nearly reaching his eyes.

I cough.

"Hello there," he says, frantically hiding the mad libs under the desk, which isn't really a desk, but more like a bunker. "Can I help you?"

"Yes," I say, placing my hands on the cool marble. A chill runs up my fingers the way a frozen car handle tickles you in mid-January. It makes me think about the first time I drove with Uncle Jones.

He had pulled me into his Porsche after driving around, following me, beckoning me to get in after I had walked nearly eleven blocks in my first Chicago December. It was one of those winters that the air would cling to your nostrils, burning you from the inside out and freezing your face to the point your skin would crack like a shattered mirror. He drove me around the city. I remember sitting in the front, my hand wrapped around the handle, my index firmly tapping with a nervous itch, ready to spring from the seat and throw myself into traffic. But he didn't lay a finger on me. Not that day anyway. We went to get lunch at a fancy restaurant with nice furniture and mood lighting, but with casual, yet somehow creative food options. Doctor B's Café. After a slight fit from the waiter, I still managed to order just a plain cheeseburger. We scanned the menus in silence, ordered in silence, and waited for the food to arrive in silence. I took my first bite of food I'd had in three days. I remember almost choking. I nearly bit off half the sandwich. I held my free hand over my mouth to wall my face, just in case my lips exploded with the overflow of bread and meat that my teeth just couldn't handle. After he had eaten a couple fries or so, truffle and parmesan I recall, he washed his throat with his iced tea mixed with heavy whipping cream, yeah, I know, disgusting, and smacked his lips as he swallowed. He always had a tendency to do that.

"Beautiful eyes," he said. "Kind. They love that." That was the first thing he told me. It's all his fault what happened to Kitty. It's all their fault.

"What floor is Hafford law firm?" I say to Lawrence, throwing away my thoughts on Uncle Jones' memory.

"Do you have an appointment?"

"No."

"Are you represented by an attorney at H&H?"

"No, I-,"

"Can't let you up." He clicks on his pen. Repeatedly. It makes me crazy. I stare, boiling inside, but only show a mask of an emotionless glare on the outside. He has a few pimple marks rotting between his eyes and on his chin. All picked. The indent from his nails scarring his skin.

"I need to get up to the Hafford law firm."

"I said that without an appointment I cannot let you up." Will a smile work? "Do you see this here?" He points to his nametag. "I am the entrusted gatekeeper for over a dozen businesses that operate behind me in this building. I cannot grant permission to people without appointments."

"Look, Larry, can I call you Larry?"

"No."

"You prefer Lawrence?"

"Only my mom calls me Larry."

"How sweet."

"I can have you escorted out if you don't leave."

"Look," I begin, deciding if I should verbally battle or maybe seduce this man to earn a ride on the elevator. I will do whatever it takes. I scan my surroundings, trying to find some type of alternate route.

Then I see her.

She's walking with someone. Close to them. Too close for it not to be Roger. Almost, entwined. As they emerge from the revolving lobby door, she pushes his hand from her ass. He pats it playfully. Of course she hides the little smirk. She's rocking that sexy long black corporate look. He's draped in designer off the rack and has rich kid wavy Tik Tok hair.

Does she see me?

I divert, trying to look small. Fuck. Abort. Abort. But it's too late. They separate, he takes the elevator. She – she didn't see me – I don't think she sees me-

"Ann?"

I'm not sure if anyone likes being recognized in public. Especially in circumstances like mine. But in this moment as I slowly turn to see Kate standing there, I'm not sure if she's here as my grim reaper or trojan horse.

"Ann?" she repeats. "Is that you? What are you doing here?" She sips a matcha with her free hand, managing to carry her black leather Prada attaché around her shoulder. Pickles pulls her along at the end of a leash, leading with a sniffing addiction for every inch of the entryway.

"Kate, oh my gosh, hi. I didn't know you worked here," I say, scratching at a fictional itch on the back of my neck. Pickles assaults my feet, yapping up at me.

"Yeah, 15th floor, not super glamorous. Richards and Richards firm." Her eyes are distant, lost in the routine of her day.

(Thank fucking god)

"So, what's going on? Pickles, stop." The dog sniffs at my feet, hovering with his tongue out and petite, but menacing, occasional yaps. I step back, trying to avoid the grotesque natural canine affection.

"Would you believe this? I went on a few dates with this guy who works at Hafford and Associates. Night goes great, but I forget my bag at his place."

"Oh, you're getting some, aren't you, girl?" She crouches to pet Pickles as she smiles up at me with her perfect whitened teeth. "Ugh, bitch that's so hot. I didn't know you were into guys, too. I would have totally set you up. How'd you meet him?"

"What's that?" I try to engage in conversation but can't get my mood off going to John Hilton's office.

"How'd you guys meet?" She stands back up, taking a long drag from her matcha.

"Oh, just a bar." I throw an invisible ball with my hand. (Casual now, Ann. Casual) "So romantic, I know," I roll my eyes. She giggles. I like seeing her giggle.

"Look, it's so crazy running into you, but I gotta go." She starts pulling out her air pods, sticking one in her ear. "This fucking day can't get any crazier. There's a ton of law students applying for internships and I have to go through all the resumes. Literally kill me."

"They let you bring Pickles to work?"

"Yeah, he just sits in my office. Days like this I just can't even function without him here for support. Plus, you know Roger is about as capable of taking care of him as nothing. It sucks because I am going away in a couple of days and I—you know, if it's not too much trouble, would you wanna possibly look after him?"

"After Pickles?"

"Yeah, he loves you. Just don't take him to school, I don't want him getting all of those kid germs. I'd owe you a huge favor." Kate folds her hands together under her chin, squeezing her eyes and smiling with a begging privation. "Please." She squeezes my hand. Oh my God how it feels. Warm. Smooth. Don't let go. Don't let go.

"Sure, I can do it."

"Oh yay!" She drops the prim façade and hugs me, still holding the leash around her left hand. I hope for something longer next time I see her. I don't hug her back. I won't be able to let go. When she releases me, her formal stare returns. Her charming disguise has been a slight deception to me. She looks at my outfit, surveying every corner of me like a military inspection.

"Something wrong?"

"No, no," she says. "I just recognized that outfit. It's like—I have almost the same one, it's crazy."

"You do?" I try to act surprised. I do a Cinderella scan of my outfit, still admiring what she wears.

"Yeah, and your hair it's..." Her head cocks to the side, her eyes buzzing in their sockets. I totally forget I'm wearing a wig. Then she shakes it off, smiling once again. "I love it. Anyways, I owe you one, ok?" She points at me, then transforms her hand into a dainty wave as she turns.

"You know," I say. "There is something I kinda need."

"Shoot," she says, halting on the second air pod.

"Would you... would you help me get up there?

"Up where?"

"Larry won't let me up without an appointment. And I lost his number."

"Bitch, follow me." She snatches my arm and leads us towards the elevators. "Oh and, that guy, when I walked in- Oliver - whatever you saw... it's just that-"

"I didn't see anyone." She smiles. I give her a wink. Oh my god, did I really just give her a wink? We strut over to the elevators.

"Excuse me," Larry calls after, "she's not-"

"She's one of my clients, she's coming up."

"She didn't sign in."

"It's fine. It's not like she's a serial killer."

What an elevator ride.

I stand so close to her. I breathe her in, sage and vanilla. Soothing and intimate. I want to hold her hand again. Pickles stares up at me the whole time, warning me off.

She bobs as we ride; listening to her air pods as if once we stepped on that elevator, we became strangers. Damn the others who ride along with us. At one point a woman in a tight pantsuit wedges between us pressing the wrong floor button. A man with a newspaper keeps sneezing and clearing his throat every ten seconds. When the ding for the fifteenth-floor sounds, she gives me a wink and finger twinkling wave.

"Later. I'll have Roger drop off Pickles." Then the steel doors close.

Hafford and Associates is a glass haven, adorned with synthetic beauty. Even the receptionist seems perfectly sculpted. The offices are floor to ceiling windows, with glass partitioning walls between them. Most partners have bookshelves set up on the shared walls of the offices. I search for John Hilton's but don't see it before making it to the front desk.

"Hello, I am here to see one of your partners," I say, hoping my tone is casual enough. She doesn't have a name tag. Classy.

Christ, I did not think this through. She sits straight, elbows back, and a bright smile eternally pasted across her face. She wears her hair up, letting a single red strand fall in front of her black rimmed Dior glasses. A blazer drapes her perfect posture over a tight, low cut top. Eye candy of the office for sure.

So that's what we'll call her. Eye Candy.

"Are you a client?" she asks.

"I am a law student. I was supposed to interview for a summer internship and was told to reach out to one of the partners about scheduling an interview, but I lost the information their assistant gave me."

She cocks her head. It's cute, sympathetic and understanding, as if this happens all the time. I doubt she really gives a shit. I study the office while she checks nothing on the computer, wondering which of these lawyers she's sleeping with.

"I'm sorry to hear that," she says, making a duck mouth with her lips. "Do you remember who it was you were supposed to meet with?"

"I think it was something Hilton. Sorry fuzzy, this week has been exam after exam."

"Oh yeah, I know. It's absolutely insane. Where do you go? I'm at Northwestern."

"DePaul."

"Oh that's so cute. You have a specialty in mind?"

"Social engineering." She lifts an eyebrow. Hey, it's my life's calling.

"Unfortunately, Mr. Hilton is out right now." I'm sure she's just pretending to be disappointed. My head's starting to ache. The room is closing in on me. This is the longest I've gone without Ativan or Haldol. I need a glass of water or something. I'm realizing what a bad idea this was. "I can give you one of his business cards."

"That would be great, thanks."

"Awesome. I'll let him know you stopped by, too."

"No."

"How come?"

"I–I, um, don't want him knowing I lost his info. That would seem kind of unprofessional right?"

"I wouldn't sweat it. What was your name?"

"Mary Bonneville."

"Ok Mary, I will let him know." She hands me a card. I sweat, trembling, studying it, reading the name: JOHN HILTON embedded in bold black ink… his face flashes in my head. Then I picture Danny.

Poor Danny.

<u>They're all Gonna Laugh at You</u>

I take off the rest of the week.

Nick calls throughout the week, but I ignore him. I know dodging work and communication threatens how they think of me. How they might suspect something. But I can't fake it right now. I'm worried that anyone I speak to might end up dead. So, I spend the week alone, imprisoned in thought, shackled by paranoia. I order every meal from DoorDash, then stop eating all together. I should probably plan a move for vice principal, but I can't focus on that. I can't focus on anything. My days are spent in darkness, the windows closed, my door locked, my records the only thing to keep me sane. I come to the conclusion that the only way to get over not killing John is to find another victim. Someone to replace this compulsive need. A sacrifice to re-harness my control. I know just the man.

On Thursday night, I receive an email from Angela reminding me that I made a commitment to volunteer at the Autumn Social Night—as she so named it—and am expected to show up or find a replacement. Any hopes of being vice principal or having any future at Pearcey rides on the dance and parent teacher conferences. I'm not going to let one snafu with a client affect my goal. John's life threatens me less than Angela Greene's potential rule over me and undoubtedly discovering the truth. It's not like he will end up on campus anytime soon. But the parent conferences encroach. Will he attend?

I promise myself that this position will change things. It will change me. I will be cured.

I need a good alibi for my plans with Oliver Miner. He was easy to find. Richards and Richards law firm has all of their associates on the website. There's no time for a whole new identity. Rush jobs never work. But I'll be fine. I'm calculated. I'm not mad. I'll find him.

Dead fake uncle or not, I'm going to the dance. At least no parents will be showing up (save the handful of volunteers that don't know John–fingers crossed). I decide to take one night off from perseverating over if and how I am to kill John Hilton. I need to regroup. I need a clean kill.

I never experienced youth socials. I'm not sure how I'd have fit in if I had enjoyed what most consider a normal upbringing. I missed out on the awkward school dances, sweet sixteen birthday parties, sleepovers, school pranks, all the stuff that made a childhood a childhood. I was excluded from what made a kid a kid, or what molded teenagers into balls of emotion and crossed feelings. It was all pressed out of me the way pulp is pressed by a juicer.

I think back to the one good memory I have as a child. It was only days leading up to what I label as the turning point– a day I don't recognize as exactly good or bad, just a day, just being a kid. That's what I guess are the good days people look back on–nothing of remembrance or importance happening, nothing happening at all–just a kid allowed to exist as they were, as they are. Hesitant? Sure. Awkward, and even a little dorky? Sure. Because that's what being a kid means. It's the days before you're devoured by the truth of humanity. Before manipulation and sex are even words of your vocabulary, and the imagination isn't like religion; a chore you spend time and time again either fighting to kill or reignite within a dying ache for magic. It's just there, the way faith was probably meant to be. Just there. Just a kid.

I would've been one of the kids at dances who sat alone, wishing I was at home in sweatpants or laying in an open field somewhere staring up at stars instead of blinding multi-colored spotlights and cheap plastic decorations that have been recycled for the same event every single year. I would have been too embarrassed to dance. Definitely too embarrassed to have asked for the hand of whomever I would have wanted to ask to dance. It was something I had missed out on but never registered missing it until now. Until the school dance.

Somehow, now, I can hear how it would've played out.

"They are all gonna laugh at you. They are all gonna laugh at you," would have turned like a broken record in my mind. Over and over as I stand behind the punch bowl while staring at the empty dance floor, the lights gliding over the tile. "They are all gonna laugh at you." Again, and again. Then laughter. The laughter of children—

"Miss Bonny!" A voice says amongst the laughs.

I snap out of it, seeing Rachel and her crew standing obediently before me waiting to be served their plastic glass of punch.

Serving punch to an army of awkwardly horny students and teachers makes me wish for the night to turn into the prom in *Carrie*. That seems like the kind of dance I would have enjoyed. It is one of the only movies I watched with Kitty that I remember liking. She wasn't a fan of the scary stuff—that's what she told me. But I always laughed during what she called "horrific" scenes. It's 'flicks' like Love

Actually and superhero crap I find horrific. It was the first time I had seen a movie before reading the book. After that, it was the last time. Now I skip the theater and public setting that offers a mildly accurate, rushed plot and underdeveloped character attempts to thrill you for an hour and forty-five minutes. I stick with the book. With the original.

I don't envy the awkward kids that surround me in their American girl dresses and barely fitting church clothes as they timidly line the perimeter of the makeshift dance floor.

Most of the boys wear bowties or clip-ons and untuck their shirts once whichever parent had dropped them off is out of sight. The girls campaign for frumpiest dress with yellow and pink frills like pixies at the bottoms. A few wear skirts, the same ones who get accosted by Angela for spaghetti straps on school days. It's a pool of awkward tension, with boys rating the girls and the girls laughing at the boys.

I stay my distance from the parent volunteers and chaperones, quietly ladling sugar filled punch. My station for the first quarter of the dance–sorry, "social night"–assigned to me by Angela Greene, who of course still won't dare admit her hand in the planning committee, even though she critiques each streamer and scoffs at the signs and decorations. She's the one who organized an entire shift schedule for each teacher volunteer.

Volunteer is a stretch.

Douglass had let me take a hit from his weed pen before I went inside when he noticed me sneaking a pre-dance cigarette. He's the only other teacher who knows I smoke on occasion.

The first time I ever interacted with him I had finished my first week teaching and needed a break after a busy lunch period. He crept up behind me and asked to bum a cigarette. I'm not sure if it's a guy thing, but having something for people to bum off you, whether it's gum, smokes, loose change, doesn't matter, is an instant way to make friends. Skip that socially impregnated way of interaction and simply move past the foreplay of small talk. "Mind if I bum one?" "You got an extra buck?" Easy. Immediate friend.

Whatever he had given me in the parking lot carries its weight. I feel nothing. It's blissful, and definitely makes the top pop 100 list that plays over the gym speakers somewhat enjoyable.

The high wears off when Angela approaches, this time standing next to me for a while, her arms folded as she stares out onto the empty dance floor.

"Heard about your uncle. So terrible." She lets an awkward silence wane between her sentences. "I called the healthcare facility you had mentioned he was staying at, the one on Maple Street. The curious thing is… they didn't have a clue who you were when I mentioned you. I thought to myself, that's just got to be the strangest thing I've ever heard." Our eyes meet in silence. We just glare, me blankly, and her, an executioner about to swing.

She's on to me. I feel her crawling up my spine – a human termite. I notice a self-satisfied, humble little grin perk from the dimple of her mouth. It's subtle, and mighty quick, just enough to suggest that the score is Angela Greene 1, Ann Bonny 0.

Now I truly want this dance to turn into Carrie. I imagine how I'd do it, if I had teleportation. I'd electrocute her somehow. I'd bring all the lights down on her and strangle her with the wires, then pour water on the circuits to send a shock through her parasitical frame. I'd chuckle as her legs twitched for the final time. Her scream, if she even could scream, would be a spark of life into this party solely needed to get everyone dancing.

"Figures," she says, looking away again. "That's why I never put my family members into places like that. The nurses are mostly dropouts and they always forget their patients' and customers' names." She's a hunting falcon. No, more like a greyhound, sniffing and seeing all without even a shift in her neck or a twitch in her peripherals. Then her gaze shifts–

"Don't use your hands Jimmy." She snaps at a crew of boys as they approach for a refill on desserts and pretzels. One with shaggy hair and a flannel goes for a cookie. "Jimmy. The tongs are there for a reason." The boy flees, no cookie at all.

"You know everyone's names?" I've never seen the boy in my life, guessing he's in seventh grade.

"Don't you, Ann?"

"I know all my students' names, of course. There's just so many kids at this school."

"Must've been a small place, Bridgeton, if you think Pearcey is big."

"I am still getting used to all the new faces. You've had a few years to learn everyone, haven't you?"

"I've taught most of these kids and their siblings. I know them. I know how they act, how they learn best, the parents too."

"And the parents are what matters most, right?"

"You said that, not me."

"Well, Amir—"

"Mr. Salem."

"–Mr. Salem, yes, he said that."

"For him, the parents are the primary concern, sure. But for the teachers, for the vice principal, the kids are the primary concern. Do you know the secondary concern?"

"Running events like this?" She didn't find it funny.

"Wrong. The staff."

"Right, yes. I was just messing around."

"If you want to be a vice principal, Ann, you don't have the opportunity to mess around. Don't you get it? Mr. Salem relies on us to make sure things run the way a school runs, and that's more pressure than I think you understand in that 'messing around' little brain of yours. It is stressful, it is no joke. It takes a long career in teaching to understand. I take my job seriously and so should you."

"I guess we will have to wait for what Amir—Mr. Salem decides."

"I guess we will."

It's the first time I'm genuinely excited to see Nick as he trots up to the snack booth.

"Hello ladies." He seems short of breath. "Mrs. Greene," followed by a head nod (or was that a bow?) "I wonder if I could borrow Miss Bonny for a task force?"

"Task force?"

"A few kids snuck out of the auditorium. I wanna do a search through the halls. I don't think you'd want kids being unsupervised." Angela nods. Anything beats spending more time with her and filling up the students' punch.

Nick leads me through the dance floor and between the tables. We pass Sonya sitting alone, staring at the stage lights as if she had been struck by a ghost.

"Sonya," I say. "Wanna come with us?" desperately hoping she will. Not sure I want to be alone with Nick.

"Hey, girl. No, I am going to just sit here." She drinks punch, although I catch a smell that tells me she must have added vodka, which has made it a faded pink color instead of the deep Hawaiian Punch red. "Want some?" She holds it up for me to smell. Her voice drawn and her words long, almost to a slur.

"Is there even any punch left in there?"

"Well, there was, but I keep adding the vodka so it kinda just dilutes after a while. Saw you talking to your pal Angela. Don't tell her, but my flask is in my purse."

"Maybe you should slow down."

"She used to be cool. Like us. One year she even brought edibles for the teachers before one of these things."

"What happened?"

"We ate them."

"No, I mean, that made her a—"

"A bitch? Well, she lost like both her parents in the same year and then there was this big prank that a few upperclassmen pulled on her after she almost got them kicked out when she found weed in their lockers. Hypocrite. Now it's tradition for the eighth graders to try and prank her before moving up to high school. Since like every fucking student had her in the past." She downs her vodka punch, knocking some stray cups off the table.

"Where's Douglass?" Nick asks her.

"Who cares, I gotta fill up." She tries standing, but wobbles. "I got another few mini bottles in my car." I catch her before she takes the tablecloth with her to the floor.

"C'mon, Sonya," I say. "Let's get you outside for some air or something."

"No, I wanna dance. Get off me!" She tries pushing me away, but her body jolts and gags, the preeminent arrival of a brewing digestive eruption.

"She's not ok, Nick," I say to him. I'm short on time, if I have any at all. "Help me walk her to the bathroom".

"I thought we were going to the hallway?" He sounds like a disappointed child.

"Nick, if Angela sees she's drunk she'll get her fired. C'mon."

We walk Sonya to the bathroom where I ask Nick to stand guard outside to make sure no students come in. I help Sonya into a stall, barely in time for her to throw herself over the toilet. I can't look while I hold her hair. I can handle blood, but I've never gotten used to vomit. When she finishes, I dampen a few paper towels and wipe along her neck and face. Then we just sit there in the stall, quietly at first.

"Nick really likes you," she finally says, her head bobbing over the toilet to make sure nothing is left. I make sure to flush it, so I only have to deal with the lingering smell of vodka.

"He's kinda…"

"Look, you don't have to say anything to me. I get it, I got it the moment I met you. Your secret is always safe with me. The thing is, Nick is um, well, just like the rest of them."

"He seems like a nice guy at least."

"Just don't trust anyone here. That's how you turn out like Angela. Your secrets come out, people treat you differently and suddenly you start bottling everything up and exploding until you are hard as stone. And what's worse, you'll start dressing like her." We both laugh. "I used to think teaching would be cool, you know?"

"You're a cool teacher, c'mon."

"I'm hella cool, are you kidding? I mean teaching in general. Don't you wish people, I don't know, respected you more for what you do? Why'd you even become a teacher anyways?"

"Well, I guess I don't really do it for anyone… I do because I have to. I made a promise to someone once, and, I think being a teacher would make her proud."

"Sounds nice."

"It was, at one time. Ready to go back out there?" I say.

"Nah, all the boys I like suck. Let's just graduate already." We laugh, quietly but enough for it to bounce from stall to stall. "Thanks, Ann. You're a cool friend." The word chokes me for a second. I can't recall someone referring to me as that.

"Look, I'm sorry about Douglass. Whatever he did."

"He's fucking the nurse is what he did. He fucks everyone. You know I'm turning 35 this year? I'm literally a dinosaur. Dinosaurs aren't sexy Ann, they are scaly and they have short arms." I inspect her pale Anglo skin. It's still quite smooth. Some speckled freckles dot her chin and nose. I never noticed them before.

"You are no dinosaur, Sonya. And if you were, you'd be a hot one."

We laugh more, sitting on the bathroom floor with our backs against the stalls as if we're high schoolers avoiding boys at prom. Though we eventually need to return to the gym, neither of us want to leave. Probably for different reasons, I'm sure she's still feeling sick. But I feel an odd sense of ease. However brief it'll be, I try to savor it. I guess I didn't miss much as a sprouting tween, because I would have probably spent my nights like this no differently. Though, I doubt back then I would have had a friend like Sonya to keep me entertained.

Nick is out of sight when we finally emerge from the bathroom. For some reason I doubt if there even were kids running through the halls. I keep trying to convince myself that Nick is in fact a good guy, and that his intentions, though flawed, are innocent. Honesty leads to questions, which I haven't the time or desire to entertain. Even someone like me with little aptitude for social interaction – sure I admit it – would've gotten the hint by now.

There's still an hour left in the dance. When I get back to the gym with Sonya, I grab her a water bottle and pretzels. Luckily, she passes as sober, and I make sure that she sits a safe distance from Angela.

My mind is untethered from the comfort of the bathroom stall. The safety of it. I sense Angela, lurking, spying. Calling Uncle Jones' fake health facility is just a start. What's next? Her looking into my past? Following me? If she finds out that Ann Bonny doesn't have a degree, doesn't have a teaching history, I'll be out on the street. Teaching is meant to be a subtle alias, but I'm beginning to think it could be a way out completely. I'm learning that not everyone is manipulative and cruel as I have previously believed. Amir is honorable, or at least pretends. Nick is, well… Nick is Nick. Even Douglass and Sonya, they both jump from mattress to mattress, but generally, they're decent people.

I wonder if things would have been different if these experiences would have occurred in my childhood years. If I wasn't uprooted from a normal life and sent away… it doesn't matter. Not anymore. I have a hunger. As I sit in that auditorium, listening to kid-proof hip hop and watching middle schoolers attempt to dance; I think of my task at hand. The killing I have to commit. Again.

What about John?

He is still out there, and no doubt when I'm done with Oliver, John will have to be next. The parent teacher conference lingers in my thoughts. Vice principal or not, John showing up and recognizing me will have me exposed. if not fired, surely interrogated, possibly even arrested. I find myself rocking. I'm dizzy, maybe I need a drink, my leg bounces as I long for the dance to just end so I can go get it over with.

Seeing Danny from across the gym fractures my paranoid swing. It's the first time I've laid eyes on him since, well, you know… his fucking dad turned out to be The Count.

I leave Sonya and go sit next to him. He's alone amongst the empty fold-up chairs that line the room. Most of the kids collect in their clusters or sit on their phones. Others congregate on the dance floor but aren't dancing. A few head bobs and subtle foot tapping, but it's organic, not subconsciously dancing.

"Didn't think you'd come." To be honest I hoped he wouldn't. But as I sit here with him now, I feel somewhat more at ease. His presence calms me. It's disturbing.

"My mom made me."

"And?"

He just shrugs.

There was one night during our relationship that Kitty convinced me to go out with her. It was a restaurant and club with three levels. The bottom level was a bar and restaurant, then the middle a disco floor with dancing and music, while the third opened up to a garden lounge that had a view of the whole city. I picture her at the dance, spinning and jumping to the music, the multicolored lights blinking from the squared light-up dancefloor. She would have gone out, sweated and taken off her shoes and never cared. That night I sat on the sidelines and just watched. It was our last night out together. Sometimes, I wish I had joined her on the dance floor.

"You know," I say to Danny. "My mom made me do a lot when I was a kid, too. Guess what?"

"What?"

"This is my first dance."

"They didn't have dances at your old school?"

"This is my first school. C'mon, let's dance." I hate dancing. I do. But something in me wants to let go, and forget the world, forget what I have to do, forget everything. And that's what dancing does, right? It makes you forget.

"No one else is dancing," he says.

"So?"

"So, if I dance, they are all going to laugh at me. And it's lame to dance alone. No girl would ever want to dance with me."

"What about me?"

"You don't count."

"I'm a girl, aren't I? And you're a boy. So, let's dance."

He shakes his head.

"How about no homework this week?"

"You know, if you're gonna blackmail someone, don't you think you should be less obvious?"

"Was that a smile, Danny?" I give him a slight nudge. "And where did you learn that word? Blackmail?"

"My dad. He's a lawyer, so he uses words like that." I begin to lose the urge to dance. "Ok fine," he pulls himself to his feet. "No homework?" he outstretches his hand. I'm frozen. "Miss Bonny?"

"Yes, Danny?"

"Do you want to dance?" A cold wind must have flown into the gym because a chill tickles my shoulders and my upper back. I am, in a moment, overcome. For the first time, and most likely the only, someone has asked me to dance at a school 'social night.'

I take Danny's hand. "Let's go."

I'm sure Danny thinks it, too. The whole walk to the dance floor I feel like all eyes are fixed on us. I'm a teenager again.

"They're all gonna laugh at you... they're all gonna laugh at you." But something eases my mind when I see Sonya giving me a thumbs up and smiling.

I picture the romcom-esque scene of Danny and I dancing together. He'll laugh as he stands on my feet and we'll be silly and do moves like the chicken dance. I'll do the sprinkler just to embarrass him. The rest of the student body will flood the dance floor seeing what a fun time we are having. Angela's orders will be ignored and there will be dancing on top of one another, all night long. Even the other teachers will join in instead of awkwardly watching from the sidelines, embracing the freedom to dance instead of munching on celery sticks and store-bought cookies.

But as soon as we reach the dance floor, I notice something.

It's a soup pot, a 'Kevin's famous chili' soup pot, perched on a rafter above the stage connected to a rope pulley system. Angela walks directly underneath it, testing the microphone to make an announcement, unaware of the danger above. I can't see whose hands are controlling the pulley, but the slack gives way, and the pot begins to shift.

All attention is on Angela, which she requests. Several times she barks for the music to pause and "everyone listen up", because she has an announcement for the raffle winner. The pot tips completely. With a splash and a gasp from the audience, Angela is covered in dark black liquid. It isn't mud, it isn't tar, although that might be fitting. It's potent. Coffee. Not hot coffee, no that would have been torture, not payback. It's old coffee, now drenched in the tissue of Angela's hair, staining her golden blonde locks brown and spotted, her beige dress the color of a rotten maple tree, and her skin a rusted marble - if marble could rust and grow transparent and brown. She is a statue frozen in time with her mouth open

and her arms cocked, like a figure in a painting who has
seen a phantom.

The room is a graveyard.

Then a giggle.

It's Rachel. Can you believe that? Rachel breaks first. Just
a short giggle, like a hiccup really, which she covers with her
hand over her mouth when she notices she let it slip.

I don't feel sorry for Angela. And I have a suspicion of
who orchestrated the prank.

The dance ends after Angela's coffee bath. A few others
had laughed before Angela stormed off the stage and
disappeared for the night. Sonya was one of them. Nick
and the other chaperones and parent volunteers handled
corralling the kids to get picked up outside. The only
person I did not see since the parking lot was Douglass.

I guess the dance really did end up like Carrie—at least
for Angela Greene it did.

I stay in the gym, waiting for the last student to leave,
and then for each teacher and chaperone to head home.
It's peaceful amid the scattered balloons and abandoned
snack plates and punch cups. Ernie is coming with a crew
to take the leftovers and clean up. I leave before he arrives,
but savor the final moments of the dance, even if it's alone.
Time to hunt.

Proud OneDer Boy

With a little digging, I find Oliver Miner's usual nightly spots. He routines three separate social media accounts. Kate has no idea how much she slipped when his name flowed from her lips.

Name, click. Occupation, click. Found you.

Oliver has an Instagram for posts with his wife, adorned with pictures of anniversaries and birthdays, sharing the joy to have married his best friend. Cringe. The same account where he posts of his dog and of the Titleist his wife bought him for Christmas that year. The other accounts are strictly for other girls, and to brag about those other girls to his friends. The girls are mostly college aged, who I'm sure he buys expensive things for and tells them he knows all the best connections in the city. Easy for a daddy who died two years ago and left you 10 million. If you ask me, it's just another form of buying someone; a lie and a handout. Payment for those desperate enough to give sex.

He and his friend group refer to themselves as the "one-der boys," alluding to their exclusive membership in the top 1% of the American workforce. Even though they aren't in the workforce themselves. More like, their parents' 1% status. The name sounds more like a sexually confused boy pop band than a friend group of douchebags with daddy and mommy's money.

When Oliver isn't sleeping around, he and his crew frequent Topgolf, hookah lounges, and sleazy bars, three of which I narrow to be his favorite. Lucky for me, I guess right on the first try. I'm heading to Hubbard Street in River North after the school dance ends.

I spot him with two of his one-der boys, sitting at the bar. The whole place is a den of sleaze under hazy red lighting and ear-bleeding covers of classic songs.

Didn't know you could ruin *Stacey's Mom*. This bar accomplished that.

I flank him from a booth in the back before making my move, observing his night out with the one-der boys. Even though they slam multiple rounds of tequila shots chased with mixed drinks, and the occasional trip to the bathroom for a line, I can't have anyone he knows be able to place me at the scene. I changed my clothes from the school dance, wearing a revealing short romper and heels and the same blonde wig from the time I saw him with Kate. A puff of my chest and the bouncer just waved me in – no need to use one of my fake IDs.

Oliver laughs louder than the music at his own jokes, smacks the bar when he isn't served fast enough, and glowers at anything younger than 25 in a short shirt while sucking the straw of his vodka cranberry. We make eye contact a few times. Just enough for him to register my presence. My potential interest. Even as a lawyer, he strikes me as more of a corporate duckling as I watch him interact with his 'friends'.

Around midnight he makes his way out the door. I rise, following him.

His Jaguar F type reeks of a freshly smoked joint. He gives me a once over as I climb in, unannounced, slouched down, dangling my legs and resting my foot on the dash. He scans my chest and legs like a hunting eagle then pulls a wad of cash from his back pocket and begins placing fifties on the dash. "Don't think I don't know a whore when I see one. You are shifty, but I like that. I do. How much?" He pours cocaine onto his key and snorts, offering me some, which I decline. I need to focus tonight.

"I'm exactly the right price," I say. "Just drive and we can talk business later."

"I like the way you think." He fires the ignition and presses on the gas.

I made sure not to wear a dress for this one. His hand is on my thigh at the first stoplight.

We skip the Saturday night traffic, taking Sheridan Road towards Ravenswood. My leg bounces and I stare out the window, hoping for the ride to end soon. Up ahead, the light turns red and he speeds up, slamming on the brakes right before the crossing line instead of flying on through. As we wait at the light, his hand reaches over the console. His fingers trail from my kneecap to my thigh. He rubs, traveling to the inside, inching towards my crotch. I stare at the light. Please just turn. He rubs his finger along the edges of my pelvis. The thin layer of cotton from my romper only provides so much protection from his uneducated touch. For a second he hits a sweet spot, a rush shoots up my waist and into my stomach, but then he loses his way, trying to rub areas that do nothing but hurt, and at a speed I can't even comprehend to guess how he thinks feels good. Why can men not understand? Circular motion.

Goddamn this is a long light.

I peek back through the rear mirror. A taxi catches my eye two blocks behind us. I saw it pass when I first stepped into his car.

His hand finally retracts, moving to himself. He unzips his pants.

"You ever give road head?"

"You got any cigarettes?" I ask. He freezes, staring at me with gaping eyes and a clenched jaw. Then the light turns green. Finally. He doesn't go until a honk from a car behind us jolts him. He presses the gas, his pants still undone, as if he's still offering me the decision to give him a blowjob.

"You shouldn't smoke you know."

"What's that?"

"If you smoke your boobs might shrink."

"So that's a no then?"

I look again into the rear mirror. We have turned twice since the light. The cab still lingers a few cars back.

We stop at a liquor store. I stay in the car, promising not to run off. With the few minutes I have, I peek more at his socials…

Oliver Miner. My newest 'client'. His profiles—the ones reserved for the one-der boys—broadcasts a list of hate speech regarding his wife. Reassuring, I think to myself. This guy isn't even trying to hide his infidelity or misogyny. At least not to the cyber world. Instead, he wears it like a war medal, triumphing over the so called "nag" who he seems to overtly spoil on Facebook. I predict the man's bedroom skill with a quick surf through his social media presence. For Oliver Miner, it will be zero foreplay and a good six minutes of his most likely average-sized dick in and out before he runs out of steam. Then he'll be done, tired; his pants will shoot back up and his belt will be on before you can ask for a smoke.

His social media also consists of far right and racist memes. There's a group photo of him and the one-der boys at Top Golf. He's in the center wearing a polo and chinos as if he just won a PGA championship, posting his score in the comments section. The caption: PROUD ONE-DER BOYS.

Another photo shows him holding the nine-iron club with a bow attached to the head. Caption: 'Best Gift. Best Wife'. The way he looks holding that thing. It's as if he's holding his wife. But he isn't. No, he's hugging a metal stick. A gift from his wife whom he loves so dearly on social media and hates so much on his other profiles that it took a simple mutual follower search to find.

Disloyal, racist, sexist... I think we can all agree on this one. I slide my phone back into my purse as he returns, a bottle of champagne in hand.

When we get to the motel–classy I know–he's preoccupied with his 'just in case I find a girl to sleep with tonight/ always prepared' box (which is filled with condoms, flute glasses, Viagra and roofies) in one hand and the bottle of champagne in the other. He is unaware of the same taxi that I've noticed following us for the past twenty minutes also pull into the lot.

He holds the bottle in front of me as if I'm a dog wanting a treat while he closes the door to our room. 'Few sips of bubbly and she's ready for sex', the classic man's approach to female anatomy. Not every man is so bad. A lot of my clients do a fair job at pleasure before I kill them. It gives me a rush of power, like I'm controlling my own roller coaster, to give and get pleasure from someone just before I end their life. Though throughout the years I've had a few orgasms, and even fewer men have treated me like a lover. Not like John Hilton. He didn't throw me around like a piece of meat to slam his hips against. Most of the men, even some of the good ones could have been just as satisfied with a plastic doll.

For a moment I wish he was John.

Don't misunderstand, there isn't a romantic attraction. But still, he treated me gently. With respect.

No, I need him out of my head.

Then why am I carrying his business card? It's smooth, skeleton white with fine black ink print, his name spelled out in all caps, his number and email underneath. What is it about business cards? They are so much sexier than contacts listed in a cell phone.

Oliver pours the champagne. I'm beginning to believe it's just as routine for him as it is for me. I quickly feel the rationale behind my previous deeds and resituate myself into the comfortably numb mindset that I'm about to kill again. He must think he is classy because before he struggles with the cork, he holds the orange bottle in my face and says, "You ever had Veuve?" It's rude to correct his pronunciation, and he seems like a guy who has a short fuse, even if he has weak hands. And I had already denied the road head, so I play along.

"Is that French?"

"The best." I present a smile of ignorant anticipation as he pours. The foam spills on the floor his first try. I sit, my hands clasped together. "Stand up," he says. I roll my eyes once his gaze drifts back to the bottle, but obey. I haven't planned my exact method to kill him yet. For someone like Oliver, I want it to be a spur of the moment type thing. Improvising is slightly more dangerous, but I need the rush.

He holds the champagne out for me, pulling back before I take it in my hands.

"Take your top off."

"It's a one-piece."

"Then take it all off." I slip the straps from my shoulders, allowing them to fall on my hips. Then I push down from the front, keeping an eye on my bra. I hope he can't see Hilton's business card wedged between my boob and bra cup. "C'mon," he urges. I quickly drift off the rest until I'm in nothing but my underwear and bra. "Good," he says, still holding the two glasses. He extends his hand again, but I wait to take it. "Tonight, you are going to refer to me as Captain. Do you understand that?"

"Yes," I squeak.

"Yes what?"

"Yes, Captain."

"Good girl." He hands me the glass. His hand digs into his chino's pocket and pulls the wad of cash. He flips through the stack. "Fresh from the ATM," he says, raising his eyebrows. The cotton and linen fibers give off an aroma of metallic leather. I half expect him to try and offer an American Express. He nods and slams it down on the TV stand between us. Then, he raises his glass. We clink and sip. The carbonation swells my stomach, and the crisp, sweet taste tickles my mouth. I wish for a whiskey. "Now," he says, parting his feet. "How about that bj?"

"Is it big, Captain?"

"You're about to find out." He points to the ground, nearly hitting me with his exaggerated overbite. "On your knees."

I hold onto the champagne, eager to throw it down the toilet. I slink to my knees. The harsh motel carpet scuffs my skin. With my free hand I unbuckle his LV belt and pull down his zipper, slowly, watching his face the whole time. He breathes heavy, biting his lips as I shuffle his pants from his waist. I rub over his boxers. He sways with his eyes closed now, as if he's already inside of someone.

"Do you like that, Captain?" His groans to answer my question. For a moment, I wonder if he's going to finish before I even pull down his boxers. I imagine him to be one of those guys who masturbates right before sex so he can hold it longer.

"Take it out. Take it out. C'mon." I reach for the elastic band holding up his boxers.

A slam thunders on the door, preceded by a cannon-fire of heavy knocks. Pounding and pounding. Then screaming.

"Oliver! Oliver! Open this door you fucking prick!"

"Fuck!" he says as the slamming bombardment of yells boom. With an abrupt metal blast, the handle bursts, breaking as the door flies open. Oliver Miner's wife (certified by the Facebook page) stands in the doorway with hellfire burning in her eyes and a nine-iron raised above her head.

Four!

She charges. Rage in her eyes.

"You cheating prick!" raising the nine iron.

I grab the back of his thigh to hold him still.

"Anchors away, Captain." I slam the champagne flute against the TV stand and stab.

"Agh!" he lets out a shrill howl as blood squirts, the broken flute stem sticking in his genitals like a dart in a bullseye. "Fuck! Fuck fuck!" He collapses backwards onto the bed, holding his leaking privates.

Incoming! The wife springs into action. I'm not sure if she's attacking me or Oliver at first. She just starts swinging, whacking the golf club against the lamp as she discharges hysterical battle cries.

I crawl backwards, away from her strike zone. She chases me with the club elevated. Is this really how I go? In a shitty motel room, clubbed down by a berserk wife while her husband bleeds to death. Not the superhero ending I've hoped for. I want to yell that I'm on the wife's side, but she's made up her mind.

I throw the television from its stand. The screen crashes down between us, giving me a split second to reach for the bathroom door, but she launches forward and corners me. I go for the bottle, the Veuve bottle. But when are the French ever good in a fight? It's the only thing within reach. I block her assault as the club drives towards my head. The nine iron explodes through, shattering the glass. A few pieces cut my face as the bottle detonates, but the club's strike has been delayed, missing me by an inch.

She has a killer follow through, I'll give her that, swinging sideways and nailing me in the leg. I fall to one knee, arresting the blow of her third stroke. I push myself to my feet, fighting for control of the golf club.

Using my own body weight, I overpower her and press her face against the wall until the cartilage in her nose gives a loud crack. There goes the nose job. Don't make me do this. Don't make me do this. But I can't say the words. No one is thinking. Reason is forfeit.

She screams and kicks me in the crotch. I drop to the floor. Before I know it, she has the club again and hands me a clobbering blow to the head.

I must've blacked out for a moment. There's a rotten taste in my mouth, and fibers from the bloody motel carpet sticking in my lips. I manage to get back on my feet, dazed but conscious.

The wife has moved onto Oliver, yelling curses as she swings at the helpless man who still lays on the bed, holding his blood gushing crotch. I pick up a shard of glass from the broken bottle, sneaking up behind the wife. I wrap one arm around her neck and stick the glass hard into her back. Then I stab again. I wedge the piece into her gut, tug, and pull. Her grip on the club loosens, and I steal it, leaving the glass inside her stomach. I pull the club towards her neck, bending the metal as I press against her throat, crushing her windpipe and snapping her esophagus.

This is not my choice. Not my plan. Casualties are inevitable in a rush job. I have no problem with her, though I do question how it took her so long to finally pin infidelity on her shitty husband. But this is war. A war she waged. I had planned on doing her a favor. But war has casualties.

She claws, and I bite back, sinking my teeth just under her ear. I use the wall for support and choke the life out of her. She doesn't deserve this. She didn't deserve him. Did Kitty deserve what she got? Mercy will only get me killed. I don't let go until her fidgeting has ceased.

My heavy breathing is outmatched by Oliver's groaning, his hands and most of his lower half soaked in red. I limp over to the side of the bed. My head swims in a daze of misty confusion. A warm trickle of blood seeps down from my temple, nesting on my bare collarbone and dripping down onto my arms and chest. I position my body perpendicular to him and raise the club, waiting for him to look at me.

"You ended a decent woman's life tonight, Oliver," I say. "Was fidelity that difficult?"

"Stop! No," he says. Waving his hand out. "Please, I'll–."

Off with his head! Off with his head!

Four!

His precious club plummets, the head smashing into his skull. A blast of blood splatters across the bed linens. Again. Smack! Again! Again! OFF WITH HIS HEAD!

I hear a noise filtering through the sound of the club squishing his brain and skull into a red and blue brownie batter. It's a giggle, then a chuckle, then total laughter. It's me. I'm laughing. Hysterically laughing as I bulldoze his head into bits with his own golf club. Truly it's the best gift ever! Fuck this man for making me kill his wife. His blood stings my eyelids and flies into my mouth as I slam down again and again, painting the sheets and comforter with his opened skull.

Finally, I stop, gazing over what is left of him. I toss the golf club onto the bed and walk over to where my romper and jacket lay, dressing myself before I gather the bodies. I need to go. Fast. The wife had yelled so loudly that someone nearby, if not the whole way across the parking lot, must have heard. Either the cops are on their way already or someone is about to show up at the door. I swipe Hilton's card from under a few shards of glass (it had fallen out during the battle). A few bloodstains, but still readable, and despite a small crease on the left corner, still intact. I shove it in its rightful place between my breast and bra strap, along with the wad of cash from Mr. Miner.

I walk out to Oliver's Jag, golf club in hand. The lot is just as dark as when we had arrived. Only a single light above the lobby building, flickering like a spastic firefly. The lobby is closed by now, and I only see one or two other rooms lit from behind the plastic shutters. I'm most likely not the only person soliciting sex at this motel tonight.

I have his keys that I took from his blood-soaked chinos, jingling them between my fingers in the parking lot. I toss the club into the back seat and turn on the car, pulling around and backing up just in front of the motel room door.

Then a car pulls into the lot.

Shit.

I slump behind the steering wheel as the oncoming vehicle showers the Jag and parking lot with its headlights' orange glow. Is it the police? I wait, refusing to breathe, anticipating the flash of blue and red lights. Nothing.

I don't budge, not until the light passes and the car, just a truck, I think, veers left and heads to the far end of the lot. I slink back up, peeking through the front windshield, watching as it pulls up to a separate room on the other side of the motel.

Slowly, carefully, I open the front door. The parking lot is quiet. So quiet I hear the sink running from inside a nearby room. I push the door open just enough so I can slip out, sneaking along the Jag back to the motel room.

I wrap the unhappy couple in the bloody sheets and lug them from the doorstep into the trunk. I don't bother with the room. Remember, I don't really exist. I'm not in the system. But still, I need to get far away from the crime scene. Fast.

As I haul them out and drop their bodies into the trunk, I hear it. A faint gasp behind me makes me freeze. I wait a good second or two before turning.

Standing outside her room two doors down from me is a little girl.

"Isn't it a bit late?" I say, praying that her parents or whoever she's here with don't walk out too. She can't be more than 7.

No response. Just a slack jaw.

"Here," I say, walking towards her, I hold out one of the hundreds from Oliver's stack, it's a little crinkled, and the edges stained with blood, but she accepts it silently.

Once the bill is in her hand, I place my finger over my mouth and give an inaudible 'shhh'. Did she just nod? I think so.

I don't have time to guess what she'll do. My time is short. I go back to the Jag and leave.

My head aches as I drive through the night. The swift crack from the nine-iron replays itself in my head like an old cassette tape. I blink rapidly, trying to stay alert. I'm drifting and my head is cloudy. I rock back and forth, my neck giving out every few minutes, my head bobbing like an inflatable punching bag. I keep both of my hands on the wheel, gripping the leather with a firm squeeze, strangling it between my bloodied knuckles. My head isn't dripping anymore, so I guess the bleeding has stopped.

At this point, I'm numb. My whole upper half is floating, paralyzed from adrenaline and blood loss. It's very possible I'm bleeding everywhere and just don't know it. Plums and blueberries dance in my eye line. A turquoise caterpillar floats across the sea in my view. Purple and white flickers splotch like watercolor paint in my vision. I squeeze my eyes once more, fighting the hallucinations. I turn off the main road, taking an unfamiliar backroad, and drive between walls of trees. A fog rises, or at least I think that's fog. Stay awake, I tell myself. It's just a little further. What is? I have no idea where the fuck I'm headed. My head rolls to my shoulder. Then pops back upright. I touch my lip, then notice my finger covered in scarlet liquid from my mouth. Maybe some music will help. I poke at the radio. Grover Washington Jr's "Just the Two of Us" is playing.

"Look at you, Ann." She's sitting next to me. No longer in the Jag. It's Uncle Jones's Porsche. The sun beams at us from the horizon of Lake Michigan. We're stopped at a light on Lakeshore Drive. I have a cigarette in my teeth, and she sits there, smiling at me with a fresh layer of ruby red lipstick and a new haircut. She got it cut short, just past her ears. It glows like golden straw with the sunbeams flushing through the car. But it's hard to focus on her beauty. There's a pounding in the back of the trunk. Something in there. But she doesn't seem to hear it.

Kitty leans across the console, her hand resting on my thigh, warm and comfortable. She gives me a quick kiss before the light turns green. I slam on the gas, flying along the edge of the city between the rows of skyscrapers on one side and the endless blue water on the other. She waves her arms in the air, holding one out of the window, and lets out a thrilling shout.

"We could just drive," she says. "We could go anywhere." Her hand grips my own as I steer with one hand, keeping my eyes on the road. "Ann?"

"We can't just... I can't leave, Kitty."

"You don't need to keep doing this, Ann." She crawls along the seat, resting her side against its upright leather, speaking to me as if she was laying on her side in bed. "You got everything you wanted. He's gone now, but that's where it stops. I could see you doing so much. You could learn to cook, get a business degree, or teach. Ann?" She returns her back against the seat. I look over at her, studying the way she slinks down, her arms crossed, staring out the window on the other side.

As she tries to sing, probably to attempt to ease the tension, I blow a cloud of smoke out the window. Her chirping along is futile. My gaze switches from staring at her, to the back, to the front where a trash bag filled with bloody latex gloves is at her feet.

"Are you going to be like this all day? What happened? Ann? What have we done?"

The song's chorus keeps repeating over itself. I press my eyelids together, trying to down it out. Trying to drown out her singing. Drown out the radio.

The POUNDING from the trunk grows. Louder. Louder.

"Ann?"

God, make it stop.

Suddenly, a horn blasts like a war trumpet. She springs to life, pointing wildly at the front window.

"Look out!"

I snap my head to face forward and jerk the steering wheel, dodging the oncoming truck at the very last second.

"No! Go away, Kitty!" I yell. Back in the darkness of the Jag. I'm breathing heavily again, wishing for a cigarette. The passenger seat is empty. I've veered off, my foot holding down on the brake on a patch along the backroad. I shift to reverse. Ok, let's try driving. I speed back on course through the night.

People talk about having an extra sense of direction. It's an ability to navigate to familiar spots. Safe spots. Areas of true power and control in the brain take the helm. It's as if the brain has a registry of locations at its disposal. That's at least how I explain how I somehow end up with the Jaguar parked in Pearcey's parking lot.

Once I get to the school, I manage to flick the key and shut off the engine. My head is throbbing. I spin, still seated in the driver's seat. I need to move, but I can't.

All I can do is panic. I think that I was followed. That little girl. She must have ratted me out. They'll be here any minute, I just know it.

But I can't just sit and wait. C'mon Ann, move. You can still be free.

I see myself from the passenger seat's point of view, slunk behind the wheel like a propped corpse. I want to nudge myself into action. I want to scream.

There's a sudden thump from the hood. I jump. Forgetting where and who I am. Is someone there?

No, it's just a fucking cat. The stray gives a hiss, showing me its teeth through the windshield.

"Go away." It doesn't move. "C'mon kitty kitty," I mumble. "Kitty. Kitty."

I open the door and fall onto the pavement. My legs are noodles beneath my waist. I pull myself up, climbing the door to stand. If I stay any longer, I'm just asking to get caught. Here in the middle of the parking lot, I'm a sitting duck.

My ears ring, and my stomach curls, warping over itself like a boa constrictor. Then my head stops spinning and I throw up on the asphalt, releasing the few contents of my stomach. I heave over the loose chunks of food and stomach acid that pile at my feet, glaring down at it as if I created a Dali. If I placed what was left of Oliver Miner's head beside it, people would think it was a collaboration with Picasso.

The bodies in the trunk are no longer important. I want them to be, but I can't control my gyrating mind or body. I limp across the parking lot towards a small hill of grass that leads to the playground, stepping off the paved concrete and onto the grass where I approach the jungle gym. My head rings in itself, commanding me with the staff sergeant of logic to turn around and go back. I have things to do. Important things.

Things like disposing of two bodies in the back of a stolen Jaguar.

But is there time? No, fuck the bodies, I need to get out of here.

My feet crunch against the loose gravel that lines the playground. I walk past the jungle gym and the monkey bars. I don't know what it is, but something calls me to climb up and go down the slide. My feet, heavy, slumping one by one as if I'm walking in mud, boom on the stairs up to the jungle gym. I pace like a zombie along the creaking bridge. It sways slightly. I hold my hands out like a tightrope walker and step across the swinging bridge of plastic-coated wooden planks. They shake as I cross, only slightly in reality, but for me it's like being shaken by a rough turbulence. I sit at the top of the slide. I remember as a kid, slides seemed like endless towers reaching up to the sky. And the thrill when you slid down, zooming at the speed of light. Now I'm jammed between the plastic tubing, slowly inching down until I pop out of the end rolling in the gravel.

After the slide, I go to the swing set. I pass on the spinning wheel, since my head already feels like it's in a washing machine cycle. The set rattles as I grip the chains and sit. The chains creak. I don't take off. I just sort of rock there, feeling like I'm soaring 100 feet from the ground, though I'm dragging my feet as I teeter on the rusting swing, my toes skimming the gravel beneath me.

Then suddenly there's a noise. I'm not alone anymore.

I turn my head so violently that I lose my balance on the swing, toppling over myself. My purse flies into the air and I hit the ground. My face plasters against the gravel, reopening a cut on my face. I crawl away from the swing, trying to escape from whatever sound is looming in the distant shadows. Police? I can't be sure. No sirens. But something or someone is getting closer.

I can't see. I'm enveloped in the darkness cast by a moonless sky. Why the hell did I come over here?

I try crawling, but my foot is stuck in the now mangled and twisted chains of the swing. Shit, I turn my body. The sound grows. Crunching on the gravel. Footsteps. I pull myself up, like a sit-up, groaning as I'm more light-headed by the second. I can't get out. My fingers are useless against the tightly linked metal of the swing set that has lassoed me in itself. I'm its prisoner. It sprouts to life, a monster of rusted brown metal, with chains for arms and a body made from the shadows of the night sky. It holds me tightly in its iron tentacles. The grip tightens with every move I make. They won't budge, pressing into my flesh and bruising my bones.

Where's my purse?

It's a few feet away. I reach, outstretching my arm, trying to expand my joints to pull the strap closer to me. I feel the leather touch my index. It draws slightly closer, close enough to rap my finger around the strap. Fatigue is setting in. My head is spinning. My consciousness drains through an hourglass. My vision blurs and a ringing stings my eardrums. I'm drowning in myself, suffocating under the waves of madness and paralysis.

I cough as I draw my phone from inside my purse. I swipe it open and go to my contact list. Who could I call? I have no one. A few years ago, Uncle Jones would have shown up. I'd have been scolded, but not hurt. Kitty would have been furious, yet again, that I got myself into trouble because I chose to continue this lifestyle.

I dial Nick. I don't think I want him. My finger just clicks down, and it happens to be his name. The phone rings.

Just as it starts, I feel a presence around me. All over me, but not touching me, figureless shadows… gathering themselves in an attack position, collected here to bring me down.

The noise around the swing set grows louder. Booming like an approaching army.

Ring. Ring. Nothing.

Fuck, c'mon.

Ring.

Louder. Louder.

Off with her head! Off with my head?

The sound escalates. Footsteps rising and rising. Laughter, chatter.

"Hello, you've reached the voicemail of Nick –

I press the red button.

Louder. Louder. My fingers disobey me. How could they? I reach into my shirt and let the business card fall right in front of my face. I dial the number.

LOUDER.

C'mon, God damnit.

The numbers rattle off into the screen. Finally, I press the small circle button with a phone on it. My world flips. I cough again. The darkness suffocates my eyes until I'm smothered in a black empty abyss, hearing the faint sound of ringing.

Breakfast with a Hooker

A lance of sunlight piercing through a half-opened window wakes me. The soft caress of a breeze drifts into a bedroom. The silky touch of warm, familiar sheets kisses my body the way a mother would, but not my mother. I nuzzle into a pillow; the linen case pampers the side of my face, holding my neck upright. I let out a murmur, cuddling myself. I'm comfortable. Peaceful. But where am I? I've felt these sheets before, just like they are now, gently draped over my half-naked body.

I shoot up. A darting pain rushes through my head.

"Woah," a voice says to me, rushing over from the doorway. "Easy does it."

My vision is still blurry, but I can make out a body gently moving towards me. I rub my eyes, picking a few stray pieces of sand from my lashes.

When my view becomes clear, I see him. John Hilton.

He hands me a glass of water and touches my forehead, scanning me like an intrigued doctor. "You have a concussion," he said. "I think."

I realize my head has a bandage wrapped around it and I'm wearing an old T-shirt over my still battered and dirty skin.

"How did-."

"You called me," John says from the side of the bed. His eyes are warm, the green in them highlighted by the sun's glow in the room. "You said you were at the playground by Pearcey. I didn't have your number in my contacts but…" He pauses. "I don't know, there was something in your voice; I just knew it was you." He chuckles, showing off bright white teeth, freshly brushed. I get a waft of mint from his breath as he laughs. "Even though I guess I don't really know who you really are."

"Who I am?"

He stands, holding his hands for me to take. "C'mon, how about a shower?" I want to ask about the others, the ones who were there when I passed out. Or did I imagine all that? I decide to stay quiet. For all I know, this is a trap. The police must be in the living room, just waiting to take me in.

I wipe away the sheets and dip my toes on the soft layer of the oriental rug between his end table and the hardwood. I struggle to stand for a moment. He keeps me upright, holding my hands like a physical therapist walking his patient for the first time after an accident. But then he lets me walk on my own, only helping me with that original step. Once I have my balance, I take the reins. One foot over the other towards the door. I notice he has hung up my leather jacket along with the dress; and my shoes are neatly left in the corner of the room. I don't mention them, I just keep walking, out of his bedroom according to his guidance and into the bathroom.

Under a flowing shower head, a heated rainstorm pours over my body. I watch blood collect at the bottom of the drain. I'm distracted by the lavender and coconut scented shampoo and body wash when the fact is, I should be worried that I left two bodies in a car trunk parked at my school.

The foam suds sink into my skin, tickling my elbows and knees, pleasant aromas that for a moment, make me feel somewhat dead.

I think of John. Did he find the Jag too? Or just me spilled out on the swing set? If he had found the bodies, I think I would have woken up in handcuffs instead of his bed.

After a shower I wish never ended, I grab a towel left for me on the sink. My head slightly tingles with a lightheaded sway as I bend over to dry my legs and feet, patting my skin before wrapping the towel around my chest. I take another from the rack and brush through my hair, gently. The bump on the side of my head where Mrs. Miner had struck me with the club is still tender.

I study the apartment now from the hallway. My suspicions are confirmed when I see a pillow and blanket draped along John's sofa in the living room. I slept alone.

The kitchen greets me with the hissing of a frying pan and the baking smell of pancakes with a hint of vanilla and buttermilk, complimented by a savory fragrance of caramelizing bacon.

The knife block remains untouched, the slit still unfilled from the blade I had stolen.

John isn't in the kitchen, but his voice gives a faint echo from down the hall. I peek around the corner and catch a glimpse of him pacing with his phone to his ear behind an ajar door to a den. Who is he speaking to? Is he calling the police? No, he wouldn't be making me breakfast if the police are coming. Or would he? It could be a trap to get me to stay, waiting for them to arrive while I stuff myself with pancakes.

Then I remember.

Danny.

I notice the same photo frame that had originally seized my attention the night I was supposed to kill John.

Who is John talking to? I want to know, but I need to be sure about Danny. Is he here? John will be out any moment. And if I'm going to kill him here and now, I don't want Danny in the next room.

Is this the morning John had hoped for after the other night? Is it a sick game? Two days prior, I was sprinting from this place without my clothes and now I'm about to be served breakfast and nursed back to health by a man I so desperately need to kill.

The oven clock says 9:30 am. The other room, I think to myself. Danny.

Could he still be sleeping in there? I'm unable to fathom how he'll react to seeing his teacher standing in a towel with a head wound in his father's apartment. How worse for John to know I'm his son's teacher. I can't imagine someone like John judging people. Besides, he's the one who hired a prostitute. Shut up Ann. Think. You might have a student sleeping in his bedroom five feet from where you're standing. I tiptoe to the second bedroom. Danny's room? I want to stop. Maybe I don't need to know. Wrong. I have to know what's on the other side of that fucking door.

I hover over the metal knob. John's voice is still a distant whisper from the den. The door handle is cool to the touch, undisturbed for a few hours, at least through the night, maybe longer. I ease the door open, just enough to peek inside. I see the top of a dresser and a small desk.

I inch the door a little more, sticking my head through. My chest cavity throbs as my heart pounds the walls of my sternum, a battering ram against a castle gate. I imagine Danny sitting on his bed, escaping into his doodles and composition notebook writing. He's wearing a black shirt and green-checkered PJ pants that go past his ankles.

But when I open the door, the bed is made neatly, firm, like a military bed ready for inspection. An ominous spirit lingers in the empty room. Not a piece of clothing unfolded or dangling from the drawers. It's stark. The only thing out of place is the desk chair, slightly pulled out. The Count of Montecristo on the desk.

I fully step into the room with a sigh. It's like walking inside a tomb, the air as empty as an unearthed grave.

"You looking for something?" I spin around, dropping the book as he glares from the doorway, his arms crossed. I'm frozen. He lightly bends, picking up the book and replacing it exactly where I had found it. "My son, he um – he doesn't stop talking about that book."

"Where is he now?" I say, my throat groggy. I cough. "Your son."

"Come with me." He offers his hand, guiding me out of the bedroom. I can't help but notice a slight tremor in his touch, a subtle shaking, doing his best to hold it inside. "Sorry for stepping away, my ex – she, well - c'mon, you must be hungry."

"Yes," I try a smile. Nothing comes.

The entirety of breakfast I anticipate a line of questioning, but John takes his time with me. I drown everything in maple syrup. The pancakes aren't fluffy enough. I don't expect much from the bachelor cook. But the bacon is the kind you have to buy over the counter, sliced in house, I guess Whole Foods. It has a smoky Applewood flavor that stimulates my mouth with a vibrant, oaky taste. I eat six pieces.

"Can I get you anything else?" he asks after finishing a glass of orange juice. I sit at the counter on a high-top chair while he hunches over on the other side of the island, propping himself by his elbow while holding his fork in the other hand, staring at me the whole time as if we've known one another for years. He allowed me to borrow another t-shirt of his. It's long enough, stretching just above my knees, so I wear only my underwear underneath.

"You don't have any chocolate milk, do you?" I say, chewing a piece of bacon.

"Chocolate milk?" I nod. He finds it funny, as if I'm joking. "I don't do a lot of sugar," he responds.

"That's a shame." I pour more syrup on my strip of bacon like ketchup on a hot dog and crunch down. It's just the right amount of crispy. Not burnt, but not flaccid and chewy.

My eyes return to the knife block at the end of the counter. I wonder if he's noticed, and if he has, when will he accuse me?

"So," he says, washing his hands. "I have all your things."

"My things?"

"Your jacket, dress, and you forgot your cash, too." He leans against the far counter, holding himself as if he was going to do a tricep dip. "From the other night, remember? You dashed out so fast you didn't even get paid."

"I um–" I haven't come up with a reason for retreating without my stuff. And if I had thought of one, the concussion has definitely sunk any ideas or lies. "I have really bad nightmares," I finally say. Really? That's what you come up with?

"Nightmares?"

"Sometimes they seem so real that I think they are. I'm so sorry I honestly hardly remember, I fled so fast. Well, I wouldn't say fled. Before I realized I was outside and didn't feel right trying to get back in to get my things."

"So, you left naked? But you came to my office? Why? So you could get paid or-."

That bitch told him.

"How'd you know –?"

"I didn't. But then I saw my business card on the ground next to you when I found you at the park. I figured it was you. So, your name is Mary?"

"I don't go by it."

"Do I get to know your real name? Since I did save you from that swing set." I laugh with him. How can I not?

He props himself against the counter. My eyes scan my tainted place setting, honing in on the fork gently resting along the brim of my plate.

"Look, I know that whatever you do can be scary sometimes. I get that and I don't judge you, but I wanna know what happened. If not now, I understand, you have been through a lot."

"Is this John Hilton, the lawyer? Or John Hilton, a concerned man?"

"Well, that depends… who am I talking to? Mercedes Valentina the prostitute, or Mary whatever… the girl I can't stop thinking about?"

I stay quiet, letting the silent lull between us grow to the point that he retreats, back to the stovetop to start cleaning up. He opens the fridge to return the orange juice. I have a split moment, taking the fork, pressing the prongs against my fingertips. Yes, I think, it might do the trick. I set the fork back in its place, holding, then, the butter knife. I run my hand along the blade. Course, but not deadly sharp.

"I got jumped, that's all." I need to change the subject. "You know," I said finally. "I remember that you still owe me a second date."

He turns, closing the fridge. He scratches the back of his neck, and tilts his head to the side, closing the gap between himself and the counter.

"I didn't think you'd–"

"Just because I ran out doesn't mean I didn't enjoy it." He looks like he's weighing his options like a TV guest on a game show.

"You feeling any better?"

"A little."

"Headache?" I nod. He pulls a pill bottle from the cupboard. I return for the fork, holding it under the counter, the way Danny hid under the lunch table, carving into his palm with his plastic knife. "Here." He plops three liquid gels to the left of my glass. "Might help." I don't touch them. I swallow the lingering pieces of bacon and wash it down with my juice.

He bites his upper lip, looking out the window in the kitchen. The curtain is pulled back, showing the city watching us from the outside.

"I took the liberty of calling a doctor. I hope that's ok."

"What?"

"He's good. He won't ask you any questions, he will just take a look at your head." I rise from my seat, rushing back towards the bedroom. I keep the fork tight along my inner forearm, moving so swiftly that he can't notice. But he follows, grabbing my arm.

"I need to go." I tug. His fingers dig into my skin.

"No, you need help."

"I don't." I tug again.

"Just let him take a look at you."

"Why?"

"You are injured. What's wrong with him just looking you over?"

"I feel fine. I'll take your pills and go. Let go." His grip wanes. I dart again for the room.

"At the very least, maybe tell me what happened." I stop. "I looked up Mercedes Valentina. I even went to that address on your ID. She doesn't exist. Anywhere. That address doesn't exist. I stood in the street like an idiot asking door to door. You made me look like a fool. Then you call me, slung out on a swing set, alone and bloody, at a school playground."

"It's none of your business!" I turn.

"You made it my business when you called for my help."

"I don't owe you anything."

"You owe me something."

I pause for a moment, weighing my options. Then I face him, removing the shirt, topless and bare. He stops in his tracks.

"Is this what you think I owe you?"

"I meant an explanation."

"Explanation?" I step forward. "Why would you need an explanation when you could have this?"

"This isn't what I meant." He steps back. "I just–"

He's turning down sex… who is this man?

"You just what? Needed to know?" I walk closer, easing my way with my shoulders cocked and my chest popped up. Toes first, fluid and slow. "Well, that depends. Can you keep a secret?" I reach a taste distance from his lips.

Goodbye, John… I think to myself. We are so close.

"Yes."

"So can I."

The fork slips through my hand to a perfect stabbing position. I plunge it to his neck. But he stops me, intercepting my wrist just before the prongs puncture his skin.

"Not the first woman to try and stab me."

"Where's your son?" I breathe heavily. His eyes narrow, his head turns from side to side.

"He's not here."

"Where's your son?"

"He's — he's with his mother, alright? Just drop the fucking fork! Jesus." Then it hits me like a semi plowing a stray deer on the highway. My heart thumps, my head swells in breath stealing pain.

"Where is he? Tell me where he is!"

"I don't fucking know! Let go!" The fork falls, clanking against the floor. His hand loosens on my wrist and I cower away, my bottom lip trembling. Keep it together, Ann. God Damnit! I collapse, kicking myself across the floor until I'm propped against the wall. Shivering, panting. I stare at nothing. He stares directly at me.

He watches, letting a moment pass without moving an inch. Then he approaches, picking up the shirt and covering me with it. I expect judgment. I expect him to tell me I'm insane. To tell me to get out. But he remains silent, inhaling and exhaling with me until my pulsating chest decreases to a minor snare beat, all the while sitting with me.

"This doesn't freak you out?" I say once I get my breath back.

"My ex was about as combustible as turpentine. We both kinda were. See that?" He points to a scar along his right eyebrow, hidden now under the dark bushes of hair that curves over his eyes.

"Candlestick?"

"Rolling pin."

"Good choice."

"You wanna know why I hired you? Even if the whole night's a performance, at least it's one I see coming. The real thing scares us. Truth often does. Material is malleable but people, they just prefer masks." I draw a long breath through my nostrils, slipping it out through my mouth and holding my eyes closed while we sit in a long silence.

"I am Ann by the way." He smiles, taking my hand in his. "Nice to meet you, Ann."

He lets me stay a little while longer, agreeing to cancel the doctor since I promise I'll go tomorrow on my own. Which I won't. I get my dress and jacket and fold them into an old duffle bag he claims he never uses anymore. I hold my tongue on my own questions for him. About his ex. About his son. I'm sure he has plenty more questions for me that stretch far beyond my entangled situation in the swing set at a school playground.

There's five hundred more dollars than I expect in the cash envelope. I hope it isn't a down payment for the next date.

Date? Is this what I agreed to? I've never gone out with a man outside of the internet-organized exchange of flesh for cash. Does he assume it's a real date? Do I? Or another hook-up with a prostitute? I haven't cleared it with him. I'm still hazy, still a little dizzy and my head aches to the point where my loosely assembled mind feels jumbled like a box of jigsaw puzzle pieces.

John orders me a cab home around one in the afternoon. I walk like a zombie, fresh and clean on the outside, but internally bleeding with confusion and disarray. I have so much pain in my head and so little grasp on my next move.

Exhausted when I get home, I plummet on my couch, passing out until six the next morning.

On Monday morning, I arrive at school well rested, greeted by flashing red and blue lights barricading the school grounds.

Red, Blue, and Purple All Over

Like I've said before, I am not in the system. The authorities have to get a sample from me to prove my DNA on the scene at the motel or from the car. And of course, they won't get that. But that doesn't matter when a platoon of police cruisers and detectives are circling the intertwined unhappy couple in the trunk of their Jaguar.

A trail of yellow tape surrounds the Jag in the parking lot. I push my way through the sea of onlooking students who finally get to see something exciting at school. Two cops wearing baby blue latex gloves handle the nine iron. They secure it inside a plastic wrap bag for inspection. Other detectives wipe the car for prints, take statements, investigate, you know, the typical murder scene hullabaloo.

All I can do is remind myself to stay calm. Look surprised. And do my best to appear disturbed.

I balletically tread along the caution tape, fingering the plastic yellow edges, tiptoeing my fingers across it like my hand is an imaginary tightrope walker. I stop a few feet away from the opened trunk. The bodies are gone, carried off in two separate tarps on stretchers to be examined and cut apart to find the cause of death, no doubt. I wonder if whoever performs their autopsy can see inside their souls and minds to find the real cause of death. Is it really blunt force trauma to the head? Or years of infidelity and a bad case of doucheness that brought this couple to be found dead in the trunk of a car, bloody and mutilated like torture victims. I don't think of myself as doing anything wrong. On the contrary, I righted their wrong. And I actually kinda like it. For once my work is on display, like a painting in a gallery. Folks from the neighborhood, parents, other teachers and peers. They all get a chance to see my real work. And in doing so, have an opportunity to know me. Finally, I think to myself, I'm on display as my truest self. So why hide who I am at all?

I'm amazed at the number of limp jaws and eager eyes gathered to get a glimpse of this. This! This that I committed. This terribly beautiful horror I directed. I guess this is how Quentin Tarantino feels after each movie he makes. For a moment, I realize that I have fans. They can't help themselves. They stare. Whether or not they despise what they see, they need to see more. They have to see it. No one can just waltz by without their attention fornicating with the gory sensation I have created. They are in awe of my masterpiece.

I take a short bow, thanking all those who have come out to support my work. Of course no one notices, and it's quite a subtle display of appreciation, because I don't do it for them, but for me. I wonder if my madness, my potential madness, is something to be accepted. A painter in my own right? An artist whose medium isn't acrylic or pastels, but blood and flesh.

I find Angela Greene standing with her arms crossed on the opposite side of the caution tape. Across the way, Sonya is crying in between sips of coffee. Amir is in the middle of the action, speaking to a few of the cops. He's the only one apparently allowed on that side.

"What is this?" I ask Angela, acting surprised.

"Some psycho killed this poor couple and left them here in the trunk of a car."

"Wow." I purse my lips together and bob my head.

"Honestly, people are so, excuse my language, F-ing sick." God, she makes me cringe. I maintain a few feet of distance from her while Amir shakes hands with a detective, making his way over to us.

"What a mess," he shakes his head, stepping under the caution tape. Angela helps, pulling up the strand of yellow for him as though he's cutting in line at airport security.

"What did they say?" Angela asks. "Are they closing school?"

Amir rubs his head, gliding his palm over the balding surface in front of his receding hairline. "They said it's up to me—"

"You're not going to, are you?" Christ, she has him by the balls.

"They want to get a statement from each staff member," he answers. "Individually."

Shit.

"What right do they have to do that? We aren't suspects, are we?" Angela asks. Why is she so worried?

"We just need to cooperate and follow whatever they say." Amir rubs his shoulder, dividing his eye contact between the two of us. "Since it is on school property, it's just protocol. At least that's what the detective said." He looks at me. A wave of surprise flushes his eyes. "What happened to you?"

"What?" I totally forgot about my own wound. He points at my head.

"Oh," I say, softly laughing it off. "I got into a small accident on Friday night. It was nothing."

"That doesn't look like nothing. That looks serious."

"I'm fine."

"The night of the dance?" Damn that bitch. Abort, I tell myself. Abort, get the fuck outta here.

"Oh my gosh, my heads all, you know, blurred up." I make a spiraling motion with my finger. "I'm just still processing my uncle's death and not thinking straight. Too many emotions. It was Saturday. Saturday night. Just a fender bender, though, nothing to worry about."

They both stare at me for a long silent span of nerve-racking seconds. Amir seems distraught, torn between an execution sentence and a one-way ticket to the psych ward. Angela doesn't seem worried or concerned at all. I've seen enough movies and studied enough people to know suspicion when I see it draped on someone's face. She wears it without shame, without any attempt to give me the impression that she gives a shit. She doesn't. I know that. So why hide suspicion? Why does she mask herself to me? She's suspicious of me. And she knows I know she can bring me down. Which is what she wants. One thing is all she needs. One slip up in my stories or my alibis and she'll have enough. Why she gives a shit is a mystery to me. I guess that's just some people. They get off by watching others fall because they have nothing else to finger themselves with at night besides the preoccupation of power over someone else's fate.

"They are going to want statements by the end of the day," Amir says, changing the subject.

"Should I arrange a meeting?" Angela offers.

"I will send an email memo out to the faculty," Amir tells her. "I don't want to get everyone worked up and waste time in a meeting."

"Good idea, I can draft one for you." She nods without a response from Amir and struts off.

It's just us two. Amir and me. And the army of cops.
And now the endless lineup of cars in the drop off lane
filled with gawking parents.

"Did they ID them?"

He shakes his head. "You're sweating. Are you alright,
miss Bonny?"

I am under control.

"Actually, I was wondering if we could speak a bit
about the VP position?-"

"You really think right now is a good time?" His eyes
wander. I can't tell who is stressed more, me or him. Men
usually can't keep eye contact when delivering bad news
or a lie. "Sometimes things aren't always up to me." What
does he mean by that?

Amir offers a heartfelt nod as he walks away, tending to
the mass of confused parents and intrigued students. I stay
there for a few moments, basking in the flashing blue and
red lights from the cruisers and allowing the murmur of
police talk and flooding rumors from the audience to
ruminate between my ears, trying to process what Amir
meant by 'not up to him'.

Sonya charges from out of nowhere, wrapping me in a
hug.

"You ok, babe?" She asks.

"I'm not sure that's always such a simple question."
How can I be ok? To be honest, at this point I feel nothing.
I'm just numb.

We head into school together. I worry about what Amir
said. Did he already make his decision? Of course, I didn't
plan on killing Oliver and leaving his body on school
grounds. But I can't change the way things went down.

A bouquet of flowers sits on my desk. White peonies.
I've never received flowers before. Are they a token of

celebration from my immaculate performance outside, like a ballet dancer or an opera singer after a flawless show? Of course not. They're from Nick, with a tag around them that says: "My Condolences."

Oh right, I remember. And so did he. My uncle "died" last week. I rummage in my head on how I should perform my ever so defeated, emotionally fragile girl self after the death of a loved one. I think of how I felt after Kitty died. A sense of shame, adrenaline, guilt, relief, loneliness, relief, guilt. Was I relieved when Uncle Jones had died? He was never my real uncle. When he actually died, I would say yes, I was relieved. It was me who killed him.

"I can show you the ropes. You can make good money. It can be just a temporary side gig to start. You'll earn more cash than you can imagine." Uncle Jones had finished the last drops of his iced tea as he sat across from me in the Doctor B's Café booth. My left knee bounced, and I hugged myself with my right arm. "No one can physically do this forever, but if you are smart, and you have someone like me in your corner, fuck, I can make you a queen. I'll get you a new name, a few if you want. Some ID's that will be good enough to show a cop. You can be registered under my name if you'd like. Be my 'niece'." He had proposed I come to work for him. He labeled the job title as a "call girl." All I had to do was act like I was on a date with rich men. They paid him, then he paid me. But it was strictly cardinal. No sex. At least not at the beginning. I would be hired as their arm candy. Someone for lonely rich white dudes to buy Hermes handbags for and take to dinner.

"I don't think I can do that."

"Tell me something. What is it you want, Mary?"

"Don't call me Mary." Mary was the last thing I heard my mother say. I never wanted to hear that again.

"Ok, new name. We will fix you up with one." He tossed a parmesan truffle French fry into his teeth and chomped. He ate with his elbow perched on the table, and a handful of fries queued in his fingers. "So, c'mon spill. Why are you here?"

"I don't know what you mean."

"Look darling, everyone comes to a city for a reason. They want a fresh start, they're running from an ex, killed their parents—"

"Yeah." It just came out. He stared at me, rubbing under his chin after swallowing the final fry. I didn't kill my parents. I never knew my father. My mother was a dancer. At least I knew she danced and was given money.

"To which?"

"New start."

"You old enough for college?"

"I like music."

"How come?"

"My mother played it for me." I looked at my knees, letting go a short breath through my nostrils.

"Where's she now?" I waited to respond. I was a nervous novice—sue me. I shouldn't have mentioned her. I shouldn't have mentioned anything. I should've never gotten into his car. Then I looked up at him. Only lifting my eyes, my chin burrowed in my chest.

"Gone."

I left Jones. But something told me I'd see him again. I spent that night in the city sleeping under the bridge along the river, just underneath New Orleans Street. The train went all night back and forth across the bridge, roaring as it soared between the buildings. The sparks from the track sprinkled me like boiling pixie dust. I wondered each time a new train came if the track would dislodge and crash on top of me, burying me under the concrete and metal.

Uncle Jones found me the next day. He pulled up again beside me. I had just found an uneaten bagel in a trash bin.

I was cold, so I agreed to join him in his car.

It was the quickest job interview ever. Pretty soon, I was on the streets, and soon after I was living more luxuriously than I could have imagined.

When I mentioned school, it was met with threats and time spent in a room he called 'the box'. Really just an empty studio with no light. Uncle Jones was the first to give me a reason to kill. It was the only way out. He had me in his grasp, or at least that's what he thought, and though he claimed it was temporary, everyone knew that girls didn't age out. Girls vanished: died of an overdose, car accident, got arrested. Not me. After I got what I needed from Uncle Jones, he was the one who vanished.

My feeling of stardom slowly fades as the school day drags on. The students have little care for learning, given the massacre outside, and keep bringing it up. Granted, I wish I could embellish them. What a great creative writing lesson that would be.

I want to tell Danny. I want to tell him so badly. To tell someone. But he isn't in class. Suddenly the excitement of my bloody exploits vanishes and melts into paranoia. I become just as distracted as my own students.

I'll be honest, my concussion is still at large. Each time I turn from the white board I get a whiplash of pain in my temples and the back of my neck. My legs ache and my back stings just above my rear pelvic bone. I know I should have stayed home from work today, but that would have only raised more suspicion, and I don't do well in tight spaces.

By late morning, I want nothing more than for the day to be over. The first three periods lag like a stalemate tennis match. I can't stop thinking about why Danny hasn't shown up to school. I'm too worried to ask Amir. He most likely has gotten a call from Danny's mom with a reason. But what if that reason is, they found out about me? How could they have? There's no way. Right? It's like looking into a tissue after a big sneeze. I want to see. I need to see. But I know it will disgust me whatever it is.

Lunchtime hits and the students file out on their own, famished, I assume, by the way they rush the door like a Black Friday sale. I remain at my desk, staring through a small window, blasting classical music to try and drown out the noise, drown out all my thoughts. My room has a decent view. It looks out onto the playground and the baseball diamond, unkempt and muddy from the cruelty of the fall-winter hybrid. A few buildings reach behind the baseball diamond and the playground, lining the horizon like tall steel colossuses watching over me at my desk, my teeth nibbling on the inside of my gums while I twirl a pen between my fingers, clicking it in and out. I watch the younger grades play on the swing set, chasing each other across the jungle gym and playing kickball on the baseball diamond.

Click, click, click. I press on my pen. The laughter and noise fills my ears from outside. The kids circle the diamond.

Circling.

I tap rapidly on the pen. In and out, in and out, playing eighth notes along with Mozart on the mechanical device. Click, click. I check the clock across the room. I want to leave. I need to get out of here. Amir will understand. Unless someone got to him first.

Where is Danny?

Then the music shuts off.

"Ann," a voice says. No, I tell myself. It's just in your head. It's just in your head. I'm not mad. "Ann," it repeats. "Ann."

Then I realize it's familiar, coming from behind me.

"Earth to Miss Bonny."

I shift in my chair. Nick stands in my classroom, a plate in his hand and chewing a mouthful from a burger clenched between his fingers.

"You alright?" He asks, swallowing. "Oh my gosh your face!"

"What?" I forgot the hideous wound I'm wearing like a scarlet letter. "Oh yeah, it's nothing. Just a small accident."

"Are you alright?" This time he says it with a sharp tone at the end of the phrase, as if the first had been ceremonial, and the second is true.

"Yes," I say, throwing my pen inside a drawer as if I'm hiding a murder weapon.

"Aren't you going to get lunch?" He holds the burger higher. As if I didn't already see it. "They got a new meat grinder and made them fresh in the cafeteria. So good." Another bite. I would typically jump on the thought of a decent burger. But today my mouth is dry, my lips chapped, and a sour taste lingers like a bad hangover.

"I'm not hungry."

"You get the flowers?" He rotates like a bobble head, scanning for the botanical gift he sent me. "I figured they were a little late, but you weren't around last week. So..."

"They are nice. Thank you."

"Why aren't they out?" I roll my chair back, showing him the flowers neatly placed in the corner behind my desk. "You just leave them on the ground?"

"Well, I didn't want the students asking questions." To tell you the truth I want to throw them out. "You know how fifth graders can be so gossipy."

"I'm sorry I didn't say anything at the dance on Friday. After, well, I would've called, but I figured I should give you space. Are you hanging in there?"

"I'm doing my best." My thigh rocks back and forth. My teeth anticipate the passage of time so much they press on the flesh inside my mouth, I taste the metallic drip of my own blood mixed with ink from chewing my pens.

"How about this mess?" he looks towards my window, even though the parking lot is on the other side of the building. "Just sickening."

"Can I tell you something?" I say, deviously leaning forward. His eyes are wide while he digs at stray burger in his teeth. "I did it."

He's quiet for a moment, letting what I say sink in, a bit lost in absent thought. Then he starts to laugh. His mouth remains shut, but he gives a soft chuckle from behind his tight lips.

"I love your sense of humor, Ann."

"Yeah," I say, turning back to Nick. "It's good therapy."

"Well, if you need anything you know where to find me." Anything, really? That's just something people say. He continues to speak, but I no longer hear his words. They grow muffled, like he's standing inside a sealed plastic container, looking at me and speaking at me, but I'm gone. I drift from myself and escape Nick's overly sympathetic lecture. His mouth moves. On and on. My eyes fix on the burger. On the meat. The brown outside, the oozing, juicy red inside. I think of the scene from outside. Their purple, rotting flesh as they laid there, motionless and dead. What would Nick look like in the back of a trunk? Anything to get him to stop talking.

"…don't you think?" It's like I zoom back from a dream. He sucks ketchup from his finger and cocks his head to the side, waiting for my answer.

"Yes, of course." I act like I've been attentively listening to whatever he was saying.

"I mean, Amir is always saying how much the parents' opinions matter." He tosses the final piece of the burger into his mouth and holds his hand over his teeth as he chews, speaking simultaneously, "I can't imagine he will be able to crawl himself out of this one. Two dead, on school grounds, damn if that doesn't kill his career here nothing will. Short of a sex scandal."

Nick waits for a response, letting a few prolonged seconds pass. I remain quiet. All I can do is nod, casually agreeing with him.

"Ok, I will get out of your hair. I guess I'll see you at the big parent conferences. You're gonna nail it." His chin rolls like a small dough ball when he smiles big.

Just as he turns to leave, a woman with milk chocolate skin blocks him in the doorway–

Blake?

It's the woman from the night I ran from John's. Only now she's wearing a police uniform. A fucking police uniform.

"Well look at this," she says. I'm paralyzed.

"What's this about?" Nick asks in some manufactured tough guy voice.

"Hate to interrupt whatever this is, but I'm sitting down with all the teachers. Relax, I have a few questions for Miss Ann Bonny here, or is it Chloe?" she says. Nick looks at me, eyebrow raised. Of course he's suspicious. But he doesn't say anything, he just leaves, giving me a final confused appraisal before closing the door and leaving me alone with Blake. Officer Blake. I sit, stiff as she pulls up a chair.

"So, you are a…"

"A cop? Yup. And you're a teacher."

"You following me?"

"Look, let's skip the awkward bullshit, huh? I've got a lot of work to do and I don't wanna waste either of our time." My leg's bouncing. Is it noticeable?

"I have nothing to hide. Whatever you need, not sure it'll be much help." I can't take my eyes off her badge. Well-polished and shiny. It gives off a shimmer from the descending sun peeking its pale orange rays through my classroom windows. On her belt, she carries a gun, pepper spray, handcuffs, and a baton. Everything suddenly feels so real. Have I been in some dreamscape all these past months. Doing this thing of mine like there'd be no repercussions? No. Settle down, Ann. We've planned for this. We aren't sloppy. Are we?

"I promise it won't take too long." She clicks a recorder and sets it next to her. A recorder? Really? "Can I get your name for the record?"

"Seriously?"

"It's for the record. Just cooperate with me here."

"I want to cooperate."

"That's good to hear. Name?"

I return behind my desk, slowly seating myself.

"Ann." I clear my throat. "Ann Bonny," I say. She pulls a small handheld notebook from her front pocket and opens it to an empty page. Her pen clicks, hovering over the lined white paper, the ballpoint end waiting to write away.

"Any other names?"

"Blame a girl for not trusting a stranger in this city?"

"Address? In case we need to reach you. I'll remind you that you aren't in any trouble here. So no need to worry. Address?"

"You know my address."

"I need this on record."

"Doesn't the school have a record book you can just take?"

"We need to gather the information from each suspect, I'm sorry, each staff member. Is that a problem?"

"Not at all. I live at 638 North Wells Street."

"You said 638 North Wells?"

"I did."

"Nice place for a teacher." Her pen freezes and she glares at me. "You live alone?"

"Are you asking if I'm married?"

"It's a really nice building."

"You said that. Does the record want to know you've been there? Can't teachers live in nice buildings?"

"Can cops?"

"I suppose that depends on the cop." Her eyes stay on me for a moment, and then she finishes writing.

"Tell me about yourself, Miss Bonny." (Miss Bonny? Really?) "How long have you worked here at Pearcey Elementary?"

"This is my first year."

"And before that?"

I swallow.

"Doesn't the school have security cameras or something?"

"They do."

Fuck.

"But they only catch the front doors and the inside halls and classrooms."

"So, places like the playground, the parking lot are just – what? Unsupervised?"

"This is your school. Not mine… Did you know either of the victims?"

"Why would I know two people killed in a parking lot?"

"This is just for our preliminary files."

"Did you interrogate every other staff member this much?"

"You feel like this is an interrogation?"

"I just want to help."

"So you've said." The pen clicks shut and she looks up at me with a less intense glare. She has to realize she won't get far with me. "Obviously we know today is sorta rough, so if there's anyone you need to talk to, we have some contacts for folks to deal with trauma like this. He's an excellent psychiatrist. He's already met with a few of your co-workers, I'm sure you'll love him."

"Trauma?"

"Well, seeing two dead bodies stuffed in a trunk isn't something most people see every day."

"Do you see it often?"

Her eyes narrow. "I've seen my fair share of blood," she says. Her demeanor holds, stiff as concrete.

"And do you feel like you need to speak to someone about it?"

"It's part of the job. I know what I signed up for."

"That doesn't answer the question."

"I'm just here to get your statement. It's only a few questions really."

"Any leads so far?" She doesn't look up at me, her eyes stay on the notebook, even though there's nothing written. It's as if she's reading imaginary words, anticipating what she's about to scribble down.

"Well, we generally only investigate the scene. Gathering intel first, then we start putting together a case and narrowing down suspects."

"So no, then?"

Her face rises, her pen clicks shut and I catch a whiff of disturbance, crumbling away her stoic disposition. I keep thinking about them scrubbing the Jag for DNA. Looking to match my DNA.

"Once we have statements from the entire staff. There could be a connection to the school. Maybe it was someone who works here – you never know."

"Maybe."

"Tell me, Ann, do any of your co-workers strike you as…"

"Dangerous?"

"I was gonna say suspicious, but I guess that works."

"I haven't been here long enough to know them all that intimately."

"I have a Mrs. Angela Greene… says you were a no show all last week. Claims you have antisocial quirks. Shady, is what she said." There's a long pause. Her eyes lock on me. I'm fighting to keep a stalemate. "Sometimes you just get a feeling, you know? Something off about someone. A little fickle of fucked-up perhaps?"

"Perhaps." She stares at me for a long time. Then she clears her throat and the pen clicks back open. "I just try my best to fit in. I think people are harder to read into than first impressions. They usually get so good at hiding what's underneath. We end up seeing a manufactured copy."

"Hmm. We play different characters? Is that it? Until you get tired of pretending. Which mask are you wearing now, Ann? Underneath that skin. There's nothing inside is there? Just… bone."

Sweat collects along the back of my neck. My jaw locks and my throat caves. The reality of getting caught is an abstract to me. At least to the part of me that can recognize reality. But now things have changed. The world is smaller. Shriveling into a claustrophobic prison. I'm Alice, locked in a shrinking room, the whole time getting bigger and bigger myself. Soon the whole house is doomed to explode.

"Can you recall what you did this weekend? Friday and Saturday?"

My head's killing me. I rub my temple. Massaging it to somehow roll out some thought or excuse. I swallow, gathering myself the best I can to appear under control. Luckily, I have some practice.

"Are you really the one who hunts the killer? Or do you just talk to suspects?"

"Is that how you feel? That you're a suspect?"

"Not at all." I smile. A calm, collected, at ease type of lawyer smile. I've seen hundreds of Kate's social media pages.

"Most of the teachers put you at the dance on Friday night."

"That's correct."

"But they didn't see you leave. Did you go anywhere after?"

"Well of course, I don't sleep at school."

"I mean out. Get a drink? See a movie? Go to someone's place?"

"I went home."

"Anyone to confirm that?"

"I have neighbors."

"Anywhere else? After the dance?"

"Saturday night?"

"Friday night."

"I was at a man's apartment."

"A man?" Her eyebrows rise from behind the notebook.

"A guy I'm seeing. Usually I fuck strangers who pick me up in their cars but - "

She shuts off the recorder.

"I think we're done with that."

"You asked."

"I'm trying to be professional, Ann. I have to ask these questions, but it doesn't look good when you conveniently show up like this."

"Show up?"

"Be honest with me. Why were you running in the street that night? You looked…"

"Looked like what?" (Like I just fled a murder scene?)

"Scared. Who's this guy? Just for the record and in case I need to follow up."

"I – I um." Her eyes roll. The pen clicks shut again, and she crosses her legs. Maybe she's starting a new tactic on me? Suddenly she looks less like a cop and more like a jealous friend.

"Let me guess. He's married?"

"What?"

"Usually when people can't give a name, they are worried it'll get out."

"Oh." God my head's killing me.

"I assure you it's confidential."

I just blurt it out.

"John Hilton."

"Something wrong?"

"I'm sorry?"

"Your nose is bleeding." I didn't feel it at first. Then as she said it, the warm trail of blood drips from my nose. I touch just above my top lip, then study the burgundy droplet on the tip of my finger, losing my attention to her.

"Shit."

"You alright?" I don't respond. In the blur that surrounds the focus on my finger, I see her reach into her back pocket and pull out a handkerchief. "Here." I wait a moment before using it to wipe the blood from my finger and face. "Wanna tell me what happened to your head there?"

"Just a silly accident."

"Was it an accident involving this, John Hilton?" My throat closes. I want to respond, but I can't. I check the back of the classroom again. Danny. He's been sitting at his desk the whole time. He peeks up from his notebook. Around his eye, the vulture brown bruise has returned, and his neck is swollen and splotched with mauve, black markings.

"Miss Bonny? Ann?"

"Yes, I'm sorry?" I jiggle my head, pressing the handkerchief against my nostril. I feel light, pumped with helium. The back of the room is empty again. The desk barren.

"Anything you wanna tell me?" I shake no. She makes a note. I don't think I can get away with this car crash lie. She seems like the type to follow every lead. If there was an accident it would have been reported. She doesn't look convinced and does one of those head turns with her eyes squinted, a small dose of her bottom lip overlapping the top with a little scrunch. "Alright."

"Are there any more questions? My students will be coming back from recess."

I don't get up to see her out. She stops just as she reaches the door, turning back around to me. "I know this might be the last thing you wanna hear, but these types of things most often go unreported. If someone is hurting you." She pulls a card from another pocket. I remain in my chair, planted behind my desk. She waits for me to come take it, but I don't budge. Finally, she leaves it in front of me. "Give me a call if you need anything. Or just wanna talk." I offer a simple nod as a thank you, never planning on using it. She hovers for a few moments, holding her empty hand out. "If you are finished with that," pointing at the handkerchief.

"Oh," I check for any more blood, but it stopped. "Here, thanks." I return the handkerchief, trying to bundle up an end that hasn't absorbed my blood.

"See you." She walks out with the bloody handkerchief between two fingers. The door closes behind her and I'm finally alone.

DEADlines

"Look, I've never done this before."

I stand in front of Sonya in the teachers' lounge while she munches through a bag of flaming hot Cheetos and grades what looks like lab reports. Her left hand is smothered in red from the artificial coloring while she grades with her right. Somehow the papers remain unstained.

Sonya isn't my first choice. But at this point, it feels like she's my only option. Her wide, excited eyes, while she sucks the red powder clean off each finger, doesn't necessarily ease my first date-level nerves.

"Look, Ann, I'm flattered, but you know I'm straight."

"What?"

"Unless you want me to run it by Douglass and you can be our third… we've never done a third before. Who am I kidding he would totally say yes… Cheeto?"

I decline her offer, not sure if the waft of manufactured cayenne is making me queasy, or the sudden flash image of Douglass naked in my head.

"Sonya, I'm not asking for a threesome."

"Then what is it?"

"I've never, well, I've never asked for help like this…"

She chomps down on a handful, to me they look like limbs, severed and twisted.

With a smile, she gasps. "Babe, what are friends for?"
Friends. Friends?
Friends.

Let's recap.

This week has been anything but normal since the 'police incident' on Monday. To be honest, I haven't been myself lately. Monday night I simply walked around the city after school, unsure where I was going or where home was. I ended up running, sprinting away as someone... a ghost... maybe no one... screamed in my ear. Then a whisper, followed by a shrill. My stomach constantly hurt, and I was sweating even though the temperature kept dropping.

On Wednesday I got hit on at a bar and went home with some young consultant who kept bragging about his recent promotion at Boston Consulting Group. I told him I'd only fuck him if he referred to himself as John the entire time. I had him repeat this after I tied him up, and then I tore each of his toes off with a pair of surgical pliers I bought on Amazon under Kate's account.

I have been sneaking into her place almost every night lately, watching her sleep and using her computer. When I killed the fake John, I thought I'd forget, but instead I left in the middle of the night and slept under the Franklin Avenue bridge.

This reverse American Psycho is pointless. I can kill every corporate duckling in Chicago, but I'm starting to think that it might not take away the fact that John Hilton still exists. And the longer he does, the longer I have a chance of losing everything. I keep hearing Tina's words, "catastrophic".

I promise myself I'm not slipping.

Now it's Thursday.

Sonya crinkles the bag of Cheetos and stuffs them in her purse.

"Ugh, these things are so fucking addicting. Supposedly they give you cancer. Do you want to go get a drink, babe?"

"Several."

Wide camera swipe and we're sitting at her favorite bar in West Loop – a tequila place where you take ice shots and throw the glass at a Prius-sized bell.

"Ok girl, shoot." Sonya digs her teeth into a lime. Then sips on the end of a spicy margarita, her arms plop on the bar top as if we're gossiping teenagers.

"You ever feel like you're in over your head?"

"Is this because of the parent teacher conferences tomorrow? Too many sexual partners? Listen, I've been there, and I've been there. As far as the conferences go, these parents will smell fear. They'll walk all over you with just a whiff of doubt."

"I don't doubt myself."

"Good, because you shouldn't."

"I have something I need to handle and I'm well… I've been avoiding it." I need to make it something that Sonya can relate to. Something tells me that letting out, 'I need to kill my student's father before he recognizes me at school and I'm outed as a killer posing as a prostitute and, by the way, the only way I can be cured is by keeping this job so I can live up to the person that my dead ex-girlfriend believed me to be' probably won't sit right.

"So, what is it? You got tea? Spill that chisme. You can tell me anything, you know that, right?"

"Can I get a shot?" The bartender obeys, and before I know it two ounces of reposado go down my throat and I'm opening up to Sonya about Kate and wanting her and not knowing how to tell her how I feel.

"This is simple," Sonya swirls her straw around in her second cocktail. "You just need to make a deadline. Whenever I have something that seems tough, I mark a day on the calendar and by sticking to it, I can't back out. Pull out your phone."

"What?"

"Your phone. Take it out and set a calendar date." I comply and before I even open the app, she swipes it – "now, when's the big day gonna be? I recommend picking something close, otherwise too much time goes by and you spiral out of control and by the time the day comes around, you've come up with too many excuses in your head and you'll ultimately back out. The first time I tried to quit drinking I ended up setting the date so far out I forgot I even did it and then when the day came, I got the notification while I was out on a Sunday Funday."

We decide on October 15th.

Do I want to kill John? I'm not sure if wanting has anything to do with it. Or does it have everything to do with it? He isn't unlike any of the others. At least I don't want to believe so. Any of the ones who were in his position before. The ones I don't think twice about killing.

Quite simply, I have to do it.

What about Danny? Does he need a dad? Did I? What will it do to him? I assume that they're already distant enough for Danny not to notice. But am I certain? I'm not sure I'm ever certain of anything. Except one. John Hilton alive threatens me. I'm so close. Why does this one man have to ruin my single shot to live a normal life. Maybe I'll feel the same once it's done. Maybe I'll stand over his body, just like I did the fake John's, and feel nothing… just an empty stomach, craving more. Is that even what I'm craving?

It'll just take one slip. One misfortunate coincidence for John Hilton to find out, for Danny to find out, for everyone at Pearcey. I can't let that happen. John Hilton has to die.

We celebrate with ice shots. Who knew throwing small cubes at a bell could be so satisfying? It feels good to laugh.

We share an uber home. I'm the first to be dropped off. On my way out of the car Sonya promises that everything will work out.

My mother always promised she'd come back. Danny promises me he's totally fine. Amir promised me the job of vice principal. Kitty promised she loved me. Google promises they don't sell personal data… I can go on and on.

When I stumble to my apartment, all worry about John, about Amir, about Angela, about everything flies out the window because why the fuck is my door open

Prince Albert

The door is ajar about two inches. I press it to open just enough to squeeze inside. My hand waits in my purse, around my knife. The room is silent. Nothing broken or stolen by the looks of things. Then I notice a small paw print.

"You want to explain this?"

I spin around and Roger Fucking Steven stands in my kitchen with his hands propped on my island. In front of him spread across the counter is, yup, the JAG KEYS.

"Explain what?"

"Don't act cute with me, bitch. Put your purse down." Roger is a big guy. I know from the expression on his face that there's little to no possible way both of us could walk away from this.

It has to be me.

I set my purse on the end table by the sofa, wishing for my gun.

"So," he says. "Explain."

"I'm lost."

"It's on the news. Oliver's death. They found him at the school you work at. I came over to drop Pickles off –"

"And you broke in?"

"It was open."

Never in my life have I left the door unlocked–

Ohhhh shit. This morning I was more than frazzled. More than in a rush. I woke up after dreaming how tonight would go. Amir had been quiet all week. I tried approaching him about the position but every time he was too busy to speak with me. Ever since Monday, Pearcey has been drab—a distant feeling weighed across the entire school. My paranoia only flourished.

Either way, Roger isn't getting away with this.

"You expect the cops to believe that?" I say "I see this as a break in and—"

He slams the counter. "Shut up and start talking!"

"So, which do you want me to do?"

"You know what I mean."

"Wow, no wonder Kate can't stand you."

"What did you say?"

"She's always venting to me about you. Don't worry, she'll be out of your hands soon."

"You have no idea what you are saying. I know Oliver. He's a dick. But I saw the car on TV. I'm going to call the cops if you don't start talking. I know she fucked him once. And now she works with him. Did you take them from Oliver... did you..."

"Does it make you upset? That she fucked someone she now works with? I bet it's not the first time, Roger."

"Fuck you. I know what she is."

"And what is that? Way out of your league?"

He slams the counter more, a child throwing a tantrum.

"Shut up, shut the fuck up!" I need to win him over. Can I kill him? No, that will just make things worse. Won't it?

Seducing him will be no good, so I try tears. It's not too hard to think of enough to make me cry. I'm not a sad person, but thinking of the conference, of John, of Angela, of Kitty...

it gives me enough artificial emotion to fabricate into a good cry.

He's immediately uncomfortable, allowing me to sit, but still wants answers. I'm on the couch, sobbing into my hands and letting out all the stress of living in a city as a woman, you know, things guys like Roger will literally do anything to stop hearing. He comes closer to me, in range, but he's too big to overpower. His guard is still up, he just wants me to stop.

"Do you need something?" Of course, let's medicate the hysterical girl. Nice. I'm sure he's a great guy to vent to. Any stressful episode just pacified by pills. Why didn't I think of that?

"My Ativan. It's for my anxiety." I wipe the tears from my eyes. "I need to go get it from the bathroom."

"I'll get it." Once he's out of sight, the waterworks shut off.

"It's in the medicine cabinet," I call after him.

He gives me just enough time to slip off the couch and grab a hammer from my closet. I rush back to the sofa and let the hammer sit between the cushions. I need him close.

"Here," he says, coming back. He takes a seat beside me. Yes. He pops the cap and hands me one. "You mind if I have one too?"

"Be my guest." I wait for him to pop his, then I swing.

Although Roger is a miscreant who stands in my way, and surely is facing death anyways, I have to give him the benefit of a fair trial.

When he wakes, a trail of blood drips from the hammer's mark on his head. A minute or so passes before he realizes he's handcuffed (yes I used his sex cuffs) to my oven. I duct tape his ankles and knees together too so that he has no chance of kicking his weight against the oven to break free.

"What the fuck is wrong with you?" I forgot to tape his mouth. Damnit.

"You broke in," I say. "This is what any girl with a right mind should do if a guy breaks into her place."

"I told you it was unlocked, you fucking bitch."

"I feel like unlocked and welcome are different. Anyways, this is no longer about me." I scroll through social media on his phone, keeping the hammer close just in case, trying to find enough wrong with Roger to carry his sentence.

My phone dings. I can never decide if I should leave it on silent or not. The ding annoys me, so does the buzz.

"One second," I tell Roger. He protests and groans, swearing and cussing me out in ways that even from a guy like him, shocks me.

John Hilton: "How's the head?"

I wait to respond, reading the text and then setting my phone on the cushion beside me. I need time to strategize. After a few minutes, I type:

"Still crazy"…

I have no idea. The 'he is typing' bubble pops up on his side of the screen. I can't breathe.

John Hilton: "Would love to see you, if you are feeling better, of course." I shut off my phone the second after reading it, stuffing it between the cushions. I want it to disappear.

Roger's griping continues. He even mentions how Kate is a lawyer and I'll never get away with this. Yup, he went there. Then he switches tactics, calling me crazy, sadistic, and sick in the head, and on and on and on.

I'm no good at juggling men. I return to Roger's phone. I need to finish him first and then I can deal with Hilton. But what do I do with him?

Do I kill him? Could this have been the lucky break I needed? He's a home intruder. I'm in the right. I'm acting out of self-defense. Even if I'm caught. Little me? Against Roger? He broke in and I fought off a predator.

What about Kate? I suspect this will work in my favor completely or terminate any chance I have with her.

No, I think. Mercy now will hurt me later. I already let one man live and he's shattering my life. If I'm going to kill John, I need to toughen up.

I offer him a drink to calm his nerves. A drink with nearly a dozen Ativan in a glass of whiskey. He takes it in one shot and doesn't last much longer after that.

I pour myself a glass of chocolate milk while I wait for him to pass out. I give him a once over with the hammer to make sure he's gone for good.

He doesn't die well.

Roger had to die. He had found out what I had done. Even for a guy as daft as Roger, it doesn't take a genius to put the pieces together and make connections. He knew before I walked in the door that I had killed Oliver and his wife. Now I need to get rid of the evidence. And I know just where to put it.

But it isn't just the fact that Roger stood in my way. Roger would have simply continued living to make Kate's life hell if I didn't end him. Eventually they would have gotten married and he would have been a poor husband and she would have been forced to find love and affection from others. He would find out, she'd want him to, and who knows, Roger would probably blow a fuse, maybe hurt her. You are welcome, Kate. I saved you from this deadbeat, harassing, dodging, low life.

Kate texts his phone: "Did you drop off Pickles?"

I don't respond. I can break up with her for him. I can tell her he's leaving, but I decide to wait. She needs to choose me on her own.

Thieving Magpie

Friday afternoon after school, I go home intending to get rid of Roger's body before I head back for the parent conferences.

Whatever help Sonya gave has dwindled away. I continue to lose all control of myself. At one point during reading time, I rush out of the classroom and curl up in a ball in the stall, fidgeting and scratching the stall walls. I chisel madness - bodies with torn limbs and stick figures killing each other - with a pen.

After all of this, I only have come to the realization of one thing. Flaming hot Cheetos go really well with chocolate milk.

Back home, I enjoy the dynamite snack combo while trying to figure out what to do with Roger's body.

Before I know it, the entire bag is almost gone. Sonya was right about them being addicting. I lay Roger over a plastic tarp, preparing to chop him up and stuff him into an oversized suitcase I found in his closet.

On my couch, Roger's body at my feet, I text John, relishing in ghosting him for a day.

"How's tonight sound?" I tap into my phone, planning on standing him up. If he's waiting at a restaurant, he'll be away from Pearcey. Two, maybe three, minutes pass before I finally press send. A few seconds go by before-

DING.

John Hilton: "Can't tonight… work thing. Thursday?"

Work thing? Why can't people tell the truth? I'm trembling. Is that 'work thing' the parent conference?

"How about the 15th?"

John Hilton: "Is that Tuesday?"

I respond with a thumbs up.

John Hilton: "Should I make a reservation?"

"Surprise me." Good, I think to myself. All done. But then-

DING.

(C'mon)

John Hilton: "I'll see you at 8."

"See you then." Ok, done. Set. No need to text again –

DING.

For fuck's sake.

I look at my phone. No text.

DING.

I press my hands over my face and ears, saved only by Rossini broadcasting from the speaker. But the DINGs don't cease. DING.

Roger's phone. It's beside me on the couch, stuck between the cushions. I pull it out. There are three separate messages in tiny green popup clouds.

Kate: "Hello?"

Kate: "Also, make sure to take out the trash."

Kate: "Can you?"

DING

Kate: "Be home around 7:45, tomorrow night."

Under Rossini's masterful The Thieving Magpie through my headphones, I tend to Roger. The plastic tarp holds the blood from Roger's body. I remove his clothes, noting that his private parts are pierced. A Prince Albert ring as it's commonly called. Even dead, he's the worst. I work diligently, carving into Roger. The bow saw is exact, cutting through the flesh and bone. But tiring as fuck.

To Kate from Roger' phone: "You got it babe. Miss you."

He fits perfectly in the suitcase but weighs quite a bit. I pull the Porsche to the front of the building and then run up to fetch Roger, skipping to the brass and strings while the crescendo heightens.

The suitcase rolls easily through the lobby and into the street, but I think my back is going to give out as I heave him into the trunk of the Porsche, the car lowering once the bag lands. As I slam the trunk a hand grabs my shoulder. I spin, tearing out my headphones-

"Ann?"

My own name paralyzes me where I stand.

"Ann!" again, cheery. More footsteps behind me. Sonya walks to the side of my car, waving inches from my face. My eyes still work, and a cloud of breath seeps from my mouth, but my body is stiff from frosty terror. Did they see?

"Did you pinch this for tonight?" Douglass circles the Porsche, snugging his hands in his pockets after tossing a roach to the curb. "Thing is fucking sweet."

"My girl has style," Sonya says. She rubs against Douglass as if they're high school sweethearts.

"You guys are good again?"

"Don't be silly, I'm married, Ann," Sonya replies in a sarcastic tone I don't exactly pick up on. They both laugh. An uber pulls up and Nick climbs out. Oh, this is great. I give him an awkward hug.

"So," he says. "We all ready for this?"

"For what?" I ask.

"Don't tell me you forgot," Sonya says. "It's the biggest freaking night of the year!"

"It's your first PTC," Douglass adds. "Sonya, did you not tell her about the initiation?"

"I did, D. Ann, I emailed you like three reminders."

"Of course," I say.

"Were you headed somewhere else?" Douglass says. "You looked kinda in a hurry."

"I thought I was picking you up," I lie.

"You are our designated driver tonight Ann, not our chauffeur for Christ's sake."

They pile in. Douglass and Sonya share the back seat while Nick sits quietly beside me as I drive to Pearcey. Having a "dead uncle" proves more helpful than I anticipated, since Douglass believes me when I tell him the car belonged to my Uncle Jones and he gifted it to me in his will. Although, he does ask a few times about the smell. I tell them my uncle used an organic car freshener, which Douglass scoffs at and asks if I had hit a skunk or kept a hobo in the trunk.

"Is everything alright?" Nick asks me. My knuckles are white on the wheel.

"Just nervous for tonight, I think." Yes, I'm nervous. Nervous that I forgot that tonight is my "initiation" as a PTC virgin and I am driving the teachers around to get drunk after the conference, meanwhile having Roger's body in the trunk. I need an excuse to leave. I need to get the hell out of here. John arriving at school has become the least of my worries—at least for now—although I keep thinking about what will happen as the maelstrom of my life comes suffocating down on itself.

When we pull into the parking lot, I'm the last to get out of the car. Nick stays behind and offers to walk me in. For once in my life, I'm glad he's there.

Before we start, Douglass summons me to the teacher's lounge where Sonya, Nick, Mr. Richardson, Mrs. Clydesdale,

Mr. Collins, Mrs. Bridenbaugh, everyone, are all gathered.
Everyone but Amir and Angela Greene. Douglass distributes
red solo cups but allots me a blue one. A bottle of Jägermeister
sits nearly emptied on the counter.

"As is tradition," Douglass begins, standing on a chair as
he addresses the teachers, broadcasting like a prewar speech.
To a bunch of educators before telling their students' parents
about the curriculum, it is a battle. A battle for their jobs. "We
gather before this year's PTC, with an honorable new
member of our Pearcey family. To Ann Bonny, who shall
with no doubt find victory in tonight's efforts. Out there our
enemy is gathering. They are here because they want to find
our weaknesses, because they think they are better than us.
But we are teachers!" A few cheers. "We are the ones who
offer intelligence, wisdom, imagination. Do not fear them. To
Ann Bonny, and her good fortune in the fight to come (here
here) and to Pearcey, and all of us! To teachers!" There's a
resounding cheer and clap.

All of them – "To teachers!"

Douglass downs his shot, and everyone follows. The
Jager stings going down, but I'm instantly loose and warm.
Sonya hands out gum to each teacher and they disembark,
off to war. She tells me good luck and to break a leg as they
march into the hall - battle stations everyone - taking their
positions in their own classrooms, waiting for their enemy
to break in at any moment.

Sonya gives me a big hug. When she lets go, I feel slow,
weightless. The room turns and her face stretches. She tells
me something, but I can't understand a word of it. I shake
myself and my vision is clear again. I'm alone in the lounge,
still and silent, waiting for something to flip my world again,
but nothing, just a slight buzzing in my head.

By the time I reach my classroom, the parents are already waiting. There are no welcoming smiles, just long, expecting faces. They have taken their own child's desks, some seated, some standing around the room. Most are quiet, few interrogate the décor on the walls, comparing their child's projects or examining–they are inspecting–searching for weak spots in my teaching. What teaching, I think.

Abruptly my world closes in and my throat swallows itself. I'm an imposter–No. I'm a teacher, I have to think of myself as one, carry myself as one, if I don't believe then they won't either.

I open my mouth, but as I do, I recognize Danny's mother. She's in the middle of the room. I doubt she knows her son sits in the back. Her arms are folded, and her face is down to her phone. Is she texting John? I don't see him anywhere.

Suddenly the same feeling from the lounge hits me again. The aftermath of a hallucinogenic earthquake. I'm spinning. I'm actually spinning. My stomach curls and my head buzzes. Is the bell ringing? Is the building on fire? They all grow blurry, stretching out like images in a Dali painting as I stare at their blank looks, unaware of where I am. Of who I am. Something is wrong with me. It isn't just the nerves. It isn't just Roger's body in my trunk or the inevitability of Angela firing me–there's something inside of me twisting my brain up and freezing my mechanisms. I've never had Jager before, but something tells me it wasn't just booze in that cup.

Then the door opens. I try to focus. My heart stops as I picture John walking in, seeing me and–

But it's Angela.

I see her in my peripherals. Except she's six feet tall and her hair is a blonde sunbeam shooting in every direction. She domineers in the doorway, her arms crossed as she stares at me with a look of, "well, what have you got?"

Back to the gaggle of parents. They grow antlers, standing like deer in a field waiting, but deer with jagged teeth and blazing fireball eyes.

I want to fall off the earth. I want everything to go dark and stay that way. My legs are caught in quicksand, I'm drowning. My arms flaccid, gooey extensions, flapping about. Stand still, Ann. All eyes on you. I sense my mind turning off and letting every muscle take the night off. But I fight back. I don't let myself faint. If I go down, I might end up at the hospital. If I go down, what will happen to the body in my trunk? If I go down here, in front of these parents, in front of Angela Greene, I will never get up.

Showtime.

The following half hour is a blur. I must have done something right, because when the dust settles, Angela is speechless. Whatever had been in that Jager is messing with my memory, because there's not a minute I recall. Miraculously the parents congregate out like sheep, a few shaking my hand as they walk out the door and others asking for my email. She just stands there. A bitter loser.

I've done it.

I don't wait for everyone to leave before heading out into the hall. All I want is to find out what the hell Douglass and Sonya and well, everyone really, had done to me.

Was 'that' my initiation?

I step out of my classroom, turn the corner and walk straight into the path of John Hilton.

Let Them Eat Cake

He stands in the hall, his jacket still on as Danny's mother accosts him for missing the meeting. She has Danny's thin black hair, but with more of a malevolent fineness.

My feet are glued to the floor. He's facing me, but has he noticed me? His eyes are switching between his ex and the ceiling. She's rambling about his constant excuses.

Inaudibly, I command my feet to turn me around and sprint down the hall. But I can't move, unsure if it's my nerves or whatever had been spiked in the Jager shot.

They appear like a cliché broken TV couple - the pitifully ignored mother and the absent, successful father (though I can tell she's far from middle class, she carries herself with corporate pride, plus, alimony doesn't buy Hermes). The single mom trying to do her best to balance her career and the child they are supposed to be raising together. I have nowhere to judge though, since I haven't the slightest grasp on how a normal marriage or parental team operates. Structure of a loving family is a stranger, a shadow, based entirely on the shows and movies Kitty used to make me watch. In her romantic comedies the couple always made it work. But not once while I observe the duo in front of me now do I expect for John and his ex to see each other as anything but enemies—at least not in this screen capture.

Then his eyes find me.

I'm able to move again, kickstarted by fright. I shift into gear and don't stop. There are footsteps behind. Keep going, Ann, keep going, don't stop.

Where is safe?

Nowhere!

I take a corner and plow through the first door. A bathroom... is it even the lady's room? No time for that. I dart straight into the stall and lock it.

He didn't see me, he did not see me, replays in my head. He won't follow me into the ladies' room.

Will he?

RINGING

My phone. Not Roger's. It's John. He's calling me.

Sirens flare in my brain. I can't silence the call, I have to just let it ring.

It finally stops. Until–

DING

As the vibration follows the message tone, I scramble. turning it to silent.

JOHN HILTON: Thinking of you.

He knows. He has to know. This is just a game now. A sick, fucked up game.

I don't respond. What is he playing? Did he really not notice me? Or did he? It was a trap. He must be standing outside the bathroom door. I just know it.

I'm finished. It's over.

My stomach constricts, boils until it shoots up through my throat and pours whatever my gut has to offer out of my mouth and all over the toilet seat.

When I finally surface, my vision blurs again. The stall door is open and staring at me from the mirror is the deer that Douglass and the others planted in my classroom. That thing is following me too. Its eyes are darts. Surrounding it is a black cloud that sucks me in and drops me years downwards. Down the rabbit hole. I'm sinking. Sinking. On and on, passing out of time and into a world of hilarious purple darkness. There's laughing and clapping and a ruckus of all sorts that blasts around, hidden in the shrouds of black that surround me while I continue to descend miles into the earth. I look up. The deer is falling too. Its antlers sharpened directly at me, falling straight to puncture and slice me in half.

Down the rabbit hole. Down. Down. Down.

I land for a moment in a backstage dressing room. No longer alone. There's a young girl on the floor, I know her. I used to be her. A woman sits in front of a Hollywood bulbed vanity mirror. Her pink leotard is torn, her lips and knees bruised. She's strung out, though the toddler is ignorant to her deceased cognizance, or at least pretends to be.

"Mother?" I say. Lost in this prison of red curtains and vermillion haze. These poisonous memories. With frail hands, the woman plays a starchy record. It spins, static at first, then letting out the sweet muddling of the distractingly beautiful Mozart's Requiem. Just in time for the men, the high rolling clients, to show up in the dressing room. To visit her once again. She shoos the child away, telling her to hide under the bed. To listen to the music. Her last dance as her child does everything she can to shut out the noise. To block out the reality.

Suddenly the vision drifts and I am again surrounded by darkness. A darkness pierced by shrilling laughter.

The laughing intensifies the more I fall. I have to be on the other side of the world by now, I think, no doubt I'll pop up in Australia or China. But I never pop out anywhere. I just keep going. Deeper into the black. Deeper. I want to scream! But I'm mute. No, I think, No! I see them around me. The others from when I was young... I'm there. I'm back years ago when it all started. They're all here, laughing, laughing...

No!

They circle around me.

The darkness fades, and I'm still. My vision is not 100 percent, but good enough to realize where I am. In the bathroom. It's Sonya, Nick, Douglass, and all the other teachers. All in the bathroom surrounding me and cheering. Laughing at me? I'm too weak to get up.

Douglass videotapes on his phone while Sonya wipes my face and helps me to my feet.

Then I realize something, they aren't laughing at me, they are cheering for me.

For me.

"What the..." I try speaking.

"Babe," Sonya says. "You did so well! No one can believe it!" She lifts my arm into the air, cheering like a schoolgirl. "You did better than anyone, ever!"

"Better at what?" I say, still pretty dizzy.

"Your initiation," Douglass tells me. "Congrats! Sorry for the whole misleading thing. No one would willingly take the magic pill and go do a conference presentation. You honestly blew me away. Welcome to fucking Pearcey!"

Somehow, I feel part of the group. For the first time. I feel like I fit in. And it's enough for me.

The teachers take turns congratulating me with hugs and high-fives as if I just raced for gold in the 100-meter dash.

I'm included in the post-PTC festivities. They play music, pull out more bottles, and transform the teacher's lounge into a college dorm. Even Angela and Amir hang around, completely fine with the majority of the staff getting hammered on school premises. Amir reminds everyone it's only because they all did Pearcey proud, and that it isn't a school night.

With Everyone gathered in the lounge, Amir calls attention to a big announcement.

Could this be it?

"Ok everyone," Amir claps his hands together. I sit straighter as I notice Angela standing behind his right shoulder. "I know this week has been extremely difficult, and even a little scary. I'm sure most of you know that there will be someone to talk to if you have anything on your mind or have some emotions to get out. We are here for you. Now, to brighten up things a bit, I do have one announcement." He rubs his hands, widening his eyes. "I am very excited to announce that our own Angela Greene will be stepping into our vice principal role!" Crickets. "So, let's have a big hand for Angela Greene, excuse me, Vice Principal Greene."

Sure, everyone claps along. But they don't care. Most of them don't give two shits about who becomes VP. To be fair, it's a superfluous position. Like any vice president. But now it's Angela Greene's position, and my intestines are squirming. What's worse is that the entire time, the entire smattering applause, the entirety that Amir brings in a cake, a fucking cake, a gluten free fucking cake, and party hats and a balloon, yes, a fucking balloon, she just stares at me, grinning, and I back at her.

In a matter of minutes, all dark thoughts of my first PTC are gone. A cake-induced sugar rush coupled with a party hat sedates my victorious high. Chocolate marble cake with a coat of vanilla icing - the perfect distraction to get over the two dead bodies found on school property and the rabble of interested parents. Anything for free cake and mingling. Sure, let's throw on some music and pass around Douglass' flask.

It's a celebration, isn't it? A celebration. A celebration for the new vice principal. A celebration of Angela Greene.

Of course, I have some cake. How can't I? I'm a little more upset that it is so good. Moist, the frosting not too sweet or too creamy. Each bite pisses me off. This should be my cake. Not Angela's.

My paper plate with the damaged square piece of cake rests on my bouncing knee while I clench a milk carton. I can't drink since I'm still DD. My eyes remain fixed on Angela, a Kubrick stare across the room. The kind of stare before a kill.

Almost everyone now makes their rounds to congratulate Angela. The small thunder I had has drifted, storming over Angela Greene now. The only ones that don't approach her are the high school "professors" who believe their job is in fact still highly superior to hers. They mingle in their own corner while the rest of us, minus me of course, join the celebration. I sit alone with my hat, my cake, and my milk.

Alone.

Nick comes next to me. I can tell he's tinkering for something to say. Before he gets out a word, I move towards Angela.

Is killing her my only option? I pass Amir, staring death in his eyes.

"Look," he says with a whisper, holding my arm. "It wouldn't have been the right time. Trust me, this will be better for both of us." And he is off.

Better for both of us? Better how? He betrayed me. Manipulated me. There are no excuses he can conjure in hope of absolution for this. Was I ever even a candidate?

"Angela," I say. "Mrs. Greene. I just wanted to say, congrats."

"There's a lot about you I don't know, Ann. But I do know you're not a kiss ass."

"I just think lately, I don't know, maybe we got off to a wrong start or…"

"We got off to a fine start. But I have a job to do, Ann. A job that requires someone with an actual background in teaching. And we both know you don't have that."

"Excuse me?"

"Save it." My hand tightens on the plastic knife left by the sink for cutting cake. "I went to visit my cousin last weekend. The one in Minnesota. She's never even heard of Bridgeton."

"Like I said before, small school."

"I don't know how you fooled Mr. Salem into getting into this place. It's now my job to actually know who is working under me. Got that?" No wonder Amir has been silent to me lately. He knew. He always knew. For how long? Or, she could be bluffing.

"I have nothing to hide, Mrs. Greene."

"No? Well, we will soon see."

Although the rest of the teachers celebrate a victorious night, I'm still DD. The pill Douglass gave me, which he never explained what kind or where he got them, wears off by the time the teachers file out. Most of them uber, but I'm tasked with shuttling the ones who live a mediocrely close distance from school.

I make three trips in the Porsche by the time I have to bring Nick, Sonya, Douglass, and Mr. Richardson, who I'm dropping off with Douglass and Sonya at another bar. They invite me but I tell them I don't feel well from being drugged. They must feel somewhat bad for the prank, because they let me off easy and don't fight me when I say I need to go straight home.

We head for West Loop with three squeezed in the back and Nick in the front. The air is close in the car, and Roger's body really starts to stink.

Nick sits shotgun again, quietly staring over at me every few minutes while the three in the back joke with each other, commenting on the night.

"Did your uncle die in this car?" Douglass says. "And what's with the opera music?"

"It's not opera," I say. "It's Beethoven."

"Why the Beethoven?"

"He knows strings."

Douglass tries lighting a joint, but I tell him not to stink up my car, to which he replies with a "it already stinks! The weed will cleanse the smell!"

"No way," I say, addressing him through my rearview mirror.

In that second, red and blue lights flash from behind us. If I haven't been through enough tonight. At this moment, I'm truly fucked.

"Quick, throw that away!" Sonya tells Douglass.

"It's legal."

"Not to drive, it isn't."

"Good thing I'm not driving." His weed is my last worry. If the officer is given a reason, all he has to do is ask to see what's in my trunk and it's over.

"Everyone shut up," that's Nick, "Ann it'll be ok. How fast were you going?" I watch through my sideview mirror now, not listening to them… just watching. Waiting for the cop to approach.

We're on the side of the road somewhere on Randolph Street. A half-mile or so up, I hear people walking from bar to bar, but on this backstreet, there's no one. No witnesses besides these four teachers if I choose to pull the handgun I keep attached to the left side of the seat. My hand lowers as the man in blue emerges. He trudges closer, practically illuminated by the still flashing lights and now spotlight behind us.

"Ann," Nick continues. "It will be ok. You haven't been drinking" –shut up, Nick or you'll be next– "where do you keep all your paperwork?"

The cop comes closer. I keep one hand on the wheel, the other hovers over the pistol. His footsteps echo as he nears, armed with a blinding flashlight.

"Evening," he says. He's probably mid-thirties, with a strong jaw and a sturdy frame. His clean-shaven face betrays no emotion as he flashes the blue light on each member of my crew. "License and registration."

"Is there a problem, sir?" Nick says. Yes, there's a problem. BODY IN THE TRUNK. BODY IN THE TRUNK.

I shoot Nick an emotionless look and he shuts up, opening the glove box for me. The policeman keeps checking the back seat.

"Where are you folks headed tonight?"

I flip through the loose napkins, pocketknife, and handbooks, looking for the right documents, the whole while too close to Nick's crotch since I have to lean over to find what I need.

"I'm the DD tonight," I say, sitting straight with what I hope is Uncle Jones' registration papers. "You know how it goes."

"This your car?"

"It's not stolen." I hand him the papers. "Can a girl like me not drive an old sports car?"

"Was that a tone, miss?"

"No, sir?" My hand lowers down the side of the seat.

"Driver's license."

I open my console; my hand is shaking. I retrieve a wallet and hand him a license.

"Says here it belongs to a Karl Jones. You don't look like a Karl."

"My uncle," I say. "He just passed, unfortunately; it's been really hard."

"I see. So, you are Wendy?" He studies my driver's license, holding it up to my face.

He sniffs the air around me, looking again at the back seat. I'm not sure if it's Roger or the booze smell from the three in the back that makes his nose curl. He stands straight and walks back to his car. I can hear my heart beating.

My fingers graze the pistol, ready to pull it up and fire when he returns. My cue will be, "could you please open the trunk?" and bang! He'll fall and I'll press on the gas, most likely needing to silence a few in the car as well.

Then he's back. Stay calm.

BODY IN THE TRUNK!

"You do know the registration is expired, right?"

"It's been such a struggle to get it done. I keep trying to make an appointment at the DMV, because I want to change the title into my name, but since there's no will… he was so sick you see, and it was really tragic–I."

"It's alright ma'am," he says. "I've had my share of issues with the DMV. Try somewhere in the suburbs. It will make your life a lot easier, trust me. Until then, I suggest not using this vehicle as your Friday night transport, lots of people on the force would've made you take a cab. Get these folks home safe, they look like hell."

He returns the papers and license. I notice Nick's eyes as I put everything into the glove box. Suspicious.

"You have a good night now and get a tag on that plate."

"Good night, sir." A few moments of relief pass before I restart the engine.

Sonya breaks the still water silence with a cheer. They all join in, except Nick, laughing and saying how they can't believe it, since the car reeks of booze. Douglass tells me that he was once breathalyzed just for driving after midnight on a Saturday.

"Why did he call you Wendy?" Sonya asks.

"My middle name is Ann," I tell her, which she buys unequivocally.

Nick stays silent the rest of the ride. I want to drop him off before Sonya, but she's in Evanston by Northwestern's campus and he lives on the other side of Sheridan Road.

When we arrive at her house, she forces me to get out of the car so I can give her a big hug. She laughs and cackles, swearing it was the best PTC of all time and she's glad I'm at Pearcey. I wish everyone was like her.

I pull up to Nick's house, but he doesn't budge. It's a quiet neighborhood, with houses spread far apart. The kind amplified with sounds of tree bristles twitching and wind scurrying down the sidewalk against perfectly cut grass.

"Well," I say.

He looks at me.

"Wanna come in?"

"What?"

"Do you want to come inside? Have a drink or something?" Or something?

"It's been a really long night, Nick."

He lets out a huff through his nostrils. Suddenly the man seated beside me somehow no longer seems like the reserved middle school teacher I know. There's some sparkle of darkness that grows in his eye.

"You know, I saw what was on that driver's license. Wendy Jones. Not Wendy Ann Bonny." His eyes grow wide, anticipating an explanation. "Who the hell are you?"

"I changed my name when I was adopted. My 'uncle' as I always put it took me out of the foster system. He gave me the name Wendy, and when I turned 18, I learned who my parents were and started to use the name they gave me. How is that so hard to believe?"

"Really? A foster kid? That's what you're going with? Angela told me that something was up with you. She's gonna fire people. Don't you want someone in your corner. I can be that. She said you were lying about your background and -"

"You don't believe me?"

He smacks the dash. "Enough lies."

I'm starting to think he's only using this ammo because I didn't go inside and sleep with him. I guess Sonya is right. Don't trust anyone.

He's panting, pointing in my face and nearly on my seat. His eyes tell me everything he wants as they scan me up and down.

"That is the truth, Nick. You think I've had it easy? Well, you're wrong. I have seen things that would make your privileged self wet your pants. You don't know me."

"That's the point."

I grab his face and plunge my lips against his. He pushes me away at first.

"What the hell?"

"Isn't this what you want?"

He answers by kissing me again. His hands fall on me, everywhere on me, eagerly grabbing, squeezing, pressing as if I'm something for him to play with.

His grip gets firm, almost pinning me down. I reach back for the gun, but it's too far.

"Tell me who you are," he repeats, coming up for air. "Who are you?" He detaches and presses my head against the window. "Who are you?"

"Isn't this what you wanted?" I reach over the console and run my hand up his leg, his grip on me loosens and he's obedient again. Just as I near his zipper, I pull away, slinking over the wheel and summoning some tears. The gun won't work here.

"I'm not a teacher," I say, pressing my head against the wheel. "I'm not a teacher."

"Hey, c'mon. Of course you are a teacher. Forget what Angela said. Lots of people lie about job history."

"I am not a teacher."

"Look, Ann, look at me. You are a teacher, ok? I'm sorry I doubted you. You have been educating your students and have been doing a great job. You are a great teacher. A great woman."

He wants me to come back. His compliments are poisonous bait for his dick. He breathes, heavily, his eyes shut as I run my hand over his jeans. As his breathing grows even heavier, I withdraw again.

"Before we do this, I want to tell you everything. I think you are special Nick. I want this to be special." He gives me all the attention in the world, only wanting one thing. "Ok," I let out a long breath. "I am a homicidal maniac who needs to kill people in order to feel whole. I have been doing it ever since I murdered the man who owned this car. It felt right. It feels right. I have no choice in the matter, and I have absolutely no control."

He doesn't twitch. He just sits there, his eyes and mouth gaping.

"Did you hear what I said?" Something tells me he'll be mute until I finish the hand job. "Nick?"

"Yes, I heard you." Then his hand is on my thigh. "You don't have to be scared and make up crazy things, Ann. I thought we were past this. My god you have an imagination." He leans closer with pursed lips, but I stop him.

"Open the trunk."

"What?"

"Just go open it."

He exits, reserved and suspicious, but obedient. Before I join him, I pull out a pen from the console. Outside the car, I lift the trunk and unzip the suitcase, revealing Roger's body. Nick gags from the smell but doesn't have the chance to cover his mouth. I jab Nick with the pen into his throat. Swift, but effective, his neck pours a piss stream of blood. He tries covering the wound, but I unload on him with the pen again and again until he's filled with holes, bloody… I then slam the trunk down on his head and throat. Again and again. Damn, Nick, for trying to manipulate me. He is just like the others. He's in my way, he is suspicious. But the worst part, he's fake. Sick, twisted and fucking awful. Hardly a shy, nice guy. All bullshit. All a cover up. I slam and cry, pressing the trunk down on him as he squirms. Then snap.

<u>Singing in the Rain</u>

The drive back into the city is freeing. I don't even bother with Nick's body. Chicago is a dangerous city. Sometimes people just get jumped. Their body left in the street.

With Roger still in the trunk, I head back to Pearcey. There's a steady fall downpour. The rhythmic thudding droplets are quite pacifying. Rain makes you forget things. It has this mysterious cleansing factor to it.

Amir's Honda still sits in his assigned parking spot. The lights are out and the car silent, but it isn't the first time he's left his car at school. So I brush it off.

Inside, I use my phone as a flashlight while navigating the stark hallways, dragging the suitcase. Walls covered with school bulletin news and art projects. Collages made from feathers and beads and macaroni shells. I sneak through the lower school wing of the campus, turning to the long hall of glass cases that hold trophies and placards.

The cafeteria is less penetrable than other classrooms; secured with a bolted lock. The kind that I can break, but I want to be in and out. And I don't want to leave any trace. So, I pick an easier door–Amir's office– to find the extra set of keys. The suitcase drifts, falling under the desk, but I let it go, rummaging through the file cabinets and drawers. I use Roger's phone for a light. I've been texting Kate as Roger throughout the night. The soft buzz his phone makes every time her name pops up on the screen makes me giddy.

Nothing is out of place on Amir's desk; a photo of his wife and a few awards and other trinkets, neatly organized and unaccompanied by littering forms or notes. Not the kind of person to leave keys exposed on his desk.

I pull open the right-hand drawer on Amir's desk. Inside is a stack of folders, a few loose paper clips, and yes, the extra ring of keys. I snatch them and no sooner are they in my pocket, the lights in the office lobby flick on.

Duck.

I sink under the desk, curling up and wrapping my hands around my knees. Someone is here.

The door opens. Two people, laughing. Then a hush. Did they see me?

"Funny." It's Amir's voice. "I thought I locked it."

"This is why it's good that you have me around at all times." Angela? "No more slipping up or forgetting." I want to peek. Just one. No, I can't. They'll see you. I hold the suitcase steady with my feet as I brace under the desk, listening to them giggle; they're hands rustling over their clothes. I'm caught between the feeling of walking in on parents having sex and a swat team raiding my apartment. Both make me sick to my stomach. I can't breathe. Don't move, Ann. Don't move.

"Let me just grab my bag and we'll go," Amir says. His bag? It's a brown leather satchel with buckles on the front, sitting directly in front of me on his swivel chair. I feel him moving towards the back of the desk.

"Or," Angela says. "We can get a little head start now?" I don't want to, but I picture what they're doing. She rubs her hands along his chest.

"In here?" he says eagerly.

"We can christen our principal partnership." Holy shit, I think. Little Miss Proper has a slightly kinky side. Amir doesn't make it to his bag. Instead, a loud thud sounds as he thumps onto the desk. Amir and Angela tear into each other. His groans. Her moans. Agh! It's too much.

Now I might laugh. I try not to. It could just be a defense mechanism. My mouth kills. I'm biting it so hard to keep everything in.

Then Roger's phone buzzes. No. It lights up. Kate is Facetiming him. Seriously? I cover the phone, pressing the power button to silence the call. Please don't hear, please –

"What's wrong?" Amir says. They stop. My heart falls out of my throat. I'm done for, I know it –

"Let's just move this." A slight click. Must have been the picture frame. Two married people getting it on above me in the principal's office. Guess they can't stand the sight of one of their spouses watching. In an instant, they're back at it.

Buzz.

Text from Kate.

I swipe the message. When it pops up, I nearly wet myself. Staring at me is a photo of her topless, bottomless, completely nude, standing in front of a hotel bathroom mirror. Then a text bubble pops up.

"Bored in my room, Facetime ;)"

I stare at the photo meant for Roger while my superiors get in on above me. My hand slips from around my knee and inches between my legs, glued to the phone. I zoom in. Yes. She's perfect. I bite my bottom lip, holding in my pleasure as I rub myself. The pounding on the desk grows. Amir's panting, Angela's moaning. God, she has an annoying little shrill. The desk shakes. Amir groans. Angela moans. I hold it all inside. It's so damn difficult. But I hold it in.

"Faster," Angela says. The pounding grows. I go faster too. Full circles, a little pressure to start, gentle, then harder. "Harder." Harder. Yes, yes.

"Hello?" Kate texts again. I don't text back. I just closed my eyes, imagining us on the desk, clawing over each other the way Amir and Angela are currently. The way Kitty and I—No, this is about Kate. Our hot, bare flesh rubbing against one another. My head presses against the underbelly of the desk as everything explodes in my stomach. It's such a rush of pleasure my leg sticks out and kicks Amir's desk chair, sending it across the room and onto its side.

"Woah!" Amir says. The phone falls on my lap, buzzing again. "Did we do that?" I hear him dismount. They giggle. No. I shut my eyes. Amir, breathing like he's just finished a 5k, trudges over to the collapsed chair and retrieves his bag. I cover my mouth again, not daring to touch the buzzing phone; too scared that any breath will ruin me. "Let's go," Amir says. His pants jingle as he pulls them up and fastens his belt. I hold my breath, waiting long after the lights go out and the door closes behind them. After ten, maybe fifteen minutes, I pop my head out.

When I finally make it to the cafeteria, I work fast, flicking on the lights in the kitchen and pulling the suitcase up to a steel prep table. The bright fluorescence reflects off the metal jungle of cookware.

Time to unpack. I carefully unzip the suitcase so as not to snag any flesh. The meat grinder sits in the corner of the kitchen beside a fridge and a warming oven. Not meant for cooking, just keeping things temperature so they're still somewhat safe to eat. Not that anything that comes out of this kitchen ever is.

I chop Roger's body into smaller fragments to fit into the grinder. The motor roars the moment I flick the small switch.

The auger and blades spin on the inside, buzzing like a revving motorcycle engine. I experiment with his fingers first, chopping them off with a butcher's knife and tossing them into the hopper. They go through easily, a small crunch here and there. I follow his fingers with his forearms, then his biceps and shoulders.

When it's over, I have successfully turned Roger into three dissection bags from Sonya's class filled with ground meat.

I carry the bags out of the school, after making sure to double up each plastic sack filled with ground guts and shredded human flesh. Most of him goes into the compost dumpster. But I keep one of the bags, tossing it into my trunk.

Under what's turning into a steady drizzle, I involuntarily whistle 'Singing in the Rain'. I have two dates to look forward to.

"I'm singing in the rain, just singing in the rain." I slam the trunk.

The boat has officially tipped. No one can stop me now.

Teacher with a Pistol

Later that night, around 4 or 5 am I'm awoken by a knock at the door.

Kate storms in, flustered, practically chewing on the end of a gas station vape pen. "It's for my nerves," she says.

When I ask what's wrong, she just huffs and puffs, throwing her purse on my couch and asking what I have to drink. She doesn't even protest the whiskey and sends it down her throat before I pour myself some. I hesitate on mine and give her another shot. The second one makes her take a seat.

She breathes, loose now. Good for me having her in the dark of the morning–that stretch before sunrise that you can still consider nighttime.

"I haven't heard from Roger for hours. He told me this morning that he was spending the night at home. He is a lot of things, but never a liar, at least… I don't know, this is ridiculous. I'm sorry for barging in like this. I literally drove all the way back from St. Louis. I was so worried." Is she worried or suspicious? She tries leaving but I keep her on the sofa with a fresh glass of whiskey. "Goddamn that's strong. Fuck, do you have anything in your fridge to chase that?"

"Let me check." I head to the kitchen while she continues to rage about Roger and his disappearing antics. Roger, who's body is currently ground meat in my fridge. Besides him, my refrigerator is pretty empty, except for a few ginger ales and chocolate milk. I bring her a Canada Dry to follow her fourth shot.

"He is just—ugh—the worst. There, I fucking said it." She isn't wearing a ton of makeup, which I like, but her eyes still bleed mascara. I help her clean up. I take care of her. Does Roger? No. "He doesn't answer his phone. He knows I'm not going to be home until tomorrow. And he just—you don't think he is with someone else, do you?"

"No idea. At least he's not doing it in your bed."

"That fucking piece of shit. I knew this would happen. I keep pushing him away. I never listen. He tells me I'm—I'm sorry, I guess I just blame myself."

"This is hardly your fault, Kate."

"Of course it is!" How dare he make her feel this way. Even in death he ruins her.

"You know what might help you?" I say, leaning down over her. This is my moment to seize. She stares at me with wanting deep in her green eyes.

"What?"

I kiss her.

"Ann!" she pushes me away, but doesn't flee.

"You have come to me when things are rocky with Roger. To me, when things are rocky with work. Don't act like you don't want this too."

"I…" I fill in the blanks for her by kissing her again, not the way I kissed Nick earlier that night, not the way I kissed John. There isn't any plan for what I'm going to do next, no move I'm going to make, from this point on, it's pure improv. The way I used to kiss Kitty. If she needs it, I need it much more.

We crawl on and shove one another, kissing and biting earlobes and necks until we are on my bed. From there we stay until dawn, diving on each other and swimming in one another's bodies until the sun peeks out from my window and the sunrise tells her to leave.

I roll over in bed. We only made out but still managed to strip to our underwear.

I feel a little cheated. Kitty and I never felt the need to wrap up or clothe ourselves after sex. But Kate sits on the side of the bed already buttoning her blouse. She reaches for my nightstand drawer where I keep a handgun.

"What's this?" She says, holding the gun up.

"It's my cure for insomnia. Don't tell me you're leaving already."

"Seriously."

"OK, I'm in my mid-twenties and live alone in a dangerous city - that's what it's for."

"A teacher with a pistol. That could be a TV show." I smile. We already have our own jokes. Soon she'll have a nickname for me, and I'll never have to tell her that I killed Roger. Soon she'll just forget him.

"This never happened, ok?" she says on her way out. I nod, lying. It certainly did happen.

And it will again.

I want her to stay, but in a moment, I'm alone again. She tells me that she's going to visit a family friend in the suburbs but will be back in the evening. I'll be waiting. Soon she'll have to make the choice between me and Roger.

Dinner for Two

She could be home any minute.

I track Kate's location using Roger's phone. She's close. By 7:30 pm, I have dinner prepared, and her apartment decorated for a night devoted to us.

A full bouquet of roses completes the table I've set with sterling silver. I strike a match, lighting two long candles in the middle of the small table dressed in a white linen cloth and decorated with silverware. The lights are dim, allowing the flickering flame of the candles to illuminate the apartment with a sensual orange hue, glowing like lanterns in a hall of catacombs.

After using her shower, I do my makeup in Kate's bedroom. It takes me back to the nights I'd wait for Kitty. The anticipation grows. I can't deny I'm nervous. She has a vanity mirror and makeup desk near the corner of her bed. Not much decorating done by Roger, I imagine, given the pillow shams and bright white duvet comforter, delicate décor that no guy would choose. It's dainty, it's girly.

I curl my hair and paint myself with blush and deep red lipstick to contrast my overly pale reflection. Roger had slight curls in his unkempt locks so there must have been something about it she likes. Once I finish with my hair, I put the curling iron back in the bathroom, leaving it plugged in, and set it on the sink. I line my eyes with her mascara, making a sharp point on the outside of my eyes, humming to the soft music playing on repeat. It's March Number One from Edward Elger's Pomp and Circumstance. Perfectly fitting. A welcoming sound for her arrival. I stay seated at her makeup bench in her room, staring at myself in the vanity. I think about what she'll say when she walks in the door.

"I know I shouldn't have," I say to my reflection. "But I did it for you." I smile as if I'm smiling at her. "Oh, how was my day?" I chuckle, tossing my hair casually. I lean in, "I saw Angela and Amir having sex in his office last night. I know, it's crazy! Should I say something? She would do it to me. Wouldn't she?"

Standing before Kate's full-length walk-up mirror, I wait for the door to open, fitting myself into one of her black dresses. The sleeve is long on my right arm, and completely absent on my left, with a nice slit in the fabric running down my right leg for mobile support. I spend a few minutes rehearsing.

"You gotta be kidding me, Kate," I say with a laughing smile, throwing a casual 'get outta here' wave. I cock my head, laughing at her inaudible jokes, chuckling with my mouth closed. "I know, right?" I say puckering my lips one final time as I check my makeup. "She is a bitch." I stand tall and run my hands down from my breasts to just below my hips, elongating my body while I grin at what I see in the reflection. I'm proud of myself. We have come so far.

Then Kate walks in the door.

Burgers A la Roger's Dick

"Roger?"A cheery, yet hesitant drift rides on her voice. Kate's footsteps echo from the front entry, halting when she makes it to the kitchen. I suppose she thinks Roger has returned unannounced. But she's wrong. He'd never do something like this for her. "Roger? Roger what is this?" There's a whiff of horror at the end of her surprised, hopeful tone.

I emerge from the bedroom, meeting her face to face, clad in her makeup and clothes, nearly as tall as her in her 3-inch Louboutin's. Honestly, these are kinda uncomfortable.

"Welcome home, Kate." A rush of pale falls like an avalanche down her forehead.

"Are-are those my clothes?"

I nod.

"How do I look?"

"You're wearing my shit. Ann, what the-?" At first she thinks it's funny, but as she studies the room, the Beethoven on the speaker, the romantic set-up, she grows silent and glares at me, fiddling with the silver Tiffany around her wrist. Is this not good enough? Do I not look right? Do I not look pretty? "What the hell is this?"

"Dinner?"

"No, I mean, what are you doing in my house? How did you even get in?"

"Would you like to sit?"

"I want to be alone, actually. I found out that a friend of mine was killed, nearly a week ago and hadn't known until now, and Roger is still—"

"Enough about Roger. Now look at all the trouble I went to, Kate. You've had a long day. Maybe you should sit and eat." I pull her a chair, signaling like a maître d. She shakes her head, tapping her arm as she hugs herself. I smile, refusing to let the panic I feel that it's not to her satisfaction betray me.

"Look, this was sweet. You are sweet, but last night was just—a mistake."

"You're wrong, Kate. Look what I got you". I run behind the kitchen island and present a bottle of New Zealand Cabernet. "Sit while I find a corkscrew."

"I can help—"

"Sit."

She obeys, finally, sitting timidly while I rummage through the drawers and make my final preparations for dinner.

"So, what are we having?"

"You will see. Ahah! Found one."

"Why are you in my dress?" Her eyes spark with subtle fear.

"I just want to have a nice dinner," I say, walking the wine to the table. Hoping to impress her, I dismember the bottle with the wine key. The cork gives a sudden pop as I pull it with the screw. Kate sits attentively; fixed on the bottle; her hands clasped together between her legs. I pour. A few droplets fall from the lip of the bottle and stain the white linen like small splotches of blood. "Oops."

I feel her tremble. Is it the velvety Cab or me? I finish pouring hers and she darts.

I catch her hand before she takes the glass.

"What?" she says.

"It needs to breathe. Dance with me."

"You're joking."

"C'mon, just one dance."

"I really don't think that's a great idea."

"Just one."

"I really want to try the food you made, Ann. I hate when it gets too cold." She takes my hand. "How about after we eat?"

"Promise?"

"I promise. We will dance after dinner."

I let her drink.

She's so fixated on her wine that she misses me slip her phone from the edge of the table and walk over to the sink and stick it in the disposal.

"Ah ah ah." I gave her a loving tap on the hand when she tries lifting the lid of the plate cover. "Be patient. I know you are hungry. Let's have a cheers." I pour myself a glass, about half the amount I gave her, and set the bottle down, then the wine key next to it, sitting across from her.

"A cheers?"

"A toast." I scoot my chair to the edge of the table. "To..." I hold up my glass. "Hm, I can't think of a toast. What would you like to toast to?"

"Um," she says, mirroring me, "I don't know, how about to friends?"

"Friends?"

She swallows air. "Yes, I guess, friends."

"Alright," I say, my grin fades, and my face goes blank with a killing stare. "To friends." Our glasses clink and we sip; hers much longer than mine.

"Let's eat." I lift the dome cover from her serving. On the white ceramic plate in front of her waits a burger. Thick patty with melted cheese oozing from the sides in a yellow goo, caramelized onion, and lettuce between two egg white buns. No tomato. Tomatoes are gross.

She looks surprised, staring at the burger and scanning every side.

"Something wrong?" I ask. I leave my plate covered. "You aren't a vegetarian, are you?"

"No, no," she says, offering the best fictional smile her law degree taught her. "It looks great. I just prefer lean meat to be honest."

"Meat is meat. Enjoy."

She picks up the burger. I made it big, so she has to grasp it in both hands. My mouth waters as the burger rises closer to her mouth.

"What about you?" she says, lowering the food.

"I'm ok with just the wine for now." Suspicion crosses her face. She brings the burger closer, stopping again before it reaches her mouth.

"I feel weird eating and you aren't."

"Honestly, I'm not hungry right now."

"At least take the cover off. It's giving me anxiety."

"Nah,"

"Why not?"

"Just eat it!" I slam my hand on the table. The silverware gives a resonant clank. Breathe, Ann. I hold out my hand like a stop sign. "I'm sorry."

"It's alright," she awkwardly looks at the floor. I hope I haven't made her uncomfortable with my anger. Finally, she takes a bite, digging into the bun and meat. A meat I heavily seasoned. She takes a full bite, chewing without breaking eye contact with me while I lick my lips, watching inventively.

"It's really good," she says, her mouth still full. She cups her hand over her face while she speaks, swallows, washing it down with the wine. "So," she begins. "How's um, how's that guy?"

"What guy?"

"The lawyer."

"He's fine."

"Did you find him?"

"Yes," I say. "Thanks again for helping me get up there. We actually have another date. Not sure if he will last, though. Most men in my life don't." I notice her hand tapping. She runs her teeth over her bottom lip, while her eyes bounce to avoid looking at me. Her finger plays a steady c minor. I take another sip of wine, sliding my hand across the tablecloth. My fingers delicately touch hers, glazing over her flesh. She pulls away, hiding her hand under the table. A silence plagues us for a moment, but then she musters her lawyer courage.

"What is this?" she asks.

"What is what?"

"I'm asking you what this is."

"Then ask what this is."

"What is this?"

"What is what?"

"What the fuck we are doing right now?"

"Dinner."

"So you don't want..."

"I don't want what?"

"To um…." She balances her wine in one hand and the burger in the other. Another sip. Well, more of a gulp, really. I'm guessing she lied about the taste. Figures. "… To sleep with me, again?"

"No, I do."

She runs her lips over each other. "What if I don't want to sleep with you? You gonna drug me?" She chuckles. "Tie me down?"

"I can if you want me to."

She's amusing herself. "I would think teachers meet plenty of other gay people."

"Not as much as you think," I say.

"Did you ever have a girlfriend?"

"Yes."

"And what happened to her?"

"She didn't like my lifestyle."

"Your lifestyle?"

"Yes, my lifestyle."

"So, she left you?"

"She didn't leave me."

"Then what happened?"

Suddenly I'm overcome. Hushed by a chill along my vertebrae. It creeps down my back, then up again up to my ears, as if someone is behind me. Kitty? Is that you? Behind me whispering into my ear. Blowing a little on my earlobes; just enough to make me shutter.

"It wasn't my fault," I mutter, soft, low. Uncertain if I'm talking to Kate or to myself. "It was theirs. It was their fault."

I look back at Kate. Meeting her eyes. She looks back at me, as if she's staring at something lifeless. Her hand reaches, touching mine. The contact is such a ploy. Her weapon against me.

"Tell me," she says. Her voice is so soft. So soothing.

"I stabbed her to death with a kitchen knife." Her face loses all color. I can't tell if she knows I'm being honest. She hesitates at first, but silently giggles behind her closed teeth. A nervous little giggle. I let out a heavy breath, a bit eased. I laugh. She joins in, slow at first, but then equal to my own.

"So, was there a funeral for Oliver?"

"What?"

"Your friend. The one who died."

"I didn't mention his name."

"Well, you talk in your sleep, silly."

But I can tell by her facial expression, I messed up.

"Where's Roger?"

"He won't be joining us."

"Where the fuck is Roger! Where is he?"

"He won't be joining us."

She takes another bite, probably out of nervousness. She chews. Then pauses. Her mouth twitches. Her teeth rub together, her eyes pop, and her mouth inverts like a duck.

"What the—"

Kate pulls a small piece of metal out of her mouth with two little beads on each end. Somehow, Roger's piercing survived the grinder and found its way into her patty. Talk about forced entry. She holds it in front of her face for a few moments, analyzing the situation, studying the small piece of metal like she found a shell on the beach. Seconds pass before she realizes. Her eyes narrow, then widen, and widen until they are gaping open, her eyelids pry apart with disgusted terror as realization sinks in.

I'm upset she's chosen Roger. But at this point, it seems like she's finally listened to him. She finally ate his dick.

Kate jerks, holding a vomit at the tip of her throat. She gags. The piercing clanks against the plate.

"Dessert is going to blow you away. Just wait," I say with a smirk. She goes limp, but instead of passing out, she grabs for the knife and lunges towards me. I shield her assault with my plate cover. She stabs; the blade goes straight to the metal cover and snaps in half. I push myself out of my chair and stand, but she's fast, swiping the wine key from the table and sticking me just under my ribcage.

I fling my plate cover against her face, knocking her onto the couch. She quickly flips onto her back, kicking the air as I close the gap between us.

"Get away from me!" she yells. "Get away!"

"It's ok," I say. "It's ok, I won't hurt you. I like you so much. I need you."

"No! Get back!"

"Please, Kate. I want to just have a nice meal. You promised a dance. Please just sit down and let me explain."

She lets out a shrill.

"Get away!"

I step closer.

She crawls across the cushions, and I follow. A small trail of blood oozes from the side of her head from where I hit her with the plate cover.

"Get back! You crazy bitch!" She kicks out again hitting the wine key still hanging in my side, the screwed end deepens. A rush of pain busts through my stomach and out my throat as the winding metal spirals through my flesh. I stumble, clenching my side, and holding the wine key steady. I tug on the end, spinning it out. Blood seeps, and an aching sting of heart stopping pain trails behind. I manage to tear it from under my ribs, pressing the wound to manage the escaping blood. My head swirls, I guess that would be from blood loss. 'Not Kate,' I think to myself. 'She wouldn't do this to me. I made her dinner. I wanted to dance.'

"You're crazy!" she yells. "You're crazy, get the fuck away from me!"

"Kate, I assure you I am not crazy," I say calmly. "Please just hear me out. He was no good for you. You and I both know that. Just think about how happy we can be together."

"Get back," she says, jumping from the cushion. But as she lands, she slips, the side of her head making direct contact with the edge of the coffee table.

Spin Cycle

I leave Kate in the corner of the bathroom while I remove my dress. She's still alive. I check her pulse every few minutes to make sure. Her warm neck slowly beats, like a faint thumping drum. Blood runs from her hairline, but I leave it.

While she's slunk unconscious in the corner, I bend down in front of her, propping myself with bended knees, staring at her face-to-face. I brush back her hair to see her small nose and plump injected lips. She's still quite beautiful, even when knocked out. Even with the now dried makeup that runs down her eyes, and the cut along her temple that adds a streak of red across her face. Gently grazing my lips over hers, I savor the fleshy contact. I pull away, noticing how dirty her clothes have become from our loving battle.

Across the room, not necessarily connected to the living room, but more within its own nook, the laundry closet holds a washer and dryer stacked on top of one another. Somehow, the laundry unit looms directly across the main living room to the bathroom. The door sings open with a loud squeak revealing a very hungry washing machine. It stares right at me, as if spying, watching me attempt a single affectionate moment with Kate.

Back to her clothes. My, they're dirty. So dirty. I sense the washing machine's drooling anticipation. Its front facing door snaps open, mouthing to me "Feed. Feed."

I take my dress. Her dress. I cut the chunk of the fabric where I've bled over. That part will need to be burned for when they find the body. Then I hear it again. The washing machine, its squeaky hiss as it whispers across the room. "Feed."

It starts to beep.

Then a peaceful silence. Temporary. Within a handful of seconds, the song returns, replaying from the beginning. My head spins. The beeping's terribly catchy beat circles in my head. Circling. Circling.

I give another attempt to ignore it. But I can't.

Beeping. The beat blasts. The sound explodes between my ears. I look at Kate. Then the washer. Ugh, that damn beeping. It spins. I start to spin. Beeping. Spinning. Beeping. Beeping. Beeping.

I can't take it.

"Off with her head!" "Off with her head!"

I feel it. It rages in my veins and flows from my fingertips. I try holding it back. I do all I can. My head grows, imploding. My face welters red and red and red and red. Spinning. Beeping. Spinning.

"Off with her fucking god damn head! FEED ME!"

I grab unconscious Kate by her feet and drag her across the floor. I don't want to do it. The machine told me to.

"I'm sorry," I say to her. But she doesn't hear. I pull her to the washing machine and stuff her inside, shoving her through the circle opening. It's harder than it sounds. At first, I'm not sure how to fit her. On the initial attempt, I try stuffing her in feet first, but then find that headfirst works better. I bend her body, rolling her up like a sleeping bag and pressing her inside. "I'm sorry," I repeat. The machine told me to. The machine told me to.

With Kate inside, I toss in the dress. I also put in the linen tablecloth. I know it's darks and whites together - minor detail when you're out of your mind.

I slam the door shut. It bounces back open.

Damnit, at first thinking that there's too much in the round washer stronghold for the door to fully close. Kate slowly gains consciousness. A slow murmur lulls out from her mouth. I try closing the door again. Fuck! Close! She's waking up. Her head bobbles. Her legs twitch.

"What the—?" she says with a groggy voice.

Her head moves as she wakes up. I finally find the problem. Her fingers are in the way. Those small, beautiful pointers and index. At one point, I longed for them to caress my cheeks, to wear that same nail polish, to feel what her fingers felt like inside of me. Maybe this way I can find out. I press harder on the door. I slam again. And then again. The door crunches against the fingers as they split off from her hand. A loud break like a number 2 pencil when the bone snaps in half. She lets out a loud, hellacious scream as her fingers fall to the floor and the washing machine door closes on her. I hold it shut with my thigh and reach for the lock button, securing her in her sealed globular prison.

A cadence of thuds and screams radiate from inside the washing machine. I leave the two fingers on the floor for the time being. My side stings with a throbbing pain from the puncture wound. I need to seal it before an infection spreads.

"Let me out!" she barely musters a full scream. I kneel in front of the machine. She presses her hand and face against the window. I think I see a tear running down from her eye. I place my hand parallel to hers, as if we're touching palm to palm.

"I just wanted to have one dance," I say to her. "Why did you do this?"

"Let me out," now it's a full-on cry. No screams left, just begging. Just like Roger. I kiss the door, crying with her, right where her face and lips are jammed against the glass. I don't want to see her go. But now she knows. I have no control. I've slipped.

I fill the retractable door with laundry detergent and set the temperature to warm, and the cycle on… let me see… my finger hovers over the 'Normal' button, but Kate isn't normal. And I had put a dress in there, but 'Delicates' might not do the trick. I decide on 'Perm Press'. I press the button. A loud BEEP echoes. That's when she starts really pounding at the door. And 'Start'. The machine rumbles to life. The water drains. Kate's screams grow muffled as the water level rises. The humming machine rotates, rocking back and forth and then fully, completely spinning. I place a cigarette in my mouth and lean against the wall, taking a long drag while Kate spins inside the machine, her body thumping against the inner walls of the washer.

As I've said, I am not mad. A mad person doesn't take these things into account. On the other hand, I am prepared. I expected at least one lover's quarrel would end with some bloodshed. Where's the fun in normal, boring, safe dates? No, no, I much prefer it this way. I like seeing the scars on the outside. That's how I know they are worth it.

I puff a cloud of smoke, holding a cigarette in my fingers as I go from the kitchen to the bathroom, snatching a bottle of whiskey on my way.

In the bathroom, I crack open the window for the smoke, leaving the dwindling cigarette between my teeth while I inspect my side wound. I'm in nothing but my underwear. The chill from the frigid Chicago night wafts through the small opening, blowing cool air over my anxious neck. I reach backward, tending to an invisible tickle that runs a chill up along my spine. I feel the hairs sticking up. Little needles, fuzzy pricks scattered over my boney flesh.

Back to the real wound. I pour the whiskey over the hole under my rib cage. The alcohol burns, like razor blades figure skating across my nerve endings. I do not flinch. I watch myself in the mirror, an audience to my own self-mending. I don't even wince, or blink, as I rub the liquor to disinfect the wound, swallowing the pain. A pain that isn't even there. The type made up in my imagination. Kate's bathroom drawer holds a sewing kit she must have taken from one of her hotel stays. The kind with just the basics - needle, thread, plastic scissors that don't actually cut. I wash away the blood and begin to stitch myself. Breathing out, allowing a soft flow of relief ease through my throat as I weave with the needle, sewing the gap in my flesh closed. I almost enjoy the needle's tickle. It's like an old friend that you are nervous at first to see again, but once you begin talking, you never want the conversation to end. It's addictive, like self-inflicted pain.

No bandages, I let the wound breathe.

After, I sit across from the washing machine as it rumbles. The screams from inside fade. I light another cigarette and drink whiskey. When the cycle ends, I hit repeat, then walk out, leaving her inside.

Just Another Manic Monday

I wake up on Monday morning in the fetal position under my desk in my classroom. The last hours are such a blur to me. How I even ended up here. What happened this weekend. Is this the catastrophe? I want to find Dr. Tina. It's too late now. I just remembered it's Monday.

John had texted me through the weekend since the date for our dinner draws closer. As October 15th, my deadline, draws closer. There's no time to mourn Kate, although I miss her. I miss Kitty. I miss the life I pictured for myself with the job of vice principal. I would have stopped killing. Now, well, I'm not sure I can stop. If there's any voluntary part of me at all that can control this violence.

THIS is my life.

When I crawl out from the desk, I see my whiteboard has been scratched and covered with markings and ramblings in red expo. Variations of "ANN BONNY... MARY ANN BONNY... OFF WITH HER HEAD... KITTY" graffiti the wall. I stand in the empty, dark classroom, percolating madness.

I don't even make it through second period before my class is visited by Angela Greene.

Her hair freshly straightened. She's swapped the cardigan sweaters for a blazer. It's her new vice principal look. Worse. Way worse.

"Miss Bonny," using her 'in front of the children,' voice. "Happy Monday." She takes a long sip from her 'AG' mug.

"Yes, Ms. Greene. What's going on?" I say, crossing my arms. I want her to disappear. Get out.

"Maybe we should step outside for a moment."

She guides me to the hallway. I feel like an unruly student about to be reprimanded.

"Here's the thing," she begins. I want to vomit from Angela's torturous, nauseating sweetness. "Mr. Salem and I were discussing you the other night and we both came to the decision that it would be best, for you, if you were to take a small leave of absence."

"Amir said that?"

"Mr. Salem. Look Ann, I know what you are. In simple terms, a fraud. Now, Mr. Salem seems to think that although you lied about your teaching history that you still bring something of value to Pearcey. I think it'll take some time, but I will get him to see the truth. He will see what you are, and after a few weeks with you gone, I am sure he will come to his senses."

"You don't know what you're saying."

"Now there is no need to get angry here at school, Ann. I know that you almost got a DUI the other night when you drove drunk with four members of our staff in the car."

"I wasn't drunk."

"And the deer. And the lies about your uncle and Bridgeton. It's just too much to even have a case in favor of you, Ann. It's better this way, it really is. I will tell people that you took a leave due to your growing responsibilities and pressure after losing a close member of your family. I will give you dignity, Ann. Not that you deserve it." She hisses into my ear. "There will be an investigation into you, Ann. When I'm done you, won't be allowed in any school again."

I want to press her against the lockers and squeeze the life from her eye sockets. But for some reason I'm weak, powerless, and immobile, boiling on the inside but cowering and closed up on the outside.

"You can't do this."

"That is precisely my job as Vice Principal, Ann. Now please excuse me, I have to take the responsibilities of our fifth-grade teacher over until we can find a temporary sub."

She turns and I snatch her by the wrist, but she spins like a whip and smacks my face.

I want to tell her I know she's cheating with Amir. God, I want to say it so badly. I figure that it would be better to whisper to Sonya. I will let the gossip spread in the school like a fire, letting Angela to burn slowly.

"Don't you ever lay a hand on me again, bitch." She points dead between my eyes like a loaded gun to my face. "Get out of my school."

Then both of us notice we are being watched. I'm back in John's kitchen; naked, cold, and utterly exposed. Douglass and Sonya stand watching from down the hallway, speechless and unresponsive when I try explaining myself. Angela struts off, unaffected, securing her dominance over all teachers. Before I can defend myself to those I had for a moment considered my friends, they retreat, leaving me alone in what feels like a shrinking hallway.

I remain there, for, I don't know, probably twenty minutes. My face stings. Angela is small, but damn can she smack. I punch the locker, nearly breaking my hand and falling onto the floor. I don't want to get up, I just want Ernie to come down the hall, mop me up and drown me in his suds and soap.

There's no way I'm going to just leave. Not without a fight. Not without giving Amir one last chance.

I barge past Mrs. Baxterly into Amir's office.

"What the hell is wrong with you?"

I slam the door behind me.

"You are letting her fire me?" I glare at Amir. He removes his bifocals and rubs them on his sweater, letting out a long sigh.

"Suspension. Temporarily."

"I'm not an idiot."

"Look, Ann," Amir starts. He slips the glasses back in place and digs his hands into his pockets. Suddenly talking down to me, as if he isn't afraid. He should be. "I don't know what you think you know, but you are wrong. I understand it seems like she has it out for you but, really, she treats everyone with the same scrutiny. You just seem to give her more to consider when she asks questions. Given your behavior of late."

"My behavior?"

"Oh, c'mon, don't tell me things haven't been off with you. And don't get me started on the situation in the parking lot. I have enough to deal with now that Mr. Jefferies (Nick) is missing. Mrs. Greene will dig and dig because she's the kind of person who needs to know everything about the people she works with, and now worse, who work for her."

"And who made it that way? I bet you love when she digs into you."

"What does that mean? If you are upset about not getting the promotion—"

"It's not about the promotion. She's manipulating you."

"Ann, you are a great teacher. But maybe this will be for the best. I know you're as clean as a whistle. People do what they have to, I accept that. (Not for long) And I don't want to see you gone for good."

"So, what do you want?"

He offers a handshake in place of any response, paired with a hopeful grin from the left side of his mouth. As if I'll counter with an understanding smile.

I notice that the picture frame of his wife still faces down on his desk. His ring is still tight on his finger. I reach towards his hand, but divert, picking up the picture frame and setting it neatly in its former place.

"Next time you fuck her, let your wife watch." And I walk out.

A cigarette screams my name.

I sneak behind the school near the gym shed. Just around the corner there's a narrow path of sidewalk leading to the courtyard overlooking the playground.

It's one of those Midwestern days that refuses to make up its mind on the weather. One moment there's a blustering chill of wind, accompanied by a gust of snow flurries, the next, sunshine peeking down from a blue sky speckled by a handful of fluffy white clouds.

Leaning against the red brick exterior of the school, I blow smoke out to mix along with the afternoon breeze. I don't bother to put my jacket on, immediately feeling the icy chill of the late autumn air suck the warmth from my fingertips. My body sinks into a cannon ball position, resting on the rough wall.

A faint sound cues from around the corner. I keep the cigarette lit, holding it between my fingers to keep it from going out as I creep along the wall, inching my way to the sharp turn of the corner.

It's a sob. Someone crying.

A shredded piece of paper blows from the corner to my feet. I bend down, recognizing it immediately. On the top of the page in the header section, the title written in bold italics: The Count of Monte Cristo. As I read, more pages follow, each slightly torn, some right from the spine, others shredded down the middle with missing chunks, torn like a shark had attacked the pages.

Danny sits with his face sunk into his arms. He weeps softly, with faint sniffling of his nose and heavy panting. The book's withered remains tuck between his knees, his composition notebook partnered to his feet. I sit beside him, waiting to speak as I take a final drag from my cigarette before squishing the butt under my heel.

"You ok, Danny?" I don't expect him to respond, but I need him to know I'm here. "Danny."

He lifts his head from the darkness of his folded body. His eyes are red from the tears and a small trail of blood runs down his lip.

"They ripped it up," he says, rubbing his nose with the back of his paw, cleaning both snot and blood from his face. "They made fun of me for reading during recess and they ripped up the book." He wipes his dripping nose with his fingers.

"Who did?"

"I'm sorry Miss B."

"No Danny. This isn't your fault."

"They destroyed it."

"It's over Danny."

"What's over?"

I just shook my head.

"The book. Forget it. It's meaningless. I don't know why I gave it to you. I don't care. I don't care about you. I didn't care about her, or any of them, I just did it because – I don't know; I just wanted to. I had to."

"No. You don't mean that. I know how it's going to end." He says with a whiff of anger in his eyes.

"What?"

"Dantes was about to kill him. It was almost over."

"You aren't Dantes," I tell him. "Dantes was going to realize something at the end."

"I don't want you to tell me how it ends," he says, "I need to read it myself." I notice his sealed fist; leaking blood. Firm, the way it had been when I spoke to him at the lunch table. He remains in a hunched, fetal position. I reach for him. He doesn't pull away as I pry open his fingers.

His entire palm is shredded, cut and bruised, with slits neatly made along the crevices of each finger, and a giant severance of flesh running diagonal across his hand. There are healed cuts and scabs, most likely from months of self-damage.

"Danny, who did this to you?" He just stares out at the playground, watching the other children swinging, running, playing, laughing. He sits, perched in stone beside me; his mouth bloody from a bully's fist and his book ruined. His demons on the brink of exposure. I know the feeling.

A small knife pokes out from his pocket. I tighten my focus on the jagged, plastic edges of the once white, now bloodstained, cafeteria cutlery.

"Danny," I repeat, slowly reaching. My hand inches along the slender strip of concrete that separates us. "I need you to tell me who is hurting you."

I go for the knife, but he pulls away before I can slip it from his pocket, coiling the way a cobra prepares to strike. I freeze.

The recess whistle blows, calling the children inside with a screeching toot. Danny doesn't budge. He just sits there, glaring at me, the color in his eyes fading away into a blank ebony. He pulls the knife and grips it between his dirty fingers, stab ready, but I catch his wrist. I'm not the blade's target.

A waft of dizziness hits me. Fuck! My head! I was spinning again.

He tears up.

"Miss Bonny, I-."

"God Damnit! What?" I release him, shrill and volatile. The knife falls. "God Damnit, Danny just leave me alone! Go find someone else who cares about your problems. Go! Go find a decent human being not some fucked up creature like me. Go!"

I swallow my breath once I register that I've snapped at Danny. His face melts and the tears break. Mine follow as I heave out my anger in gusts of heavy breathing. He steps away from me, as if suddenly I too, am his enemy.

"No, Danny," my voice calm again. "No, I am sorry I-"

But it's too late. He retreats and darts off leaving his composition book behind. Just like that, I've alienated myself from both my school and the only person I connect with. It breaks my heart, if that's the thing you call that pumps blood throughout the body. At this point I'd say it's some nameless organ that fills its biological role but refrains from any of the emotional personality gifted to humanity.

Danny is out of sight. Soon it's just me standing alone between the playground and the school building, unwelcome on both sides.

I pick up Danny's notebook, tucking it under my arm. As far as I'm concerned, the notebook is the only thing that really matters to him. The remnants of the book I gifted Danny still linger by my feet. I don't bother cleaning that up. A few pages blow along with the breeze, scattering themselves across the sidewalk and onto the grass field.

All I can think is that I should run after him. I should fix this. But I can't. I don't know how. Breaking things, killing things, that's what I'm good at.

I tap my finger nervously against my leg and stare at the playground. I focus on one of the swings. It rocks, letting out a metal croak from the suspended chains. I think of the night when I killed Oliver Miner and his wife and came to the playground in ridiculous delirium. I hate myself for being such a fool. As I stand alone in a post drinking-like state of regret, I wish John never saved me that night. It would have prevented so much pain.

I run home, unsure of my next move. I won't allow Amir and Angela to get away with this. I have to handle John first. But as I approach my building, I'm caught off guard. The police cars parked in front of my building are not a great sign.

Officer Blake

The lights are faint, their sirens silent, but still, I know they must be here for Kate. I should run. And go where? That would just look suspicious.

Amanda posts at the front desk, her forehead sweaty and her face pale with a soft pink trying to break through her dark skin. She speaks to a man with a green striped sweater over a collared shirt. His glasses sit on the end of his nose and his hand rubs his patchy beard. He's definitely not a cop, even though a few stand beside him like armed guards while he sits next to Amanda, listening to her as she barely manufactures a complete sentence, stuttered by shock.

I do my best to avoid making noticeable eye contact as I scurry straight to the elevator. Thirteen... thirteen... c'mon. The elevator doors slide open.

More cops in the hallway. Fuck.

But they aren't here for me. My door is closed, my apartment undisturbed from when I had left it. Next door, uniforms step in and out of Kate and Roger's yellow-taped apartment.

A bald man in blue stops me just as I reach my apartment door.

"Excuse me, ma'am," he says approaching with his hand up. "Do you live here?"

"Yes."

"Might I ask you a few questions?"

"Did something happen?"

A woman pokes out from behind the tape. It's Officer Blake. Again. God fucking damnit. She lifts the tape and slips out from the doorway. Our eyes meet from behind the shoulder of the bald officer. I switch her for the carpet, but she remains in my peripherals. She sets him aside.

"I'll take over from here," she says "Thanks, Nelson." Office Nelson gives Blake a complimentary nod and walks off. "Can't be coincidence, can it?" she says to me.

"You must really like me. Where's the uniform?" She's in a turtleneck and suit now.

"Promoted to detective." she says, unfazed. "Can we chat?"

"Are you making an assumption based on coincidence?"

"Let's do this somewhere else than the hallway, huh?"

I slip the key in and turn. Trying my best to keep my hand steady. "Would you like to come inside?" It opens with a swinging cricket.

"Thank you," she says, stepping into my apartment.

I follow her, dropping my keys at the front entry table and head straight to the bathroom.

"Can I get you anything to drink?"

"I'm ok, thank you." Her voice travels from the living room as she makes herself welcome. I lean over the bathroom sink, taking in a deep breath before staring at the mirror. Get it together, Ann. I'm shaking.

I imagine her standing beside my couch, taking a look around, a real long look, appraising each inch with a suspicious prowl, like a collector at an art show, judging, scrutinizing, looking for something nonexistent. My place is spotless. I cleaned it recently. Since Roger. She won't find the Oliver Miner's Jag keys. She won't find anything.

"Make yourself at home," I say to Blake as I head to the kitchen. She remains in the living room, awkwardly shifting, studying the pillows and the walls for the tenth time. She pleasantly nods, taking a seat near the sofa. Again, she unsheathes her notebook and pen from her front pocket. It seems like only a moment ago I sat with her in my classroom.

"It's very clean," I hear her say.

I open the fridge, pour chocolate milk for myself and swallow it in one gulp. "So, detective? That's big." I say, clapping my lips. "I'd take you out to celebrate, but I have plans." I walk into the living room.

"I'd really like it if we stuck to being professional for this. Is that alright with you?"

"I'm here to help. What's going on?" I slink on the sofa across from her, trying my best to distract her the way Kate had distracted me on that same couch.

"Well, the lobby attendant—"

"Amanda?"

"Yes, Amanda. She was called about a disturbance on this floor and when she heard nothing from your neighbors, she went inside and found a woman dead in her own washing machine."

(Time to perform)

"How terrible," I do my best to act surprised. To act disgusted. To act horrified. Deep down I'm thrilled yet another person has been an audience member to my crescendo. "That's so incredibly awful. My gosh." I borrow one from Angela Greene's playbook and hold my hand over my chest.

"Yes, it is." She takes a note. I'm acting my heart out. And she gives me a note? How dare she! "Can you tell me…" she's one of those people who takes long pauses in the middle of her sentences. It makes me anxious. "How well did you know Kate and Roger?"

"How well does anyone really know their neighbors?" I begin. "I mean, I pass them in the hall when I come home sometimes or run into them in the lobby. It's hard to get to know a person when the majority of the time you exchange meaningless small talk in order to seem socially polite. Kate was always friendly. Roger was, well, distant, a little rude. Kind of the jealous type. I guess like most guys."

"Did they seem happy?"

"I would often hear them fighting. These walls aren't too thick if you know what I mean."

"No I don't. Please elaborate."

"Well, they would fight a lot. I'd hear them argue. They'd scream and they'd shout, and then their make-ups were just as loud."

"Elaborate for me, please."

"They'd fuck really hard." Her eyebrows raise and she nearly chokes on her own air. Hey, she asked.

"And when was the last time you saw the victim?"

"Victim?"

"Kate."

"Oh. Yes. She asked me to watch Pickles."

"Pickles?"

"Their Shih Tzu."

"Where were they going?"

"It was just Kate. I honestly didn't ask. I just know she had to be out of town for a few days. Maybe she needed space from Roger."

"This Roger. Tell me more about him."

"What's there more to say? He was an ass if I'm being honest."

"Was?"

"What?"

"You keep using the word was when you refer to Roger. Usually, people only use past tense when someone's no longer around."

"Oh well, it's just a silly tense. Not really something I pay attention to."

"You teach English, right?"

"Is he a suspect?" A lull passes again, this time under a wave of heat and leg bouncing as I try avoiding eye contact.

"So would you describe Roger as...violent?"

"I think everyone has the capacity to be violent."

"What makes you say that?"

"We live in a violent world. Violence makes violence." Thank you, Anthony Burgess.

"Well put. What about Kate? What can you tell me about her?"

"Good girl."

"Good, how?"

"Independent, I suppose. She had a good job."

"Surface level. What kind of woman was she? In your eyes? Was she flirty?"

"With me? Is that jealousy?"

"On her computer there was a selection of private videos and photos. Kink toys and bondage equipment in their nightstand. The couple seems, well..."

"Unfit?"

"I was going to say promiscuous."

I shrug. She jots down some more notes, waiting a few eternally prolonged seconds before she resumes questioning. My leg bounces set to rapid fire as it shoots up and down. My side aches. The adrenaline from running home aggravated the wound under my rib cage. Kate's final impression on me. I haven't checked if it reopened, worried that Officer Blake will question that too.

We stare at one another for some time. Her dark brown eyes study me with mysterious intent, trying to break through my outer shell and read my insides. I do my best to give her nothing, keeping my defenses upright and strong.

"So," she finally says, breaking the silence. "Did you hear anything last night or the night before?"

"Nothing out of the ordinary. What do you think happened? You don't think-," I play the role perfectly, swallowing my breath with a shivering fear and worry. "You don't think Roger could have done this?"

"In most cases things like this are done by a partner. Plus, if he's nowhere to be found then he might have skipped town. Or worse."

"Or worse?" I ask.

"There's something strange about finding one double homicide, a man and wife, at Pearcey, and then this. I wonder if Roger's body is somewhere. This could be linked."

"What are you suggesting? Don't serial killers leave traces? Or order their victims' bodies in the same way each time."

"Sure, in movies."

"So you don't think Roger did it?"

"It's too early to be certain." As she inches closer to the door I feel the need to stand and walk her out. "You still seeing that same guy? What was his name, John?"

"Later tonight, actually."

"I see. Look, this might not mean shit coming from me but… it can be a pretty painful road, all the lying."

"I'm not lying to John about anything."

"I don't mean lying to John." She rises off the couch. This time I walk her to the door, counting the minutes until I'm alone. Before she leaves, she says "Enjoy your dinner tonight. And oh, Nick Jeffries. He's a teacher at Pearcey isn't he?"

I nod.

"His body was found in Winnetka this morning."

I make sure to bolt the door once it closes behind her.

Synthetic Bermuda

Sonya calls me shortly after Blake departs. She must have heard about Nick, because she's sobbing on the other end. There's nothing for me to say. I don't bother responding. My time of plastic emotions has ended. My instruments are tired. My falsities at their end.

"You know," I say to her when she's finally calmed down. "You were really the closest thing I ever had to a friend." And I hang up. I have to get ready for my date.

Hilton's knee bumps against mine as we ride in the back seat of his private car. We've hardly spoken since we met up. It's unusual, but I'm too focused guessing where he is taking me. Will my plan work at our destination?

The car smells like pine and leather, cruising like an eel through the stoplights. The driver wears a hat and says nothing more than a "how are you this evening ma'am."

The night breathes an overcast of violet darkness. In the stillness of the car, we make little conversation. I'm fixated on Danny. I should be concerned about where he'd gone after our exchange, regretful that I had snapped at him. It's a strange thing, regret. We assume we can pick and choose the moments in life when it will hit, but this can't be farther from the truth. In fact, it's the times I least expect, or even resent, that are filled with the most regret. I have only felt this once before. When I lost Kitty. Every time I glance over at John, I see Danny, diligently scribbling in his bleak notebook.

For a pre-date, downtown cruise, the drive proves rather quiet. John has barely looked at me. He complimented my outfit, one of Kate's sleek dark purple dresses, but that was the last thing he said to me before and during the car ride. Now he stares out the window while we sit in traffic, his face so close to the glass his breath forms a cloud on the window. I'm not really worried or interested in small talk, so I don't mind, although it feels unusual. There's a preshow attitude to the air outside, a certain stillness of cold before a winter downfall.

My insides coil as we pull along the curb. We are in the center of Viagra Triangle. A stratosphere of movement and noise surrounded by fancy sports cars and neon signs. The aura chokes on the lingering perfumes of Miss Cartier chasing Mr. Rolex. A siren wails in my mind. No, I think to myself. Not here. But there's no need to worry. I have no ex's, no spouse to catch me cheating, and no business associates that I have to schmooze. The Triangle is a storm of people. A flooding crowd of couples out to spend, out to socialize, out to be seen. It's everything I'm not. It's an endless, three angled madness.

"Relax," he says with a sly whisper to my ear, squeezing my hand. "I hate these people, too."

I curse him behind my impassive mask, silently pleading, 'then why the fuck are we here?'

In the restaurant, the hostess guides us through the maze of tables. A tempo of silverware fills the room, clicking against plates like worn bones cracking at the joint. The place erupts with white noise of human chatter morphing into one loud trumpeting inflection of seemingly meaningless banter. I drown in it all, though nauseated by the contrasting potion of steaming entrees and expensive cologne filling the restaurant.

I catch a whiff of the hostess' perfume. Sage, a little rose petal, and of course anise. Sexy, provocative, a nice mix with her short black dress and 5-inch heels. Her legs are thin, too thin. Her skintight dress presses her boobs to near explosion. Her hair is straight, bright and golden blonde. She is "perfect". The pinnacle of social taste. Perfect to greet you when you walk in the door of a restaurant where everything from the watch you wear to the wine you order is a competition. It's dark enough, the tablecloths low enough, for men to get a little preview, or give one, during the lull between entrees and dessert. It's a place where slipping a hundred dollar bill gets you a table on a busy Friday night. Where club owners and politicians trade favors for well-rated escorts. A trip to the bathroom promises a nice tray for tips and a friendly face offering a towel to dry your hands. Gum? Sure. Cigarettes? Yes, please. Condoms? I think I have a chance. If you say the magic word, they might even have something to stick up your nose. Something to dull the pain when he breeches inside you tonight? We've got you covered. Something to make you last longer? I swear it works most of the time. Everything has a price tag. Everything, and everyone, is for sale.

We walk by a table of ducklings accompanied by a handful of girls. I watch two of them in particular, the future Mr. and Mrs. Miner. She plays with his chin, tickling his neck and begging for his worthless attention while he gawks at women in low cut tops and short dresses. Customers holler at their waiters, impatient and uprooted by the slightest mistakes. Couples clink glasses in toasts, some new relationships and others old. Men spy down the waitress' shirt offering a taste of the wine, while women on reluctant dates sip a chilled martini glass in need of a Tanqueray saving. It's a full spread of reptiles and vile monsters, the tapestry to my violent motivation.

At the table, I let John Hilton remove my jacket that covers the new dress I stole from Kate's closet. She hadn't worn it yet, so it lacks the same smell as the dress I wore the night before, which I miss.

John hands the jacket to the hostess, along with his own. He pulls out my seat and gently caresses my arm as he guides me into my chair.

When he sits across from me, I search the catacombs of my database of social practice to find the right thing to say. I'm like a kid stranded in a library struggling to find the right book.

"Nice place," I finally say.

The busser approaches and fills our water glasses. John nods with a short "thank you." He folds his hands in front of himself, eyeing his surroundings while we sit in utter silence. I don't want to speak. I don't think I know how to. I can barely hear in the chaotic concert of noise and commotion that fuels the dim lit restaurant. "I'm guessing you haven't been here before?"

"What gave that away?"

"Look, it's actually not that bad." He sighs, letting down his firm façade and allowing the vulnerable man I had spared resurface. "Maybe this was a mistake, we—we can leave if you want."

"No, let's stay."

"I brought my wife here once. She loved this shit, and probably still does. Like over there," John props his elbow on the table and pointed with an imaginary finger gun. "That's the same judge having T-bone and lobster with the prosecutor and defense attorney for a high-profile murder case. On the other side, that's Max Hatfield, he brings a new girl here every week, hands the maître d a hundred bucks and then brings his wife on Valentine's Day. No one says anything." I realize I'm not in a restaurant. No. It's a haven for high-end hypocrisy and secrets. I could kill each one of them.

"And you? You bring your wife and hookers?" He straightens himself, letting his hand fall to his lap, then lets out a slight sigh before responding.

"No. I only—and I don't see you as that."

"As a hooker?"

"Yes… I mean, no."

"Then what do you see me as?

A waiter in a white blazer and a black bow tie interrupts us.

"Welcome back, Mr. Hilton, how are you two doing this evening?"

"Wonderful, thank you," John says. The waiter pops a bottle of champagne, filling two flutes and setting them in front of us.

"On the house. Would you like me to run through the menu with you or is there anything else I can get you started for you right away?"

"We're alright for now," John says. "Thank you."

The waiter nods, motioning for a quick escape, but I stop him with a question of my own.

"Are there any specials tonight?"

"Yes, there's a beautiful Chilean Sea Bass with a delicious mascarpone sauce and fingerlings. Also a porterhouse steak with mushroom ragu and roasted spinach—"

"Two Macallan 18's. Neat." The waiter looks at John, as if he needs to approve of my order. Typical. "Thank you. What was your name?"

"Greg."

"Thank you, Greg," I say with a hearty smile as I let him go.

In the back of the restaurant, a woman in a black gown sits at a grand piano. She's been diddling on the keys to produce a pleasant background whisper of musical interludes, something to blend the constant flow of chatter into a harmonic uproar. Then I hear it, a change in keys. The altering tempo goes from some piano school booklet of noise to pure melodious heaven. She begins playing Beethoven. I watch, awed as her fingers dance over the singing keys.

"You enjoy that type of music?" John must have caught my wandering eyes.

"I'm somewhat in love with more old-fashioned stuff," I say to him. "My mom would play it for me."

"Quite the enigma you are, Ann. I bet there's a lot to learn about you." I don't respond. He no longer exists. No one does; the maître d, the waiter, the ducklings, they've all suddenly vanished as the ninth symphony flows through the air like a wafting spring breeze. Then his voice chimes in above the music. "Tonight is a special night," John says. "Just wait."

As if on John's cue, a violinist walks beside the piano, directly across from the graceful angel who continues her momentous play. Have I escaped Viagra Triangle? No. I'm on a cloud, completely subdued as the violin strokes his bow along the strings, adding to the piano's anthem, complimenting it with peaceful perfection.

"How'd you know I would enjoy this?" I ask John, finally breaking my eye-contact with the two musical performers.

"Does this ever happen?"

"Does what ever happen?"

"You going on a second date with a man who hired you?" He fingers imaginary quotation marks around the word 'hired'.

"You could say it's our third if you count saving me in the park and making me breakfast."

He chuckles, taking a sip of champagne.

"How did you end up there again?" I look at him, confused.

"I already told you that. Can't we talk about something else?"

"Ok. You never told me about your ex," he says.

"Is this how second dates usually go? You sit and bullshit until the truth about past lovers comes up?"

"C'mon. I'll tell you about mine. I'm not saying you have to tell me your whole history. I just think it's interesting hearing about old flames."

"I hardly asked." He does one of those head bobs, silently pleading 'c'mon, play along with me.' I figure what the hell. "She was more of a Roman candle than an old flame if you know what I mean."

"She?"

"Yes, she. Does that—"

"Bother me? Heavens no. So, whatever happened to her?" Greg saves me upon his return to the table, flashing a fresh smile as he places our Scotch in front of us. We send him away and take a pause in talking to look over the menus. They are those vintage laminated folded ones. They remind me of the manila folders teachers have students set on their desks during a test to make anti-cheating partitions. I hide behind mine, holding my whiskey as I pretend to study through the list of overpriced appetizers and entrees.

Then Hilton tries to break the silence.

"So, you were telling me about–"

"I can't decide between the specials," I say, dropping the menu from my face. "Steak or fish?"

"We could get both and share?"

"I don't really do the whole sharing plates thing. Maybe fish? It's better for me. Every time I eat steak something has to die."

"Well how is that any different when you eat a fish? They get caught in a net and practically get strangled."

"Yeah but fish aren't the same as land animals. It seems like more of a humane way of killing."

"I don't know. If you ask me, killing is killing."

"Yes, but if you need to kill, what would the most humane way of doing it be?"

"I don't think there's anything humane about killing."

"So it's a necessity? Part of human nature to kill, but not a humane way of behaving?"

"You kill a fish, and you kill a cow. What's the difference? You have two carcasses. Two things to eat. Once you kill them they aren't animals any more, they are just meat. Justification won't make the taste any better or worse. So if the question is how you kill them then it's the same answer, but if it's trying to make one animal more valuable alive than the other-."

"Then it's the fish" Sounds an awful lot like a vegan ad…

"Well, maybe. Which would you rather have die in this instance I suppose? A fish or a cow. But here's the problem with your logic, Ann. They are both already dead."

"Did you have any questions?" Greg returns. His foot taps and his upper lip twitches while he leans over the table.

"I will have the steak special," I say.

"Excellent choice. And how would you like it cooked?"

"Bloody."

John orders the fish. Another lull of silence passes after we hand the menus to Greg and drink our whiskey.

I do a quick study of the restaurant, eyeing how the waiters at the end of the bar pick up the drinks. A similar process goes for the entrées. There's a window at the front of the kitchen with those heating lamps where rows of expo workers in black uniforms wait for the food. I have two options. Food or drink. He'll order another whiskey. I'm sure of it. Or he'll pop off to the bathroom. That'll give me plenty of time. I know it's crowded. The last place for a murder. But why not make the finale somewhat of a spectacle? Focus, Ann, no mistakes.

"Have you ever read Alice in Wonderland?"

John lets out a throat-clearing giggle, swallowing a sip of whiskey before answering. "A long time ago."

"What character would you be?"

"What character?"

"If you could choose."

"I'm not really sure."

"If you had to choose."

"I don't remember most of them."

"If I had a gun to your head and said you had to choose or die, who would you choose?" I offer a few laughs after threatening him. He wears a blank stare at first, but then joins in.

"So, in this life-or-death character choice…" he looks at the ceiling, closing one eye… "I guess Alice."

"Alice?"

"Yes, Alice."

"Why?"

"She's the hero."

"So, you think you're the hero?"

"No, you asked who I could be." He pauses, drifting slightly, tapping his finger on the tablecloth. "I wish I could have been the hero at times in my life, I suppose."

"Did something happen?"

I see Danny in his eyes. That same look. Wanting to say something. Wanting to share truth. "I wasn't always present. I wasn't there enough."

"Are we back to ex's?"

"No. No. Forget I said it. Your turn."

"I wouldn't be anyone."

"What do you mean? You can't do that."

"I wouldn't," I repeat, hiding behind a sip of whiskey.

"What a jip," he says. "C'mon."

"Fine. I'd be Carol."

"Who?"

"Lewis Carol."

"Wait. Didn't he write it? That doesn't count."

"Why not? In a way, isn't every person in the book just an extension of himself? You write characters, create characters, live as them... trying to find the one right face... or just an accumulation of all of them."

"I suppose so, but..."

"So I am all the characters. Just pieces."

"That's not a good thing," he says.

"How come?"

"Because then you aren't a person at all. You can hide behind whatever faces you like, but in the end... you can't change what's underneath. Only how you see yourself."

The pianist changes her tempo and begins playing Camille Saint-Saen's Danse Macabre. Her delicately rapid fingers mesmerize my attention away from John. But in my staring at her, I then notice something from the corner of my eye at the other side of the restaurant.

My intestines strangle my stomach. A knot in my organs closes my windpipe. Code red, I think to myself. Code fucking red. Why are they here?

Danse Macabre

Across the room, a hostess escorts Amir Salem and Angela Greene. For a moment, I don't even recognize her with curled hair and hoop earrings dangling from her ears. But the simple layer of mascara and foundation can't hide her scouring face. It's the first time I've seen her wear blush or eyeliner. She actually looks good, filling out a yellow dress with a shawl draped over her exposed, brawny shoulders. Amir doesn't look like a K-12 principal in his jeans, sports coat, and white button-down. It isn't the fanciest outfit in the room, but he sure looks more country club than lead educator.

"Ann, what is it?" John asks, noticing my drawn stare of concern. I need to disappear. I try to suck myself within my body. Maybe if I make myself extremely small? Fuck, why doesn't Alice's Wonderland exist. At least in that world the pills actually help. They're getting closer. I try to guess which table in the dining room the hostess will place them. Please don't be near us. Please don't see me. "Ann," he repeats, "… is everything ok?"

They get closer. Closer. I curse the hostess. Damn her. Take them somewhere on the other side. I shoot up from the table, knocking a champagne glass. It shatters on the floor. A few bussers rush to the rescue, assaulting the sharp mess.

John stands.

"Ann!" His voice starts high but lowers. In a harsh whisper, "what the fuck is going on?"

"I just need to go to the ladies' room." I turn away from the table, showing my back to Amir and Angela as they take their seats only three tables away from John and me. I escape for cover, feeling the eyes of judgmental fellow diners and yes, Angela Greene, on my back, spotting me with her buzzard eyes. I feel them follow me to the far end of the restaurant. I pass a wine wall, turning to hide on the side that makes a short hallway opposing the main dining area. I crouch, staring through the rows of Spanish cabernets.

"Ma'am," a voice asks from behind me. "Are you alright?" A concerned waiter stares down at me. I rise, trying to keep my composure.

"Yes, sorry. I'm not crazy."

"You trying to avoid someone? People do hide over here all the time when they're trying to avoid their date."

"No, I–" I fumble around in my head. "I was just looking for the restroom."

"Ah," he says, offering directions with his outstretched arm. "You go straight that way and the second right is the ladies." I give him a thankful nod and rush to the bathroom.

I sit confined in the cold bathroom stall like a prisoner waiting in a cell on execution day. The anticipation grows as my thigh bounces faster. Faster.

I sift through my purse, retrieving the orange bottle of Kitty's Ativan. I give it a nice shake and pop five, (no, six should do it,) into my palm. Plus, one for myself, make it two. I slip the six into a hollowed out ChapStick capsule that I keep hidden in the breast of my dress. I need Hilton gone. I need to finish the job. It's either that or my paranoia will swallow me whole. It has already begun. The ship is tipping and my mind lapsing into mad darkness. If I wait to go home with him, I risk running into Danny. At least if the pills don't kill him, they will suppress him, and he'll be an easy finish in an alley somewhere.

John seems upset when I return to the table. I sit without an apology, trying to avoid looking in the direction of Amir and Angela. I wonder if I offer Greg enough money, he will slip them something for me as well.

"Are you feeling better?" John asks.

"I will be soon," I reach for my drink, downing it. The golden sting of the whiskey soothes my nerves.

Her eyes are on me. I know it. Staring at me like a vulture eyeing down a wounded animal, waiting for that perfect moment. Just circling. My eyes twitch; tempted to fix away from John and over to check Amir and Angela. But I keep them glued on him. God it's painstaking. The longest eye contact I've ever given anyone.

"I think I might hit the restroom before the food comes." He stands, chewing his gums. "You'll be here when I get back, right?"

I nod. For a second, I feel sorry for him. He's giving me the perfect opportunity. So thoughtful, John. My eyes follow him as he shifts between tables to the restroom. I wait a minute or two once he's out of sight. Now's my chance. Now might be my only chance.

I pull the ChapStick capsule from my dress, holding it in my fingers, and glancing over my shoulder again. Coast is clear. No John in sight. Hurry, Ann, this is your only shot. Just drop them in his drink. Go ahead. No one's looking.

Now!

"Is that Ann Bonny?" My heart falls out. Standing at the table is Amir and Angela. My hand recoils, hiding the ChapStick in my tight fist.

"Fancy seeing this," Angela Greene says. I close my eyes.

"Was that Mr. Hilton who was sitting here a moment ago?" Amir says. My foot is bouncing. Snap out of it, Ann.

"Yes," I say, turning with a smile.

"He's a big-time donor," Amir beams. Angela's mouth remains shut, her hip tossing to the side and her arms crossed.

Pleasant bitch.

"Date night?" I say.

"Just a platonic outing, of course. A professional celebration."

"For the vice principal promotion," Angela chimes in.

"Is it just you two?" I ask. "Didn't want to include your spouses at the professional celebration dinner?"

That shuts them up.

"Look, Ann," Amir finally continues. "I know today was hard. We both really want what's best for you. We would also appreciate it if you kept whatever you saw, or think you saw, to yourself."

"Sounds like an admission of guilt to me."

"Miss Bonny—"

"It's alright, Angela," Amir says, calm. At least on the outside. "Ann, what is it you want from me?"

"I want you to look me in the eyes and tell me you lied to me. Tell me you manipulated me and that you are sleeping with her."

"You bitch." It takes her a second to get the curse out.

"You know everything I do is for the school's sake." I didn't realize it until now, but he's a terrible liar. I should have seen it before. "If you are willing to play nice, then who knows, maybe the suspension will be lifted early." I sense a catch. Then I see him approaching. No. John is on his way back.

"Made some friends?" John says as he swoops in.

"Hey," Amir's smile grows, shaking John's hand. This is what he really wants from this uninvited exchange. "John Hilton, right? Amir Salem, principal at Pearcey, remember?"

"That's right, yes. I'm sorry I didn't recognize you at first. My ex-wife usually handles all the school stuff. I wish I could be around more." John's grin fades, replaced with a somber downpour. I'm watching my world crumble. Nero before a flame-engulfed Rome.

"You can't blame yourself. We at Pearcey are with you still. And we thank you for staying with us. Your donations go a long way, they really do. Every child who shares our roof has the best academic opportunities because of men like you."

"Men like me." Something about that makes John scoff, then giggle to himself. His hands fall into his pockets and suddenly he seems more uncomfortable than I am. Why wouldn't he?

He's a pro at faking it. They all are.

"So, you are out with our lovely Ann Bonny?" Shut up. Amir. "This is Mrs. Angela Greene."

"How wonderful," John says, extending his hand to Angela. "Nice to meet you."

"Pleasure," she responds behind her pasty smile. "How do you guys know each other?"

"Oh I—" I stare.

"We met at a bar," he says.

"Yes."

John is all smiles. The smile he must have practiced for the courtroom because it's one I haven't seen yet.

"Just still getting to know each other," he says. "I only learned a bit ago about her work. Still such a shock."

"We are looking forward to having you back in a week, Bonny. At least you have something good to spend your suspension doing" Angela gives me a snake grin. I return her favorite gesture with a cold stare. I want to swipe the butter knife from the table and plunge it deep into her throat.

"So, you're all teachers?" John says pointing. John's face leaves him, replaced by a distant, colorless façade of human form. "That's amazing," he says.

"It really is," Angela continues. I want her to shut up. Shut up! Leave! Maybe I should faint? Or just snap her neck in front of the whole restaurant. "Fifth grade. Danny is one of her best students."

I avoid looking at John at all costs. I don't know where to look. Everything is spinning so fast.

"Look," Amir says. There it is, that usual hand motion while he is in deep thought. "I would be so remiss if I didn't tell you about the new project. I sent a mass email to all the big time parents last week but—"

"You know what," I say, placing my hand on John's shoulder. "We should get back to dinner. It was great to see you guys."

"This will only take a second, Ann."

"No," John says, "she's right. Maybe another time. Give my office a call." Amir's eyes don't budge from mine. It's over. Pearcey that is. But I'm pretty sure John sees through Amir's prosthetic amiability too, so I'm not too concerned with shooting his pitch for more money from my wealthy date. "Great to see you," John gives Amir another handshake.

"You've got a terrific kid, by the way. He seems happier and more grown every day."

"Could've fooled me. Haven't seen the boy smile in probably a year. He must be a different kid at school."

"Well, that's because he's got our best, Miss Bonny."

"If she is the best, then why would she be suspended?"

"We really should be getting back to our table," Angela pipes in for a final word. She takes Amir by the arm.

"Enjoy your dinner, guys."

We remain standing as they retreat to their table. Amir hides behind his menu, finishing his glass of wine in a catfish-sized gulp. I enjoy watching them flee, but then I remember I now have to face John.

At first, we sit in silence. A dark, rain cloud silence. I try to open my mouth, but my jaw is locked, my throat clogged. He seems normal, rearranging his silverware and table setting as he waits for the main course to arrive.

I reach for my whiskey, but it's empty.

"Look," I begin.

"You don't have to explain anything to me."

"I don't?" My brain zigzags from relief to suspicion. My leg bounces under the table so rapidly that the water trembles in the glasses.

"I get it, I think. You want more on the side? Is that why you do it? My biggest question is like, how do you go from that to teaching? Or teaching to that? I mean it's two things that just don't mix."

"Because I am an escort?"

"Give me a break. You're no more a real escort than I am a good father."

"Then why?"

"Was anything real? I mean, if it wasn't, wouldn't I be a corpse by now?"

Then the food comes. We stare at one another while Greg watches the food runners set our dishes in front of us.

"Ok, you two, is there anything else I can get for you this evening?" We stay silent. "Ok, well just let me know. And oh yes, enjoy your dinner." I chew on the inside of my bottom lip, trying to hold a firm demeanor, trying to remain calm and reserved.

"How do you justify it? You have your own reality of guilt and innocence? What happened to you? Bullied? Parents beat you? Raped, or something?"

"Look, I don't know what you think you might know-"

"Make no mistake, I have an unlimited amount of emotions inside right now despite how relaxed I may seem." There's only one explanation. Blake must have got to him. Then I remember - the handkerchief. How stupid was I? How could I let her take that back when it had my blood on it?

"Guess we both are good at wearing masks."

"You know there's an investigation into you." His voice turns to a harsh whisper. "You are a suspect for murder for crying out loud."

"The lawyer and the killer at dinner together," I joke, taking another sip as I let my situation, shocking as it is, sink in. "This is the perfect place for that. Right?" He didn't like the joke. "Everyone's always looking for a reason. I forfeited reality a long time ago."

"So, what? You do the world a favor?"

"Some were just a bad fuck."

"You like deflecting from the truth."

"The truth? The truth is I learned how hideous men's hearts were. All it took was something sharp to get a closer look."

"You're mad-"

"And you are just like them. A manipulator."

"You assume too much."

"Accept it. You, my victim. I, your whore. Did you really expect this to be a love story? We were each other's experiment. Each a body on a slab."

"I am guessing I was just one of those men who deserved what was coming to him, wasn't I?" I don't answer. "But you could've done it at any time? Why not? Why not right now?"

I don't have an answer for him. I eye the steak knife. He notices, but the silence is severed when his phone rings. I want to run, or stab, but something in John's eyes screams worry and terror. His voice trembles on the phone—not the built voice he usually has, but one with a tremor of loss. I stay in my seat, waiting for my fear to be certified.

"That was Danny's babysitter, damnit his mother was supposed to have him tonight, but she had a date. I need to go-

"What happened?"

"Nothing… he," John's confidence trembles a bit, his voice breaking. "He… he is not responding and locked himself in the bathroom."

"Then let's go."

"No. You aren't going near my son. I am calling the police to come pick you up. They can deal with you. I've had enough of this."

"An ambulance won't make it in time for your son. We are close enough, but we need to go now."

"An ambulance, he's—"

"This isn't about me or you anymore, this is about Danny!"

"Fine, but I'm not letting you out of my sight."

I should run. I should take my steak knife, cut John's throat, and leave him to bleed out, slunk over his sea bass. It would be a long shot, but I could escape to some kind of on the run freedom.

But Danny needs me.

Carnival of Animals

When the car pulls in front of John's building I don't hesitate or wait for John to follow. I know what's going on. I've seen it before. And it's my fault. I jump out without a word and rush through the revolving doors past the attendant and right to the elevator.

With a ding, I arrive on John's floor. Inside, the lights are all off except the kitchen. I ignore the frantic, teary babysitter. I yell at her to not call anyone. She isn't prepared for this. She's a teenager. I, on the other hand, am well prepared.

John runs in behind me and starts banging on the bathroom door. My legs are frozen for a moment while I take some form of a mental image. A tail of hair dangles over John's bloody red eyes. His shirt now untucked and wrinkled, his jacket thrown on the floor like a used rag, and his face—that face that turns to me as I step into the hall—well that's a face that you scarcely see on a man like John Hilton. It's hellish and desperate. His control surrendered, only the worst thing imaginable.

A face of pain.

"Do you have anything in the medicine cabinet in there?"

"I think some prescriptions. I don't know, why?" He repeatedly yells Danny's name, hoping it will beckon an end to this nightmare. To just open the door. Useless.

"I need you to get me a pen," I say. I kneel to his eyeline. "And a screwdriver if you have one."

"What?"

"Did you hear me? John. Do you have a pen and a screwdriver? Hurry!"

"Yes." His eyes track a thought that drifts above my shoulder. "In the laundry room."

"Go. Go get them." He nods but needs my help to bring him to his feet.

"Ann I—"

"Go!"

He darts down the hall.

"Danny." I slap the door. "Danny… can you hear me? It's Miss Bonny. Danny." I fear that he isn't just ignoring me.

When I finally break through the lock, I see Danny sprawled on the floor. His eyes roll to glimpse the back end of his skull. With a flash, Danny vanishes, and Kitty replaces him. The image is too similar, as if Danny is just a copied version of her, laid across the bathroom tile; one arm at her side, the other outstretched, inches from a now empty orange pill bottle. I react nearly the same as I had when I walked in on her like this. I stand, helpless for a moment, my body frozen, my joints seal with concreted disbelief. A familiar horror infiltrates my veins, igniting life back into my body as the desperate anxiety and the realization that every moment counts hit my brain.

Kitty had owned Naloxone. A drug for when you take too many drugs. But it didn't always work. If you ask me, it's nothing more than make-up sex between a toxic couple—temporary salt on an ever growing, infected wound. Seldomly a permanent fix. Throughout our relationship, she had overdosed twice. She tried covering the marks she gave herself on her wrists with long sleeves and stacked bracelets, but I always knew. The night she died, she threatened to kill herself. She used that against me. I suppose that's one of the reasons I justified it to myself; that whole self-preservation nonsense and the fact that deep down Kitty wanted to die seems to make it alright. Bullshit, all of it. Excuses and justifications are just party favors to get guilt to leave the ceremony of bad thoughts in your head.

The amount of pills Kitty had taken compared to Danny is like comparing the Mongol Empire to Rhode Island. I recognize some of the containers: Advil, Ibuprofen, and a crinkled punch card for Dayquil. Unlike Kitty, they aren't completely emptied into Danny's system. Dozens of white and blue capsules litter the floor around Danny, most likely spilling from when he finally swallowed enough to collapse. If he's lucky, it won't be enough to stop his heart, just knock him out.

I rush to Danny's limp self and prop his head back. His skin is clammy and somehow paler than before. The type of opaqueness you see when you give a final look at a dead relative laying in a casket. I lean over his mouth. He isn't breathing.

"Here," John says. "Here are some towels." He rushes to the bathroom door, tossing the towels to me and propping himself on the doorframe to balance, stunned and teary eyed. "Is he alright? Ann? Ann, is he?"

"I need you to relax, John."

"What can I do?"

I take the towels and roll Danny on his side.

"Look away," I say to the father as my fingers dig into Danny's throat.

Finally, with a violent gag, Danny jolts to life. I guide his head, gently, the same way I had guided Kitty's, over the trash can and let Danny do the rest as he throws up. "Let it out."

I cup the back of Danny's sweat-damped head, and run a towel under the sink, letting it rest on his neck to cool him. I wipe his face as he bobs over the trash can. John remains petrified in the doorway, every so often running his hand over his face and rubbing under his eyes.

"You're alright, Danny, I'm here" I say, running my hand down the side of his face. I'm not sure if he even realizes it's me. "It's going to be alright, kid." I rock him slowly, trying to sooth his jitters as he coughs and pants. Red circles form under his eyes. With a few spits of whatever lingers around his mouth from the vomit, he's breathing normally. Well, not completely normal, it's that kind of breathing after a rollercoaster or a car crash. A hesitant, what the hell is happening to me? Is this even real life, type of breathing.

"You should have someone check on him. A doctor perhaps?" I ask John. No response. He's gone.

A few minutes pass before John comes back.

"The sitter already called 911." He says walking back into the bathroom. "I am sorry, Ann. Cops will probably come, too. They know you're here."

I ignore him, aware of my situation, but focused more on Danny's.

After helping Danny wash his face and change, I lay him on his side in bed.

"I'm so sorry, Miss Bonny."

"Nonsense," I say rolling the clothes he's been wearing into a ball for the trash. You don't keep clothes you overdose or attempt suicide in. You just don't. "Don't ever apologize to me, ok?" I sit on the edge of the bed and slowly rest my hand on his shoulder. "You'll be ok, Danny."

A few long moments of silence pass. At least they seem long. Probably only a handful of minutes. But you know how when you're in the dark and things seem alright, time seems to do this thing where it stands still. I notice a stillness I've never felt before. An ease, you might even call it a sense of peace, as I sit with Danny in the darkness. It's a first for me, sitting motionless, absent eyes fixed on a lingering nothingness while my head whispers empty thoughts of reassurance.

Flashes of red and blue reflecting off the window curtains interrupt the serenity. I peek through the window curtain to see a squad of police cruisers forming in front of the building below. No doubt they're here for me. I'm not worried about getting caught. I surrendered that when I chose to come here anyway. But it hits me, that spring of survival, when I see the lights and uniforms storming from below.

When I turn to say goodbye to Danny, it's too late. He's drifted to sleep. Good, I think, breathing a sigh of relief. I know for the first time, whatever I do, Danny will be ok. I savor the instant and spare a second to remember his face, his living, peaceful face, before heading out.

I close the door to Danny's room, keeping the knob turned so it doesn't give a loud click when I shut it the whole way. Then I head to the kitchen to get a knife.

I need to end what started this circus of chaos in my well-balanced life. While Danny sleeps safely in his bed, I curse John, squeezing a blame into my mind that he is responsible for everything that has torn down the perfectly executed life of execution I constructed. Before him, no one suspected me, before him, my lives were separate, and there was never a scant scent of police or doubt that I did this because they deserved it. They deserved to die; not that deep down I'm sick and enjoy the slaughter.

I pull the first that catches my eye and brush my fingers along the edge to gauge its sharpness. Satisfied, I tiptoe down the hall, struck by a cloaked déjà vu as I creep in the dark of John's apartment wielding one of his kitchen knives. This time it will be different. This time I won't be spooked by the picture of my student. This time he will die.

I pass by Danny's room, quiet as I can, and head straight for the main door. He will wake up, fatherless, better for it. I figure John was in the hall, negotiating with the cops how to bring me down.

Then the door opens.

John stands in the doorway with his phone in his hand and a shocked look on his face. I glance over his shoulder. The hallway is empty.

I stop in my tracks and hide the knife behind my back. John swallows before returning his phone to his pocket. He coughs, the throat clearing kind, and drops his hands to his sides. He had to have seen the blade.

"That was his mother. How is he?" He exhales and bites down on his bottom lip. I don't blink. I don't let him move or even breathe without me catching it. "She is on her way. She told me it was smart not to call an ambulance. Danny was lucky, I guess. They would've been too late so it's good you came. Though, if I am going to be honest, I really didn't expect you to—"

"Enough." I let the knife show, holding it out and pointing the blade to his face as I step closer.

But he doesn't budge. He doesn't flee or fight. He just sighs.

"Look," he starts. The red and blue law enforcement light show dances in the window of his living room. I press the knife to his throat.

"You don't have to—"

"Shut up!" I yell. I don't have time for dialogue. I probably don't have time at all. I figure I'll cut his throat and the cops will reach his apartment, their guns pointed at me while I stand holding the knife over him bleeding out on the floor.

"Go ahead then," he says. I hold the knife steady, the steel just kissing his skin. "I'm probably to blame for all this. Maybe I deserve it." I press harder, not too hard, but enough that red trails down. "If you were a real killer, I wouldn't have a son tonight. Whatever you are, you don't have to stay that way. You need to hurry." I fight the urge for a moment. Something inside me wants to stab him over and over again right here and now. But the knife lowers, leaving behind a thin paper-cut sliver of opened flesh.

"What?"

He cuts me off by pressing a finger to my lips. Then guides my hand to his chest, reaching between the upper buttons of his shirt revealing a wire taped to his chest. Blake's smart. What more could she have needed? A confession would've guaranteed my position on her butcher block. But John rips it from his chest and throws the mechanism of wires into the toilet.

"They'll be using the elevator and the main stairs. But the top floor has a separate flight that leads to the back of the building. Into an alleyway."

"Why would you tell me this? Even if I get out of the building, by now, I won't get far enough for them not to find me."

"You're running out of time, Ann." He wraps his hand around mine.

Our eyes lock.

"I didn't fake all of it," I say. "There just used to be someone—."

"Just go." His dimples perk. They're child-like. I nod, not engaging the same half-smile he gives me.

Without savoring a second, I bolt through the still opened door.

I race out into the alley without the slightest idea of what to do next. The cops will be here any minute. How far can I really get on foot? It doesn't matter. I don't think; I just run.

With sirens in the distance, I keep my pace sprinting back into the heart of downtown. Barefoot. I toss my shoes over a chain-linked fence that barricades the drop down into a metro train stop. I'm in such a rush I don't get to say goodbye to them, I just slip them off and chuck them as hard as I can, not waiting to see where they land, just lugging them into the black air and spinning into full retreat.

And I run.

I don't dare take Michigan Avenue. I sprint through the alleys and side streets. In no particular direction. Nowhere is safe. My apartment must be swarming with cops. Without it registering, I head towards the river. I take the stairs from the top of the bridge to the Riverwalk. All the way down, under bridges and pushing through couples and drunk friend groups. All the way to the boardwalk on Lakeshore leading to Navy Pier.

I might be mad. I might be bat shit fucking crazy. But at least now, I own it.

At this point, I don't feel the sting of the cold anymore. In fact, I don't feel a thing. At this time of night it's desolate; darkness from side to side. I'm alone with the river rolling over itself as the wind blows along its rocky surface. For a moment, I allow myself to catch my breath, walking steady. Silence looms save but a faint call of sirens.

I pull out the remaining Ativan pills and let them fall into the water. It's not just the pills I throw in. No. I throw in Mary Ann Bonny. I throw in the 'innocent female teacher,' the 'calm neighbor,' the passive girl. I throw in every mask I've worn over the years, the engines that drove me to this insanity. My pure reflection remains. Finally, I recognize the image, and madness smiles right back. The water is so inviting, a mysterious opaqueness that beckons.

I think about what John had said about the ducklings. How they pretend to be friends but would so gladly smile putting a knife in their co-workers' back to get ahead. Am I any worse than them? If they killed each other's careers so they could be promoted, destroying reputations and stealing jobs, how is that any separate than taking life? To me, they're just another horse poled down, spinning, climbing over one another until they wear out and die.

It makes me wonder, what's the point? If everyone is just in a loop of their own, wouldn't we all be mad? Then me, too? Do I exist like the rest? No, I can't begin to accept that. I know I am different. As is Danny. He lives outside of their loops, unwilling, if not refusing, to ride life's carousel of decisions and choices. He's shown me that.

Isn't love just another circle? Just another loop in life? It begins; it ends. Either by death or by choice. Every time love sprouts, it lives for a time to be beautiful, growing into a colorful, natural work of art. Each seems unique, with its own blossom, petals, and configuration. But what's so unique when they all have their happy moments; they all have their unhappy disasters that result in a solution, temporary of course, or annihilation. Love is patient, love is blind, love is nothing you will ever find. Because it doesn't exist. Nothing exists in this world but the world itself, spinning and spinning until it, too, will decay and fall out of its own loop.

If there's a possibility that someone could save me completely, she died. I sit alone now, listening to the noise of the city, mostly sirens, stuck on that carousel, mad as the day I mounted the ride. Then suddenly I feel somewhat at ease, as if part of me has escaped. As if a gust lifted part of myself from me. My masks melt in the dark abyss of the lake.

As if my mind is a record box, Camille Saint-Saens' Le Carnival de Animaux begins playing. Loud.

I know this one by heart. The harmonious melody drowns out the city, the crashing lake water, everything in the distance. I wonder, at first, if it's another ploy. Another distraction, like when my mother would play these tunes. But I submit. It conquers each fiber, taking my body and twisting, almost pulling me by a slew of ghost marionette strings. The violins run over each chord in perfect vicious, balletic fashion. And here, alone where the bleak fringe of the city meets what seems to be endless black water, I start to dance.

I'm elevated and swayed, subdued by such chaotic serenity, that the police assault has vanished from my mind. If I have a world of my own, everything is nonsense.

My world is finally built.

The pending crescendo of uniforms dissipates from my mind as I reach the merry-go-round. The sirens softly sing in the distance while I trail deeper into Navy Pier, racing over to where things began. Everything is so bright. An illumination of colors and lights, with a whole carnival of animals to keep company. To dance with. They all seem so still as I climb over the carousel gate with a big sign in front saying OUT OF ORDER.

Made in the USA
Monee, IL
17 February 2025

12486023R00194